"I think it's me... you're Santa Claus...."

Seven-year-old Erin glared accusingly at John. "I think the real Santa Claus wouldn't like that at all. I think he'd be very mad at you."

Unable to come up with a defense, John laughed. "You're right. But I'd explain to Santa that as a police officer, I'm doing a good thing by making sure your baby-sitter stops robbing his mom. And I think Santa would forgive me."

"Look, where are we going with this?" her father broke in.

John had no intention of charging the twins with anything. If he was very lucky, they would have had the spit scared out of them so badly they'd never get into trouble again. "I'm going to release your children, Mr. Murphy," he said. "I think we've got enough to get the baby-sitter into juvenile court."

A smile of gratitude crossed Murphy's lips. "I appreciate how you've handled this, Detective. I'll make sure the kids understand how serious this situation is. By the way, what was Erin talking about, that nonsense about Santa?"

John smiled. "Ask her."

Dear Reader,

I remember the first time I left my husband alone with our first child. The baby was one week old, and an order I'd placed at the maternity shop had finally arrived. I asked my husband if he could handle our precious newborn by himself during the half hour it would take for me to drive to the store and back. "Of course I can," my husband boasted. "He's my son. I'm his daddy."

So off I went—and came home to quite a scene: my husband and the baby on the dining room floor, surrounded by diapers, baby wipes, wadded tissues, waterproof pads, cotton balls and a damp undershirt or two. My husband was out of breath and glistening with perspiration, but he'd never looked more proud of himself. Drowsy and content, the baby was nestled in his lap. "I had to change his diaper *five* times while you were gone," my husband told me. "By the third diaper I knew what I was doing. I'm his dad, after all."

My husband has always been my hero, but that afternoon fourteen years ago, when he valiantly changed five diapers in thirty minutes, his hero rating rose about a hundred points. To me, fathers—devoted, loving fathers—are the greatest heroes of all.

Father Christmas is dedicated to all the heroic fathers in the world.

Judith Arnold

FATHER CHRISTMAS
Judith Arnold

Harlequin Books

TORONTO • NEW YORK • LONDON
AMSTERDAM • PARIS • SYDNEY • HAMBURG
STOCKHOLM • ATHENS • TOKYO • MILAN
MADRID • WARSAW • BUDAPEST • AUCKLAND

ISBN 0-373-70767-3

FATHER CHRISTMAS

FATHER CHRISTMAS

CHAPTER ONE

JOHN RUSSO'S DAY BEGAN with a murder-suicide. After that, it was all downhill.

He stared out the window in the upper half of the kitchen door. Behind him the room lay in shadow. He'd turned off the light so he could see the night through the panes of glass. A slow, chill rain was falling. The moon looked like a ball of gray lint behind the clouds.

He took a slug of beer from the bottle he held, counting on it to subdue the throbbing in his temples and muffle the noise from the den. Michael was waging World War III in there, one brave boy against the entire population of a Fisher-Price airport. It sounded as if Mike were going to win the battle, which wasn't surprising since the Fisher-Price people were two inches tall and unarmed, in every sense of the word.

John wished he could hear the rain instead of his son's rebel yells. He wished he could go outside, stand beneath the drizzle and let it wash away a day's worth of emotional crud. But the back porch thermometer read thirty-eight degrees and the rain was mixed with sleet, tiny pellets of ice ticking like grains of sand against the rear wall of the house. Too cold a storm for a smart man to stand in.

If he weren't the sort of person to take responsibility for things, he'd call the day's disasters a pileup of bad luck. But he was too smart—or maybe not smart enough—to blame anyone except himself for the fact that the hairline fissures in his life were suddenly expanding into fault lines, causing the earth to shift beneath his feet and the fragile world he'd built to tumble down around him.

Mike's shrill voice tore through his brain. The kid whooped and hollered, sounding like a cross between a coyote and a squad car siren. How could a two-year-old be so loud? John couldn't recall ever being that loud as a child. Of course, in a family with seven kids, one voice, no matter how loud, wasn't going to get heard. John had learned not to waste his vocal cords, not to fight his way into the conversation unless he had something worth saying.

Evidently Mike believed it was worth saying that airport security in the Russo den stank. "Uh-oh! Uh-oh!" he shrieked gleefully. "It's a bomb! *Boom!* All blowed up!"

John took another pull of beer, closed his eyes and rested his forehead against the cool glass of the window. His conversation with Norma replayed itself in his mind, warning him that he was in deep trouble and he was going to have to do something fast. Damn. He didn't want to do anything about Norma. He'd been very happy with the way things were. Mike loved Norma. He trusted her. So did John. And she was so convenient.

But she was leaving, and if John didn't make other arrangements...

That wasn't an option. He *had* to make other arrangements.

There wasn't enough beer in the world to drown out the raucous play of his son, the insistent patter of the rain, the constant murmur of his conscience telling him that everything he'd counted on was more or less gone and he was going to have to deal with it somehow. He was going to have to put his losses behind him and move on. For Mike's sake if not for his own.

Maybe Norma's news, and then the letter waiting for him in his mailbox, wouldn't have bothered John so much if he hadn't started his day at the Balfour home, responding to the anxious call of a neighbor who'd sworn she heard what sounded like gunshots coming from the modest split-level house. The scene hadn't been particularly gruesome; John had seen worse. When you were a cop, you got used to viewing the horror violence left in its wake. And while from a moral perspective, murder-suicides were tragic, from a cop standpoint, they were easy. The crime came ready-solved, all tied up except for the paperwork. No sleuthing required, no loose ends, no arrests, no trial, no D.A. on his back, no jail.

But this one was sad enough to break the devil's heart. Edith Balfour had been wasting away with Lou Gehrig's disease, and she'd pleaded with her husband to end her misery. He'd responded by putting a bullet between her eyes, and then he'd turned the gun on himself. The note he'd left behind explained it all: he couldn't bear to watch her suffer and he couldn't bear to live without her. They'd been married for forty-one years.

The sight of them lying side by side in the bed they must have shared their entire wedded life, their hands clasped and their pillows drenched in blood, had been depressing. John wasn't crazy enough to envy them, yet he recognized that that kind of love, that kind of dependence on each other, must have been a beautiful thing. He couldn't imagine loving a woman so much he would rather die than go on without her. The idea overwhelmed him.

Still, he was a professional, and he'd handled the investigation the way it needed to be handled. The most difficult part had been talking to the Balfours' thirty-six-year-old daughter, Mary, in Ohio. Once he'd found her number in the leather-bound address book by Edith Balfour's bed, he'd telephoned the local police department in Mary Balfour's town and asked them to send an officer over so Mary wouldn't be alone when she got the news. Even with a patrolman and a neighbor by her side, she'd fallen apart. John had had to listen to her sob, long distance. "Why?" she'd wailed. "Why?"

If that had been the worst of it, he would have gotten through the day all right. He wouldn't be staring out at the sleety November rain, polishing off his second beer of the night and contemplating whether he should put his son to bed before he opened a third.

Norma was leaving. Talk about not knowing how to survive once someone was gone...

When he'd stopped at her house to pick up Mike after work, she had been frenetic, her eyes as wide as a speed freak's, her hair standing on end, her cardigan buttoned crookedly over her plump fifty-year-old body. "Oh, John," she'd babbled, ignoring Mike as he smashed a towering construction of Waffle Blocks across the floor of her finished basement, "Oh, God, what a day. My daughter had her baby, John! It's almost a month early! The good news is the doctors say the baby's going to be all right. But I need to fly to San Jose right away to be with my daughter. I mean, everything's so unexpected, nothing is ready. They haven't even bought a crib yet. I've got to be with them. You understand.''

John understood about things being unexpected, and he understood about not being ready for a baby. He also understood that if Norma went to San Jose to be with her daughter, she would no longer be in Arlington to watch his son while he was at work.

"I'm leaving this weekend. And I figured, since it's just one week till Thanksgiving, I'm going to stay in California through the New Year. I was already planning to go for Christmas, but they need me there now. I'm sorry to leave you in the lurch like this. I made a few calls today—stop that, Michael! Pick up the blocks, sweetie!—and my friend Harriet Simka might be able to help out with Michael for tomorrow, at least. I wrote her number down somewhere.... Mike, pick up the blocks *now*."

John didn't know Harriet Simka. He'd known Norma for years. She lived seven houses away from him, and she'd raised three kids of her own, and Mike adored her. She charged John a reasonable fee for her baby-sitting services, she was flexible when John had to work late, and the arrangement had met everyone's needs. But one thing, one little snafu, the premature birth of a grandchild—and John's precarious life collapsed like Mike's tower of Waffle Blocks.

"Mike, come on, now—your daddy's here," Norma had said. Mike had responded by crawling under the couch and giggling.

What am I going to do? John had thought, swallowing his panic while Norma got down on her knees and peered under the couch, cajoling Mike to come out. John worked full-time as a detective in the Arlington Police Department. Sometimes his cases demanded more than a nine-to-five shift. He needed reliable child care, and until now Norma had been reliable.

"I don't wanna come out," Michael had shouted. John couldn't blame him. More often than he'd like to admit, he wished he could crawl into a safe, dark place and not come out.

Norma had lured Mike out with a cookie, handed John a slip of paper with her friend Harriet's number on it and sent John and Mike home. John had pulled the mail from the box before driving into the garage. Mixed in with the advertising circulars and bills was a letter from Sherry's lawyer. It wasn't unexpected, but still... There it was, in his face, the reality of it.

Just one more reason he wanted to step out into the sleety night, start walking and not turn back.

But John took his responsibilities seriously. He would never walk away. Instead, he would do what had to be done, which for the present meant getting Mike ready for bed.

Sighing, he turned from the soggy evening and set his empty bottle on the counter by the sink. Then he steeled himself and entered the den.

The carnage was impressive. Bolster cushions from the sofa had been combined with the coffee table to create a fort, the toy airport was upside down on the rug and plastic toy people beamed their flat smiles at him from outposts all around the room. In the midst of the mayhem, Mike balanced an airplane in both hands and swooped it through the air, humming like a motor. "I fly the plane!" he shouted joyfully. "Daddy, look! I fly it!"

"Time to land it," John said, sidestepping a misplaced cushion and venturing farther into the room. "It's cleanup time."

"No."

"Yes." As Mike zoomed the plane past John, he reached out and swiped it.

Mike's face crumpled into a grimace, and then he howled. "No, no, no! No cleanup time!"

"Yes cleanup time." One of the things that bothered John about being a father was that his verbal skills frequently deteriorated until he was speaking like a toddler. On the job he talked like a normal adult. But at home, where there were no other grown-ups, he found himself mimicking Mike's speech patterns. It made John feel as if a part of his mind shut down when he was with Mike, the part that knew how to construct sentences and paragraphs.

"No, no, no!" Mike stormed across the room to where a trio of Fisher-Price people lay in ambush behind the CD rack. He swung his foot, sending the brightly colored, grinning figures in three different directions with one kick. Not bad for a soccer player, but unacceptable for a two-year-old a half hour past his bedtime.

"Clean up now," John said, his voice dropping in volume. The angrier he got, the quieter he got.

"No! I want Mommy! I want Mommy!" Mike barreled past John and out of the den, leaving the mess behind like a tornado seeking new trailer parks to destroy.

Hearing Mike beg for his mother raised John's anger to such a level that he couldn't speak at all. He simply stood amid the ruins of Mike's toy airport and gulped in deep breaths of air.

So Mike wanted his mommy. Well, of course he did. What two-year-old kid didn't?

But Mike's mommy had been gone for six months,

and the letter John had received that evening from her lawyer announced that she was gone for good. A person could still get a quickie divorce if she wanted one, and Sherry had wanted one. She'd wanted one so badly she hadn't given a thought to the innocent son she'd left behind.

Which was also John's fault, he told himself, feeling the ache return to his temples. He gazed about him at the disorderly room, the scattered sofa cushions, the war-torn airport, and decided the mess was his fault, too. Everything, with the possible exception of Norma's grandchild's premature arrival, was John's fault.

He stalked out of the den in search of his son. Mike had slammed himself inside his bedroom. Evidently he could hear John's footsteps in the hall, because he shouted through the closed door, "I want Mommy!"

"Mommy isn't here," John shouted back. "How about a bath and then some milk and cookies."

"Mommy give me a bath."

"Mommy isn't here." He could say it a million times. He could chant it like a mantra, recite it like liturgy. *Mommy isn't here.* Sooner or later Mike was going to realize it was true, she wasn't there, and he was stuck with Dad for better or worse, for baths and cookies.

"Where Mommy go?"

"To Las Vegas." As if that was going to mean anything to Mike. "It's just you and me. Open the door."

Mike waited a long time before saying in a tremulous whimper, "I want cookies."

The hell with the bath. John would give him cookies. It was the least a boy needed when he had to confront the fact that Mommy was in Las Vegas and wasn't coming back. Cookies for two-year-old boys and beer for thirty-two-year-old boys.

"Okay," John called quietly through the door. "No bath. Just cookies."

Mike made him sweat it out for a few minutes. Then he opened the door. John could have opened it himself—he'd removed the lock a long time ago—but honoring a closed door was a way of showing his respect for Mike. Maybe in time Mike might show some respect for him, too.

Tearful and wary, Mike slid his tiny hand into John's and accompanied him down the hall to the kitchen. He kept his gaze on the burgundy carpet—not the shade John would have chosen, but Sherry had decorated the house according to her tastes. In the kitchen, John switched on the light and lifted Mike into his booster seat at the table. "Cookies," Mike said. It sounded like a warning.

"Chocolate chip or sandwich creams?"

"Choco-chip."

John pulled the bag of chocolate chip cookies from a cabinet and counted out three. He filled a toddler cup with milk, snapped on the lid and set it before Mike. Given the kid's mood, if John had asked him whether he wanted milk, he would have said no. Being two meant saying no a lot.

While Mike glowered at John and ate his snack, John pulled a cold bottle of beer from the fridge. On the tile counter next to the fridge lay a cream-colored business envelope containing the letter from Sherry's lawyer. John had read it twice, then refolded it along its creases and tucked it inside. He wished he could seal it and mail it back to the lawyer. But that wouldn't change anything.

And really, he didn't want Sherry in his life, not at this point. It was too late. Too much damage had been done.

"How are the cookies?" he asked, wrenching the cap off the bottle.

"Okay." Mike couldn't sulk when he was eating cookies. It was physically impossible. He looked as if he were trying to pout, but each nibble forced his mouth into a smile. Above him, the Tiffany-style lamp—another of Sherry's decorating choices—sent a cone of amber light down onto the table, teasing reddish highlights out of Mike's brown hair. A year ago, his hair had been a honey-colored reflection of Sherry's blond tresses, but it was growing progressively darker. In another few years it might be as black as John's.

He took a sip of beer. The sour bubbles nipped at his tongue. Behind him on the counter, the lawyer's letter nipped at his conscience.

He waited until Mike had devoured his second cookie before saying, "Michael, I know this is going to make you sad, but Mommy isn't coming back."

Mike fixed his round brown eyes accusingly on John. His eyes were already as dark as John's, and his jaw already hinted at the angularity of his father's. In time, once the baby fat melted from his face, he would have the unmistakable face of his father. All traces of Sherry would be gone.

"She had to go off and do other things," John explained delicately. "I told you about this when she left. Remember?"

Mike began to pout.

"I got a letter today that says she's not coming back. I'm sorry, Mike. I don't know how else to tell you."

"Mommy coming back?"

"No."

"How come?"

"She..." *She was having an affair, remember? She found a man who could give her what I couldn't, and she fell in love and they ran away. Remember, Mike? Remember that day I came home from work and found a note on the door saying Mommy took you to Norma's and then ran away with that guy—the stud from the auto-body shop.*

Maybe it was just as well if Mike didn't remember. John would remember for both of them.

"She decided she needed a different kind of life," he told Mike.

"When she coming back?"

"She isn't." John heard his voice crack. He wasn't feeling any grief for himself. Just for Mike. Just for this little boy who couldn't believe his mother was gone.

Mike sucked on a cookie. A chocolate chip smeared the corner of his mouth. He chewed, swallowed and said, "I get a new mommy?"

"I don't know about that." Hell, he didn't even know where Mike was going to get a new baby-sitter. "For the time being, it's you and me. Just Daddy."

"You're police," Mike stated.

John nodded.

"I got a police. I need a mommy."

Well, that sure summed it up. John shrugged and took another drink. "I don't know. We'll see."

"I need a mommy and a plane."

"You have a plane," John reminded him. "It's in the den." Upside down in the middle of a toddler-size crash site.

"I need 'nuther one. Two planes. Norma can be my mommy."

"Norma—" Oh, God, he couldn't do it. He couldn't tell Mike that Norma was going away, too. "Norma's taking a vacation."

"What's that?"

"That means she's leaving Connecticut for a little while. She'll be back, though."

"She go with Mommy?"

John had conducted less complicated interrogations with serial rapists. He didn't believe in lying to his son, but he didn't know how to phrase the truth in words Mike would understand. "Ladies go away sometimes," he finally said. "Some ladies come back and some don't. Maybe it's best not to get too attached to them." Cripes. John ought to keep his cynicism to himself. Mike was too young to start distrusting women.

Yet how could Mike keep from becoming pessimistic? His mother had left him. His mother had decided that John was never going to be what she needed in a man, so she'd found someone who was. And once she'd found that other man, no one—not even her own son—mattered anymore.

Well, Mike mattered to John. He had obviously been a lousy husband, and he wasn't going to win any awards as a father. But at least he was there, in the kitchen with milk and cookies, answering the world's toughest questions as best he could. If he were the sort who ran from his responsibilities and fears, he would never have survived police work, let alone earned **his** detective shield. He would never risk what cops risked every day. And he sure as hell would never have married Sherry after she'd told him she was pregnant.

He'd married her because he believed in taking care of what was his. He'd married her and given their son a name and a home, and now that she was gone, he would have to give Mike more, although for the life of him, he didn't know what to give or how to give it.

All he knew was that even if he gave Mike everything he had, it would never be enough.

"THERE YOU GO," Molly said, smoothing the adhesive strip over Keisha's elbow, where she'd knocked off a scab while jumping around in the foam pit. "How does that feel?"

Keisha sniffled and flexed her arm to test the bandage, which was bright red and adorned with stars. "Okay."

"Do you think it's going to heal the way it is? Or should I apply the super-secret-magic cure?"

Keisha's eyes, tearful just moments ago, glowed with excitement. "The super-secret cure!"

Grinning, Molly reached into the first-aid cabinet and pulled out a hollow plastic tube filled with pink water and glittery confetti. She kissed the tip of the wand, then touched the tip to Keisha's bandage. "Super-secret-magic!" she chanted. "Make Keisha's elbow better!"

Keisha erupted in giggles. "It feels better already!"

"Of course it does. The super-secret-magic treatment works very fast. Okay," she said, clamping her hands on the little girl's waist and swinging her down from the counter. "Go eat your lunch. And take it easy next time you're in the foam pit."

Keisha didn't stick around long enough to listen to Molly's lecture. She romped out of the back room at a gallop, leaving Molly to put away the first-aid supplies—and the super-secret-magic wand.

As she straightened out the back room, she hummed along with the Sugar Plum Fairy's dance from Tchaikovsky's *Nutcracker,* which wafted down the hall from the main room. Molly always had the teachers play music at lunchtime, sometimes classical, sometimes folk songs, sometimes jazz or Calypso rhythms, or even rock music, as long as the lyrics were clean. One of her professional journals recently published a report about the value of harmonious music to the intellectual growth of young children. Molly was thrilled to contribute to the intellectual growth of the students at the Children's Garden Preschool, but mostly she played the music at lunch because it kept the kids from throwing their food around.

Closing the cabinet, she turned—and flinched when she found the doorway filled with a tall, lanky man. She hadn't heard his approach, and his sudden appearance startled her. He wasn't one of the fathers who dropped their kids off or picked them up from the preschool. Nor was he the mailman. Molly had never seen this man before.

If she had, she definitely would have remembered.

It wasn't that he was outrageously handsome— which he was. Molly just wasn't the sort of woman who went to pieces over a handsome man. It wasn't even his height, which might not have been all that tall; *everyone* seemed tall to Molly, who stood five-foot-three in her sneakered feet. He wasn't heavyset or muscular. His clothing—casually tailored khaki slacks, a gray wool blazer, a forest green shirt and a gray tie loosened at the collar—didn't shout wealth or high style. His hair was too long to look neat but too short to look pretentious, and his face was a stunning arrangement of stark lines and gaunt angles. His eyes were dark and deep-set, so piercing she practically felt stung by them. When he shifted one arm, his jacket gaped open enough for her to see that beneath it he was wearing a leather shoulder holster with a gun in it.

Her heart pounded double time. No stranger—especially one carrying a firearm—was supposed to get past the front desk. But Molly's assistant, Cara, often helped the teachers during lunchtime, and Molly had had to abandon the front desk to bandage Keisha's bleeding elbow. No one had been standing guard at the entry to prevent this man and his gun from invading the premises.

Swallowing, she squared her shoulders and stared straight into his eyes. "Can I help you?" she asked, her voice deceptively firm. Heaven knew, she didn't want to annoy an armed man. But she had to get him out of the building as quickly and quietly as possible.

"I'm looking for Molly Saunders."

"Let's go to the front desk," she suggested, risking a step toward him and trying to pretend she hadn't glimpsed that revolver under his jacket.

He stepped back, allowing her to pass through the door and lead him into to the reception area. From the main room came the high-pitched chatter of children and the familiar strains of the *Nutcracker's* "Waltz of the Flowers." Watching the stranger's face, Molly eased herself behind the L-shaped desk, though she didn't dare sit. At her right hand the computer monitor's screen saver showed fish in colorful outlines, blowing bubbles. At her left stood the telephone. If she could reach it, if she could dial the three-digit police emergency number before he drew his gun and pulled the trigger...

He remained on the opposite side of the desk, studying her. "Molly Saunders?" he repeated.

"I'm Molly Saunders."

He shifted his weight from one foot to the other. His jacket rearranged itself, draping over the gun so she could no longer see it. "I got your name from Allison Winslow," he said.

Her nerves subsided a degree. Allison was her best friend. She wouldn't give Molly's name to a murderer—at least not intentionally. "Do you know Allison?"

He shook his head. "I got her name from someone whose case I handled. James McCoy."

Molly's tension dropped another notch. Jamie McCoy, Allison's fiancé, had discovered an abandoned baby on his porch last June. If Molly wasn't mistaken, he'd contacted a private investigator to locate the child's mother. Private eyes carried guns, didn't they?

If this man was a private eye, his gun was understandable, even if it made her extremely uneasy. "What can I do for you, Mr....?"

"John Russo." She thought he was going to shake her hand, but he only stared at her with his disturbingly dark eyes. "I have a son."

She nodded, waiting for him to elaborate.

He seemed to give his words a great deal of thought before he spoke. "His baby-sitter had to leave town, and I'm..." His mouth twisted into a smile, or maybe it was a grimace. "I'd like to enroll him here."

Molly caught herself before informing him that the Children's Garden was full to capacity, with a few names on the waiting list. Of course it wouldn't be fair to let him jump ahead of others on the list, but he looked desperate. A desperate man with a gun had to be taken seriously.

"How old is your son, Mr. Russo?"

"Two."

"And his mother—?"

"Not in the picture," he said laconically. Something hardened in his eyes.

All right. A single father of a two-year-old, with a gun and without a baby-sitter, an acquaintance of her best friend's fiancé... She really shouldn't let him skip ahead of the others on the waiting list, especially since the Young Toddlers class was already full. And yet those eyes...

"I'm sure you must have some questions about the Children's Garden—how our program works, how we pick our faculty—"

He shook his head. "No questions. Can you take Mike?"

"Don't you even want to tour the facilities?" She knew that if he did, it would only confirm that he was right in wanting his son to attend her preschool. The Children's Garden operated out of bright, clean rooms, abundant with wholesome stimuli and learning activities, arranged with play spaces where children could burn off energy, an outdoor playground and bathrooms equipped with everything from changing tables to toilets for the older children. The head faculty all had college degrees, and the adult-to-child ratio was much better than the state's licensing board required. Molly believed, without undue modesty, that her preschool was the best in Arlington.

Either John Russo knew the school's reputation or he didn't care. "Can you take him?"

"Do you want to know about our fee schedule?"

"I can afford it," he said. "Can you take him?"

She *really* shouldn't be so willing to ignore the waiting list, at least not without meeting the child, observing him in action, getting a sense of how he would fit in with the other children in the Young Toddler class. "When did you want to have him start?"

"Monday."

Monday? Today was Friday! "Usually, Mr. Russo, we like to have a child come in and get a feel for the school. Our program is an excellent one, but it's not appropriate for every child."

"He'll do okay." A muscle fluttered in Russo's jaw, the only sign that he wasn't in complete control of himself. He held his long, lean body very still. If she hadn't glimpsed his gun, she would never guess that he was armed.

"I'll tell you what," she said, refusing to consider too deeply why she was willing to accommodate this man. "On Saturday mornings I run a special program for fathers and their children. I call it the Daddy School."

"That's what your friend does," he said. "Allison Winslow."

"That's right. She teaches classes for fathers-to-be and fathers of newborns. Once the children get older, their fathers have different needs, so she graduates them on to me." Molly smiled. Russo didn't smile back. "Anyway, I open the Children's Garden from ten to twelve for fathers and their children to come in and play. My teachers and I observe, offer suggestions, answer questions. Sometimes I'll provide more formal instruction while another teacher takes the children off to play. Why don't you bring your son tomorrow so I can meet him?" And so she could see how such a reserved, self-protective man could possibly relate to a two-year-old boy whose mother was not in the picture. So she could develop an idea of what she was getting herself into by allowing Russo's son into her school. And so Russo himself could see if this was really what he wanted, what his son needed.

"Meanwhile," she continued when he didn't speak, "I'll give you a folder of information about the Children's Garden. Also, some forms you'll need to fill out—health forms, emergency forms, insurance and so on. And—" she pulled a prepared "Welcome to the Garden" folder from a drawer in the file cabinet behind her "—a list of our tuition costs for the half-day and full-day program."

He barely glanced at the fee schedule before sliding it back into the folder. "I'll be here tomorrow at ten," he promised, his dark eyes boring into her for a long, quiet moment before he turned.

She watched him stroll out of the reception area and through the front door. Moving around the desk, she approached the door and spied on him through the glass sidelight. His legs were absurdly long, his gait as graceful as a dancer's as he crossed the parking lot to a nondescript Ford. Seemingly impervious to the November cold, he yanked off his jacket and tossed it onto the passenger seat before climbing in.

Seeing the thick leather shoulder strap of his holster—seeing his gun—she shuddered and turned away.

Why on earth had she agreed to let his son attend her preschool?

His eyes, she acknowledged. The dark power of his eyes had made her say yes.

CHAPTER TWO

"I DON'T LIKE HARRY," Mike announced for the zillionth time.

The raw morning air nipped at John as he strapped Mike into his booster seat in the back of the car. "Forget about Harriet, okay? It was just for one day."

"I don't like Harry. I like Norma," Mike explained.

John clipped the seat belt into its lock. "That was yesterday," he said, straightening up and opening the driver's door. The sun was milky white and cold, reminding John that winter was only a few weeks away. He zipped up his leather jacket, then lifted the Children's Garden folder from the roof of the car, where he'd temporarily left it, and tossed it onto the passenger seat. Inside, along with a half-dozen forms he'd filled out delineating the state of Mike's health, his vaccination history, John's phone number at work, his cell phone number and the phone numbers of three other neighbors, none of whom were planning to fly off to San Jose in the foreseeable future, he'd enclosed a check covering one month's tuition as well as an enrollment fee, a supplies fee and an insurance fee.

Police work paid pretty well, thank God, and John didn't have much in the way of expenses. His check wasn't going to bounce, even though the number he'd had to write next to the dollar sign was a whole lot larger than he would have liked.

He closed Mike's door, then got in behind the wheel and started the engine. "No more Harry," he told Mike. "Except for emergencies. If everything works out today, you're going to go to school."

"What school?"

"A school for kids."

"They got cookies?"

"Probably," John fibbed. One of the brochures in the Children's Garden folder discussed nutrition, urging parents not to pack their children's lunch bags and boxes with sweets, and describing the healthful snacks—fruit, cheese, crackers and the like—the school provided. But maybe every now and then they'd splurge on cookies. If they knew anything about children, they'd recognize the value of cookies as a behavioral tool.

"Norma in the school?"

"No. There'll be other teachers there. A lady named Molly."

"Molly?"

"Molly Saunders." An image of the woman flashed across John's vision, nearly obliterating his view of the modest residential street through the windshield. *Molly Saunders.* Glossy brown hair, amber brown eyes…and the fullest, sweetest lips he'd ever seen on a woman.

He hadn't wanted to notice her lips. Or her eyes, wide-set and direct, or her hair, stick straight and blunt cut in a sassy shoulder-length style. Or her figure, a delicious array of curves proportioned just right for her petite frame. He hadn't wanted to notice that she was young and fresh and pretty. He didn't want to think of her as a woman.

She was a teacher. A preschool administrator. A

first-aid expert who had been applying a bandage strip
to a little girl's elbow. John had lurked just outside
the door to that small storage room and watched as
Molly spoke to the fretful child, consoling her as she
washed the trickle of blood from the girl's tiny scrape,
dabbed a no-sting ointment on the girl's skin, ruffled
her hair and regaled her with a story about a snowman
who lost his bowtie and wound up with a scarf instead.
And then Molly Saunders had touched a magic wand
to the girl's elbow.

Twenty-four hours after John had walked out of the
Balfours' bloodstained bedroom, he'd found himself
transfixed by a woman with a gentle voice and a magic
wand. He'd been thinking about that woman ever
since.

He didn't want to think about her. He just wanted
to know he could leave his son in a safe place while
he was at work. If Molly Saunders was part of that
safe place, so be it.

"I wanna cookie," Mike said.

At last he was off his I-don't-like-Harry kick, but if
the Children's Garden was really hard core about re-
fined-sugar treats, Mike was going to be as disappointed with this child care arrangement as he'd been
with Harriet Simka.

A dozen cars were parked in the lot outside the
square brick building on Dudley Road in a neighborhood that straddled the undefined boundary separating
urban from suburban Arlington. A few blocks north
placed a person in the downtown business district, but
the preschool building sat at a comfortable remove
from the city's hustle and bustle. Several leafless trees
bordered the small parking lot. Beyond the chain-link

fence that surrounded the rear yard, John could see a sprawling outdoor play area surrounded by dead grass.

Mike noticed the play area as soon as John let him out of his car seat. He raced over to the fence. "I go on the swing!" he yelled. "I go on the swing!"

John joined his son by the fence to check out the play area: besides the swing set there was an expanse of sand and a complicated wood-and-plastic jungle gym featuring slides, bridges, tunnels and a small raised platform that children could reach by climbing a rope ladder on one side or a sloping pile of tires on the other. It looked like something an imaginative kid could turn into a house or a fort or an airport under siege by two-year-old guerrillas.

He should have inspected the outside play area yesterday. He should have inspected the rest of the school, as well. But he'd only had an hour for lunch, and he'd wasted half of it visiting another preschool, where the kids had been wandering the halls aimlessly while the teachers huddled in a staff room puffing on cigarettes. John might not be an expert when it came to preschools, but he knew he'd rather quit his job and stay home with Mike, collecting welfare if he had to, than send him to that dive.

He took Mike's hand and pulled him away from the fence, ignoring his top-volume protests about wanting to go on the swings. Around the building, they entered through the front door. Warmth enveloped him, and he loosened his hold on Mike, who seemed to have forgotten the swings the instant he noticed the equally exciting enticements inside. Without waiting for permission, he charged down the entry hall, passing open cubbies labeled with children's names printed on construction paper teddy bears. John chased him, then stumbled to a halt when he reached the room at the end.

It was large and so glaringly lit he had to blink. Waist-high dividers broke the room into smaller areas, each gated and bearing a sign: Young Toddlers, Older Toddlers, Pre-K and Tiny Tots. John knew the school must serve a reasonable number of children, yet everything was incredibly clean and neat—the art supplies, the bookshelves, the fabric-covered mats rolled into cylinders and stacked against the partitions, the construction blocks sorted into bins, the dolls seated in tidy rows.

John's house hadn't been this orderly since the day Mike was born.

What was even more startling than the neatness was that the room was empty. Noises filtered down through the ceiling, though—voices, thumps and laughter. Evidently all the action was on the second floor.

Before John could locate the stairs, a door at the rear swung open and Molly emerged, carrying a tray laden with bottles of apple juice, paper cups and a box of whole-wheat crackers. Seeing John and Mike, she smiled.

God, what a mouth. Her lips were a natural coral shade, full and wide, designed for smiling. Or kissing.

"Oh, good," she said. "You came."

Oh, good. He'd come. As if there had ever been any question that he would.

"Now I can lock the door. We're all upstairs, and it's so noisy I wasn't sure I'd hear the buzzer if you rang. So I took a chance and left the door open. Let me go lock up."

As she drew near, John lifted the tray from her

hands. It was heavier than he'd expected. Her smile intensified once he divested her of her burden.

Mike trailed her down the hall. "You have cookies?" he asked hopefully.

"Crackers," Molly told him. "I'm Molly. Who are you?"

"Michael Russo. I wanna cookie."

They vanished into the hall, leaving John holding the tray. Would Molly condemn him as a bad father because his kid was hooked on cookies? Well, hell, he'd never claimed to be the perfect father. Cookies had gotten him through a lot of tough times with his son.

The cookie addict and Molly reappeared from the hallway. Mike pranced ahead of her, apparently energized by the room. "I don't like Harry," he announced. "Daddy says I can come here and no more Harry."

Still smiling, Molly glanced questioningly at John. She made no move to retake the tray, which was a good thing, because if she had, he would have insisted on carrying it for her, and nowadays some women considered a display of chivalry sexist. As a cop, John had learned to be sensitive about the fact that some people were touchy, taking offense when none was intended.

"Harry?" she asked.

Her eyes were as spectacular as her mouth. They were brown, but they looked as if someone had sprinkled gold dust into them. They sparkled like her magic first-aid wand.

"Harriet," he explained. "A baby-sitter. He didn't like her." Molly smelled of baby powder and something else, something spicy. Ginger, maybe.

"Well, let's see how he does here. Would you like to come upstairs, Michael?" she asked, abandoning John and the tray and snagging Mike before he figured out how to unlatch the Pre-K gate. "There are other children upstairs, and lots of toys to play with."

When she turned her back to John, taking Mike's hand and escorting him to a rear alcove, the room seemed to grow dimmer. John followed her as if she were the only source of light in the world. She bypassed a door opening into the backyard and headed up a flight of stairs. The sounds of children at play drifted down from above.

Mike scampered up the steps ahead of Molly. When he got to the top, he let out a whoop and vanished into the room. John could understand why as soon as he reached the top of the stairway. The second-floor room was as well lit and colorful as the first-floor room, but it lacked walls, dividers and gates. It was wide-open and beckoning.

One corner held a play kitchen, another a collection of plastic blocks as large as the children who scampered around the room. There were also cartons of dress-up clothing, a sand table, a collection of simple musical instruments, a fleet of wheeled toy vehicles. At the opposite end of the room was an enclosed pen, maybe twelve feet square, filled with what appeared to be foam rubber balls and scraps. Several children were in the enclosure, jumping up and down and throwing the balls at one another. Standing to one side, a young woman—a teacher, John surmised—kept an eye on the children in the pen.

Mike didn't give a second look to the cars and trucks, the dress-up corner or the sand table. He raced directly to the enclosure and wiggled between the ropes that fenced it. In no time he was giggling, leaping and flopping among the balls.

"I guess he feels at home here," John murmured.

For the first time since Molly had entered the room downstairs, her smile faltered. "Here, let me take this," she said, reaching for the tray.

He shook his head. "Just show me where to put it."

She gestured toward a side table out of the way of the flow of activity, and he lowered the tray next to another tray holding a stack of paper napkins and plates filled with cubes of cheese. "We'll have a chance to talk later," she promised. "Right now, I've got a class to run."

He surveyed the room, this time observing not just the toys and his son but the other people present: at least six adult men, dressed casually and trying to find a way to fit into the bedlam. A couple of fathers hovered anxiously over their frolicking offspring. One had taken a shovel and was attempting to lure his kid toward the sand table. Yet another was on the floor, pushing a toy fire engine, ignoring all the children.

It didn't look like a class to John. More like a free-for-all, the kids pulling one way and the fathers the other.

He stationed himself near the snack table, watching as Molly ventured into the fray. He expected her to call the group to order, maybe have the men sit in some sort of formation from which they would be able to hear her as she lectured on a topic. But there was no order, no formation. She simply walked over to the man and child at the sand table and started talking to them.

When it came to observing, John was a pro. He remained where he was, mentally recording everything he saw as if he were searching a crime scene for evidence. He couldn't hear Molly's voice above the din, but he watched as she nodded toward the father, then bent down to confer with the child, getting on her knees and urging the father to get on his so he would be at the child's eye level. Molly said something to the father, who said something to the child, and they began to collaborate on the construction of a sand castle.

Molly rose to her feet and moved on.

John frowned. That was it? A little father-child matchmaking? He'd heard about the Daddy School from James McCoy, the syndicated humor columnist who'd wound up at John's desk last summer when he'd been trying to track down the woman who'd abandoned a baby on his porch. McCoy had mentioned then that he was taking a Daddy School class from a nurse—Allison Winslow, the woman who'd put John in touch with Molly. From what John had gathered about the nurse's class, it had been a more structured program, with students meeting weekly to discuss issues in child rearing.

Evidently, Molly Saunders had a very different idea of what a Daddy School should be. She ambled over to the father playing with the fire engine, sat on the floor and engaged him in such a serious chat that he tossed aside the fire truck and gave her his full attention. John noted their body language—the father gesticulating with his hands, frowning, shaking his head, and Molly leaning toward him, speaking softly, patting his shoulder.

Some class.

At least Mike seemed to be having a blast. John sauntered across the room to the ball-filled pen. The young woman overseeing the children sent him a smile.

"Is it safe?" he asked, motioning toward the penned-in area with his head.

"The foam pit? Sure." She turned her gaze to the scrambling children. "They love it in there. Is your boy going to be attending the Children's Garden or are you just here for the Daddy School?"

John wasn't sure if Mike would be attending the preschool, but he certainly wasn't here for the Daddy School. "I'm hoping he'll be a student here."

The woman extended her right hand. "I'm Shannon Hull," she said. "I teach the Pre-K class. What's your boy's name?"

"Michael Russo," John told her.

"He's, what? About two years old?"

John nodded.

"That would put him in the Young Toddlers group. His teacher will be Amy." Shannon watched the children in the pen for a minute. "Your son is a bit aggressive, isn't he."

John studied Mike's behavior in the foam pit. Mike repeatedly stood up and hurled himself down onto the soft balls, shrieking and making exploding noises as he hit. He wasn't aiming his body at any of the other children, though. He wasn't even throwing the balls at anyone. "No," John said quietly. "He isn't."

"Watch the way he moves," Shannon suggested, following Mike with her gaze. Mike struggled to his feet, then let out a roar and catapulted himself back into the balls. "He isn't aggressive in the sense of wanting to hurt anyone. But the way he flings himself around, the way he just pushes himself through space... He's letting off a lot of steam."

John shrugged. Why shouldn't Mike be letting off steam?

"That's one of the things we use the foam pit for. The kids think it's just for fun—which it is. But when a kid has a lot of tension inside him, we'll bring him to the foam pit and let him work it out. This is a safe place to vent physically without hurting yourself."

"You think Mike is tense?"

"Just watching him, I'd say there's a lot of stress inside that little boy. A lot of anger. Feel free to correct me if I'm wrong," she added with a knowing smile.

John ground his teeth together to prevent himself from telling her that she had a hell of a nerve critiquing his son's emotional state. Two-bit psychology wasn't what he wanted out of a preschool. All he wanted was for Mike to be safe and under supervision while John was at work.

If he weren't desperate for child care, he'd haul Mike out of the pit right now. He'd be damned if he was going to leave his son to the mercies of some twenty-three-year-old Freud wanna-be who was going to take the kid's psychic temperature and report on Mike's anger level.

She'd invited John to correct her, but he didn't. Slowly, gradually, as his rage over her instant diagnosis waned, he forced himself to admit that she might have a point. Of course Mike had a lot of anger, of course he was aggressive. What little kid wouldn't need to let off steam after having gone through what Mike had gone through in the past few days, the past few months?

Rattled by the teacher's perceptiveness, he turned and stalked away. He felt her eyes on him for a moment, but by the time he reached the center of the bustling room, he heard her addressing the children in the pit. He reined in what was left of his temper. The teacher had just been showing off, that was all.

Before he could make it back to the snack table, Molly emerged from a group of fathers and children in the music area. With the deftness of a cop seizing a suspect, she curled her fingers around his forearm and eased him toward the play kitchen. "Let's talk," she murmured.

He caught a whiff of her ginger scent again. The top of her head barely reached his shoulder, and as he gazed down he saw the silky thickness of her hair, the tip of her nose, the gentle swell of her bosom in a cream-colored sweater. Her hand arched around his forearm, warming him right through the lined leather of his jacket, the flannel of his shirt.

It wasn't appropriate for him to feel that kind of warmth from a teacher, a woman to whom he was entrusting his son. Frankly, John didn't want to feel any kind of warmth from any women right now. Women would only complicate his life and consume his dwindling reserves of trust. He didn't need that.

As soon as they reached the kitchen Molly released him. He flexed his hand as if restoring sensation to his arm and took a safe step back from her. He knew he'd have to spend the next few minutes with her if he wanted her to accept Mike into her school. Ordering himself not to think of her scent or her full, soft lips, he surveyed the miniature kitchen in search of a place to sit.

Molly fit reasonably well on one of the pint-size chairs. She gestured for him to sit on one, too, but there was no way he could do that without breaking it, or dislocating half his joints, or both.

"Sit on the table," she suggested. "It can hold your weight."

Nodding, he lowered himself onto the sturdy kitchen table, the surface of which was as high off the ground as a regular chair's seat would have been. He had no place for his legs, which bent sharply at the knees as he tried to squeeze them into the narrow space between the table and Molly's chair.

She peered up at him, her gaze unflinching. "I'd like Michael to attend this school," she said. "I think he could really benefit from our program."

He was so relieved, he forgot all about Shannon's freeze-dried evaluation of his son's personality. "Thank you."

"But..." A hint of a smile traced Molly's lips and vanished. "I confess to being a little worried about him."

"Why?"

"Well, for one thing—" her lips thinned and her chin rose defiantly "—his father brought a gun into a preschool filled with children. That makes me very leery."

John took a deep breath and returned her steady stare. If she was going to judge Mike because his father carried a gun, he'd skip this school. He'd make other plans. He'd beg Harriet Simka to take Mike on and he'd beg Mike to accept Harriet. Because, damn it—

"In order for us to work successfully with a child, we need to know what's going on in that child's life. It's not that I want to know your personal business, Mr. Russo. But as it is, we'd be pushing our enrollment limits to let Michael in. I'd really like to help you out—and to help him, too. I think he'd be very happy here. But...your gun makes me nervous."

She had guts, he'd give her that. She knew her mind and she knew her school. "I know gun safety."

"Gun safety doesn't include bringing a pistol into a preschool, Mr. Russo. Guns are weapons. They're deadly."

"I know exactly how deadly guns are."

"Do you?"

"I'm a cop."

Her brow creased in a frown. "If you're a—a police officer, you ought to know better than to bring a gun into a day care facility."

"I was on my lunch break yesterday," he told her. "I had an hour to check out day care options. I kept the gun holstered and hidden. It's not like I took it into your classrooms for show-and-tell."

"Thank heavens for that," she muttered, a hint of her smile returning.

"Mike doesn't touch my gun. I'm not even sure he's ever seen it. It's kept unloaded and locked up when I'm home."

She held his gaze for a moment, then glanced past him. He turned but saw nothing in particular going on where she was looking. When he turned back, she was studying her hands. They were small, not much bigger than a child's.

"I've seen what guns can do," he remarked. "I don't need a lecture."

"I'm sure." She seemed fascinated by her clear, shiny nail polish.

"You don't like cops," he guessed.

She glanced up again. Her eyes seemed to take up

half her face, and the thick dark lashes fringing them made them look even larger. "I never said that, Mr. Russo. And I'm sorry if you think I'm a busybody. But this is my school and I'm concerned about children's safety. And violence. And weapons."

"We have the same concerns," he told her. He didn't like civilians passing judgment as if they knew more about violence and weapons than cops did. When it came to children, she was the expert. But safety? That was his profession.

Her steady gaze was pleasantly neutral. "I suppose one concern we share is your son. To get his enrollment in place, I'll need to have the forms I gave you yesterday, plus a tuition payment."

"I left all that in the car." He twisted to view his son hurling himself around in the foam pit, then eyed her again. "So he's in?"

"Yes." She smiled reluctantly. "He's in."

John didn't return her smile. He knew how Mike was in: with an asterisk next to his name. With a question mark. With a note from teacher Shannon Hull mentioning his aggressive tendencies. With a red flag on his file because his father was a cop and carried a gun and couldn't possibly be a good father.

But John already knew that being a cop knocked him off the Ideal Family Man list. That was why Sherry had left—because John was too busy being a cop, saving the world, to notice that the most important part of his own world was falling apart. Because cops worked late and thought too much about the abundance of evil in the world, and because it was easier to lock up a service revolver than to lock up a career's worth of doubt and despair at the end of the day. Because sometimes a cop spent his shift mopping up after a murder-suicide, and by the time he was done with that, he didn't have the energy to fight with his kid over a bath.

The Children's Garden Preschool was free to blame John for all the mistakes he'd ever made, and all the others he had yet to make. But the school had better not blame Mike. He'd been through enough, and none of it was his fault, so Molly Saunders had better not take his father's sins out on him.

CHAPTER THREE

"HE'S A COP," Gail muttered. "I can't believe you bent the rules for a cop."

"I didn't bend the rules. I just..." Molly sighed and reached for her wineglass. "I decided I could squeeze his son into the Young Toddlers class. That's all."

"Ahead of the everyone else on the waiting list." Gail shook her head and clicked her tongue. "What do you think, Allison? Does that sound fair to you?"

Allison Winslow laughed. She and Molly had been friends forever, and Molly knew she was too smart to intervene in a squabble between the Saunders sisters, especially on Thanksgiving Day.

They were seated around the Shaker-style table in Allison and Jamie's dining room. The tablecloth was nearly invisible beneath an overwhelming array of food. Molly had eaten enough to feed the entire Arlington High School football team for a year—and as the smallest person at the party, or at least the smallest person able to digest solid foods, she suspected that all the others at the table had eaten even more. But the turkey platter held enough meat for another formal dinner, and the bowls of stuffing, yams and butternut squash were heaped high with leftovers.

"I don't want to talk about your nursery school," Allison announced, moving to the head of the table, where Jamie's five-month-old daughter, Samantha, was finger-painting with a glob of cranberry sauce on the tray of her high chair. Allison deftly wiped the tray and then Samantha's fingers with a couple of paper napkins. "I want to talk about my wedding."

"No! Not again!" Jamie, the male half of Allison's impending wedding, held his hands up in protest. "You promised we were only going to talk about it three times a day!"

"Today's a holiday, which means I can talk about it as much as I want," Allison said placidly. She unstrapped Samantha from the high chair and lifted her out. Samantha gave a squeal of delight and pawed at Allison's face. Once Allison and Jamie were married, Allison was planning to adopt his daughter. But it looked to Molly as if Samantha already considered Allison her mother.

"Today's Thanksgiving," Jamie complained. "Which means I can talk about football—"

A loud chorus of boos from everyone at the table—including Samantha—greeted his remark.

Allison resumed her seat, arranging the little girl on her lap and smiling at her fiancé. "We've already talked about football," she observed. "Remember? You said there was a game on TV at four o'clock, and I said we'd be sitting down to dinner at four-thirty so you'd have to miss the game. What more needs to be said?"

"Well, actually—" Jamie glanced at his watch "—I could catch the last quarter."

"Now, Jamie, if you really don't want any input into the final plans, that's your choice. I'm sure we women can come up with the details. Molly, remember that lime-green tuxedo with the matching ruffled shirt we saw at the mall? Don't you think Jamie would look great in lime green? He could even wear green dress loafers to match."

"Absolutely," Molly played along. "Although I also like that raspberry-pink tux with the red velvet collar—"

Jamie groaned good-naturedly. "Okay, okay" he surrendered. "I really didn't want to watch that game. There's a better match-up starting at seven thirty, anyway." He took a sip of wine and gazed around the dining room, pretending to be disgruntled. "There's nothing quite like being outnumbered by women, five to one. All that stuff we were giving thanks for—our health, the baby, being with friends—"

"Our wedding," Allison added with a grin.

"That, too. But I'll tell you, one thing I would have given a lot of thanks for is another guy at this table. I for one could have used a little more testosterone here tonight. You should have brought along your favorite man in blue," Jamie said to Molly.

She felt a flush of warmth in her cheeks—from the overabundance of food, she told herself. John Russo wasn't her man in blue, favorite or otherwise, and he never would be. He was, as Gail had pointed out, a cop. He was cold and shuttered, and much too tall. And besides, he had that gun. And those eyes that seemed just as deadly.

Across the table, she could see her sister bristling. "I still don't know why you took his son into the school," Gail muttered. "Why did you cut him such a break? Did he threaten you?"

"Of course not," Molly said. But she knew Gail didn't trust policemen, and with good reason. She knew what Gail had gone through, thanks to an officer of the law; Molly had been the one to put her back together afterward.

Gail might have honed herself into a tough-as-nails lawyer as a result of her experience—a lawyer who went up against the cops every chance she got. But she still saw cops as a threat. Whatever threat Molly might have sensed in Russo's lethal gaze, though, she'd also sensed that he needed her—or his son did. Observing the boy at the Children's Garden over the past few days had only validated her suspicions. Michael Russo was a bright, affectionate child. But he was troubled, with deep wells of sadness inside him.

"You know, Gail," Jamie interjected, "Detective Russo's a good guy. He was terrific when we were trying to find Samantha's birth mother." Jamie turned to study his daughter, who leaned contentedly against Allison's bosom and sucked her thumb. Last summer Jamie had found the baby on his back porch, strapped into a car seat with no clue as to her mother's whereabouts, only a note proclaiming that Jamie was the father. When, at Allison's urging, he'd gone to the police, John Russo had taken the case. Jamie had filled Molly in when she'd called him last week after accepting Russo's son into her school. Now Jamie defended Russo to Molly's sister. "He got the job done. He was smart, he was organized and he considered every possibility before he acted."

"Any cop could have found her birth mother. They've got computers and networks."

"Another cop might have scared Sam's mother into hiding—or into running off with Sam so I'd never get legal custody of her. Another cop might have scared me away, too," Jamie admitted. "Russo did everything right."

"Well, hooray for him." Gail pushed away from the table and lifted the turkey platter. "Bottom line—he's a cop. I hope Molly has the wisdom to watch her step around him."

"It's not as if I have much to do with him, anyway," Molly called to her sister's retreating back. She waited until the kitchen door swung shut behind Gail before exchanging a glance with Allison. Besides Molly, only Allison knew what Gail had been through years ago when a policeman had pulled her off the road over a broken taillight and come close to destroying her life. Gail and Molly had never even told their parents. It had been too awful—and by the time she'd regained her bearings, Gail had realized there was nothing she could do about it.

Except hate cops forever.

Molly sighed. One part of her—the loyal sister part—empathized with Gail's resentment. But another part—the devoted director of the Children's Garden Preschool part—wanted to reach out and help any child who could benefit from her program. She'd known, even before meeting Michael Russo, that he would benefit. She'd known just from spending a few minutes in the company of Michael's father.

The fact that she hadn't stopped picturing his eyes, his rangy body, his thick, black hair, his large hands and long, graceful legs...that had nothing to do with his son. The fact that she could lie awake at night and wonder about this man whose son's mother was "not in the picture," wonder about whether his mouth ever shaped a smile, whether his eyes ever grew soft with love, whether a woman other than Michael's mother *was* in the picture...

The fact that Molly's thoughts about a boy's father

were totally inappropriate had nothing to do with her desire to help that boy. Nothing at all.

JOHN COULDN'T COME UP with much to give thanks for.

Except for the usual stuff, and none of it trivial: his son's health, his own. His job, his income, his house. His family, even though Russos were scattered from New Hampshire to New Jersey. They'd all journeyed to his parents' home in Rhode Island for the holiday—sisters, brothers, in-laws and offspring. His mother ruled the house, ordering everyone around and basking in the clamor of voices, the revival of old arguments and the excess of love.

But late Thursday night, John had had to strap his bleary-eyed, hyper son into the car seat and depart for home, making the two-hour-plus drive back to Arlington because he'd pulled a Friday shift.

The preschool wasn't open Friday. John had managed to hire Harriet Simka for the day. Mike wasn't pleased, but John had no alternative.

He arrived at the precinct house with Mike's voice still pounding in his head: "I don't like Harry! No, no, no! I don't like her!" He felt guilty, but what could he do? Bring Mike with him to work?

He was tired—from the round-trip drive to his mother's house yesterday, from trying to settle Mike down to sleep, from trying to wake him up this morning. Tired from Mike's raucous protests regarding Harriet. Tired from having to juggle child care arrangements so much. Tired from having everything pressing down on him, every decision, every responsibility. Tired because the weight was all his, because he'd created that weight and couldn't—*wouldn't*—unload it.

So much for Thanksgiving.

"Russo?" Lieutenant Coffey called into the squad room from the doorway of his glass-enclosed office two seconds after John had hung his jacket over the back of his chair. Coffey had probably been spying on the squad room through the glass, waiting for him to arrive.

He crossed the room to Coffey's office. Coffey hovered near the door, a bespectacled man in a wrinkled suit, with a jowly chin and hawk-sharp eyes. "I've got a job for you," he said, gesturing toward one of the worn vinyl chairs that faced his desk.

He didn't close the office door behind John, which meant it wasn't going to be a sensitive case. The sensitive cases were usually more interesting, but John was a pro. It was his job to take whatever assignment his commanding officer stuck him with.

He took a seat and Coffey smiled faintly. Coffey wasn't exactly short, but when they stood side by side John towered over him, and he suspected the height discrepancy made his boss uncomfortable. Coffey liked people looking up to him, and John was kind enough to do that as Coffey circled his desk. Reaching his own swivel chair, he remained standing until the silence grew awkward, then sank into the chair, which squeaked at its joints.

"How was your holiday?" he asked.

"Fine." There was camaraderie, and there was camaraderie. John would take a bullet for any of the guys in his squad. But swapping small talk about family gatherings made him uncomfortable.

Coffey knew that, and he moved on to business.

"One of the branches of Connecticut Bank and Trust has a problem."

John frowned and shifted in his chair.

"A burglary through the ATM. Twice this past week, some unauthorized person managed to withdraw a total of five thousand dollars from a private account. Two thousand the first time, three the second."

"A bank robbery." John's frown deepened. He leaned forward, rested his forearms on his knees and tapped his fingers together. "Am I in trouble?"

"You?" Coffey's mild brown eyes widened and he laughed. "Of course not."

"Then what's going on? I don't do bank robberies."

Coffey's smile grew cagey. "Yes, you do."

Russo raced through his memory, trying to recall any cases he'd screwed up recently. He hadn't been given a diddly case like this since he'd earned his detective's shield two years ago. During those two years, he'd handled murders, assaults, domestic violence, a kidnapping—and James McCoy's baby. He'd worked backup on a couple of drug cases; he'd waded into gang situations. He'd saved a few lives.

An ATM scam? No way Coffey would assign him to such a Mickey Mouse case unless someone had him in his scopes for some reason. "Is IAD looking at me?"

"Have you done anything the internal affairs department needs to know about?" Coffey laughed again and shook his head. "I'm giving you this case because you need a break."

"What break?"

"You've had a run, Russo. The Balfour case last week—a heart-wrenching tragedy, am I right? Fol-

lowed by the gay-bashing incident this past Monday.
Two arrests Tuesday. A nice collar, by the way. You
did a good job, and the D.A. was real happy with how
you put it all together for him. But it's a lot to deal
with.''

Russo pressed his lips together. He had a hunch
where Coffey was going with this conversation, and
he didn't like it.

Coffey leaned back in his chair. Atop one of the
four-drawer file cabinets behind him stood a framed
photograph of his family—three fresh-scrubbed kids
and a wife. Atop one of the other four-drawer file cabinets stood a six-inch-tall porcelain Christmas tree.

''I know things are hinky at home for you,'' Coffey
continued. ''I got word from HR that your divorce
came through last week. They said you went in and
removed the ex from your health and life insurance
forms.''

John nodded. He kept his private life as private as
he could. But the day Sherry had made the end of their
marriage legal and permanent, John no longer wanted
her name on any of his policies. And while the human
resources department was supposed to maintain the
confidentiality of employee files, police work was intense enough that if a commanding officer called down
to HR for information on a cop, HR didn't hold back.

''You've got the kid—a motherless son—and the
holidays are coming up. You've got a lot of things
going on in your life right now, John.'' Coffey's voice
grew gentle. ''And you've dealt with two ugly cases
over the past week. I don't want to see one of my best
men crack, okay?''

''I'm not going to crack,'' John said quietly.

"I know you're not. You're going to investigate an ATM robbery."

John could have protested that he was as capable as anyone in the squad room—*more* capable than anyone—when it came to dealing with ugly cases. But why argue? He'd learned long ago not to let his ego get in the way of his work. If Coffey wanted him to investigate an ATM robbery, he would. Maybe a few days away from blood would put him in a holiday mood.

Sure.

"Do they have a surveillance camera on the ATM?" he asked.

"They've got everything. Videotapes, computer printouts, all the data on the transactions and a record of the time and date. The weird thing is, they don't have pictures of anyone doing anything when the phony withdrawals are being made. The camera shows a blank. Like someone is blocking the lens."

"Hard to do that without being conspicuous," said John.

"Okay, so you're dealing with a genius or a contortionist or both. Either it's an inside job or you've got some sort of computer freak who's figured out a way to outsmart the PIN system without starring in the bank's video. It's the C.B.T. branch on the corner of Dudley and Newcombe. Have a look around, see if you get any ideas. They're waiting for you with the tapes, the computer data and an army of bank tellers waiting to prove they're innocent. The manager's name is—" Coffey lifted a slip of notepaper and read from it "—Evelyn Fong. She's expecting you."

"Okay." John stood, deciding that if Coffey was going to stick him with a dull assignment like this—

regardless of Coffey's noble rationale—John didn't have to respect Coffey's hang-ups about his lack of height. He plucked the notepaper from Coffey's fingers and strode toward the door.

"John?" Once again Coffey jolted him by using his first name. He paused and turned back to his boss. "Go easy on yourself, huh?"

He pivoted and left the office, moving without pause to his desk to pick up his jacket and notepad. He would figure out this stupid ATM theft. He'd deal with Evelyn Fong and her bank and the thief who'd somehow disabled the surveillance camera. He knew how to solve crimes, with or without blood.

But go easy on himself?

That was one thing he didn't know how to do.

THE FIRST DAY of school after the Thanksgiving holiday was the first day of December, which meant Molly had to attend to a monthly flurry of paperwork. She sent vague smiles and nods at the children who trooped past her desk, most of them clinging to their mothers' hands, a few escorted by fathers dressed for work. They clomped through the entry and down the hall in their unwieldy rubber boots and thick-soled sneakers, hung up their coats and stashed their lunches in their cubbies, then raced the rest of the way down the hall to the first-floor classroom. Molly heard the giggles and squeals of children settling in for their morning activities. She smiled again as the parents retraced their steps down the hallway, pausing at her desk to drop off their December tuition checks.

"Cara?" she called to her administrative assistant, who was sorting through four days' worth of phone mail.

Cara pressed the pause button on the answering machine. "You want me to take the checks to the bank?" she asked, eyeing the bulky deposit envelope in Molly's hand.

"I'll do it today. You can hold down the fort, can't you?"

Cara rolled her eyes. "As if you had to ask."

If Molly had been in a less unsettled mood, she would have grinned at her young assistant's attitude. Cara was twenty-one, a recent graduate of the local community college. She was as sweet and pretty as spun-sugar candy, and the children adored her. What the children couldn't appreciate nearly as well as Molly was that behind her spun-sugar demeanor was a sharp, efficient mind.

Molly knew that when it came to finding a dependable assistant, sharp and efficient were more important than sweet. To operate a successful preschool, Molly had to be on top of everything, from health inspections to insurance to the latest theories on child development and education. She had to be a financial whiz, too. Setting a tuition the market would bear, paying her staff more than they'd earn elsewhere so they wouldn't quit the minute a more remunerative offer came along, maintaining the facility and meeting the bills... Molly had learned that a degree in Early Childhood Education wasn't enough to run a school like the Children's Garden. She'd had to go back to college at night to take courses in marketing and management.

Depositing the tuition checks was a simple enough chore, though. Ordinarily she was happy to let Cara drive the eight blocks to the local bank branch with the deposit envelope. But today Molly yearned for the exercise a brisk walk would provide. She was restless, anxious to clear her head.

She slipped into her down parka, pulled on her leather gloves and slung the strap of her purse over her shoulder. "I'll be back in a half hour," she promised.

"I think we might just survive without you," Cara said, waving her out the door.

The wintry sun was cold but bright, the stubbly grass crisp and pale with frost as she cut a diagonal path across the lawn to the sidewalk. The Children's Garden was situated in a mixed neighborhood, private homes side by side with small convenience stores, a café, a cottage with a neon hand glowing in the front window and a sign where the wrist should be: Readings, Predictions, Tarot. Madame Roussard, Licensed Palmist. Molly wondered how one went about getting such a license.

The house with the electric hand in the window was one of the few buildings that didn't have Christmas lights strung up along the eaves, a giant candy-cane placard taped to the door or a fat plastic Santa perched on the roof. The convenience stores, ecumenical in spirit, had electric menorahs standing in their windows, and foil-wrapped cardboard depictions of dreidels were displayed alongside foil-wrapped cardboard wreaths and fireplace stockings.

Molly tried to downplay the holidays at the school—not because she didn't absolutely love this time of year, but because the children received an overdose of holiday commercialism everywhere else they went. She allowed for class time to discuss different seasonal traditions, but the children didn't need religious symbols at the school. They got more than enough holiday cheer the instant they stepped outside.

Although there was no snow on the ground, the air was Christmas-cold. Molly needed that cold air to cleanse her mind after having spent every night of the four-day Thanksgiving weekend thinking about cops…about one cop in particular.

She hadn't seen him that morning. She must have had her nose buried under a pile of tuition slips and checks when John Russo brought his son in. Not until she heard Amy, the Young Toddlers head teacher, sing out, "Good morning, Michael!" did she realize he'd arrived, but when she glanced up and surveyed the hallway, Michael's father wasn't there.

Just as well, she tried to convince herself, ducking her head as an icy breeze slapped her cheeks. John Russo's child might be her concern, but Russo himself wasn't. She'd invited him to continue attending the Daddy School program, but he hadn't seemed terribly comfortable at the first one.

Of course, Michael hadn't been an official student at the time. But even so, his father had held back.

Molly had the feeling holding back was something John Russo did a lot of the time.

Damn! Why was she so obsessed with him? She'd volunteered to hike to the bank to remove him from her thoughts, not to waste even more energy thinking about him. She ought to use this time away from her desk to figure out what to buy Gail for Christmas, or Allison and Jamie. Samantha would be a cinch to shop for. She suspected Jamie would get his daughter something totally impractical—an electric train set, probably—and Allison would get the little girl something totally practical—clothing, teething toys, a walker.

Molly would get her a set of classic unpainted wooden blocks, and then she and Samantha would sprawl out on the floor and build a palace with them.

She would never buy wooden blocks for a child like Michael Russo, since he'd be likely to throw them. Hollow plastic blocks were all she would trust him with.

She wondered if children were more prone to aggressive behavior when their fathers carried guns.

She wondered what had happened to Michael's mother, whether she'd walked away or Russo had driven her away. She wondered how a woman could find the strength to walk away from her own son, and from a man like Russo.

She wondered why she was even wondering. Russo was the father of one of her students—and she swore to herself, as she'd sworn to her sister on Thanksgiving Day, that she'd made room in her school for one more child because of that child, not his father.

Another block brought her deeper into Arlington's business district. Convenience stores and palm-reading parlors gave way to more densely packed shops and offices. Across the street, at the corner in front of the bank branch, a fellow dressed up as Santa Claus stood by a kettle, ringing a bell and collecting donations for charity.

Molly dug in her purse for a dollar bill to toss into his kettle. Tucking her wallet back into her purse, she shook her head and grinned at the Santa impersonator. He was much too lanky to be a proper Saint Nick. With his back to her, he looked lost in the Santa suit, his shoulders broad but bony, his legs long and lean. If only the tunic top of his costume were a bit shorter, she'd have a nice view of his buns—and she bet that view *would* be nice.

He had his gaze fixed on the bank building—no doubt hoping that people emerging with hefty cash withdrawals from the automated teller machine would be moved to drop a few bills in his kettle. If he really wanted to raise some money, she thought, he ought to ring his bell with a bit more vigor. He moved his hand listlessly, causing the clapper to hit the brass with a muffled clank.

Some people just didn't know how to be Santas, she supposed.

Chuckling, she waited for the light to turn green, then stepped into the crosswalk. The charity Santa turned to observe the flow of traffic, and Molly stumbled to a halt in the middle of the street when she saw the face partially hidden beneath a woolly white wig and cottony puffs of fake beard. The artificial hair, the red stocking cap, the pillow-stuffed tunic...none of it detracted from the intensity of his dark, searing gaze.

Detective John Russo was Santa Claus. The most uncannily sexy Santa Claus Molly had ever seen.

CHAPTER FOUR

HE FELT LIKE an idiot in the Santa suit. It wouldn't have bothered him quite so much if he could have avoided being seen by anyone who knew him. But to have Molly Saunders, of all people, make him, right in the middle of the crosswalk at the intersection of Dudley and Newcombe...

Not good.

The synthetic fiber of his beard tickled his chin, and the fleecy weight of his wig and hat caused his scalp to sweat. The cushion he'd belted around his waist under his jacket made his motions clumsy and oafish. He'd been reluctant to wear the costume for his surveillance on the bank's ATM alcove, but he'd agreed to give it a try, consoled by the thought that even if it proved futile, he would end the day with something to show for his efforts: a kettle full of money donated by generous pedestrians. A sign above the kettle announced that the money was earmarked for Higgins House, a homeless shelter in town. It was one of the police department's favorite charities.

But John wasn't a fund-raiser. He was a detective on a case.

Apparently, that was the last thing anyone would take him for if Molly's eruption in giggles was anything to go by. With her cold-kissed cheeks and sparkling eyes, she looked more in tune with Christmas than he felt. Her smile seemed to convey the spirit of the season.

This ATM case wasn't coming together. He'd thought he could psyche it out in a day, but Friday evening, after reviewing branch manager Evelyn Fong's records and videos, all he'd accomplished was to figure out that someone was deliberately blocking the lens of the video camera before withdrawing cash from the machine. Someone incredibly tall, given that the camera hung from the ceiling in the bank vestibule. The tapes showed no one that tall entering or leaving the vestibule within an hour of either of the two withdrawals in question.

The woman from whose account the money had been withdrawn was of average height, and she swore her ATM card was stored safely in a dresser drawer in her bedroom whenever she wasn't using it. Her husband was on crutches after breaking his ankle in a basketball game, and since it was a joint savings account, he wouldn't be likely to steal money from it—although John hadn't completely ruled out the possibility. But it would be difficult for him to disguise his crutches on the video.

Their fifteen-year-old son had an after-school baby-sitting job. Both times money had been taken from the account he'd been baby-sitting for his neighbor, who had confirmed his alibi.

The bank's insurance would cover the woman's loss, but a crime had been committed. John figured he had nothing to lose by giving this Santa gig a shot—especially since Lieutenant Coffey seemed to have no intention of assigning him to anything more substantial.

So there he was, dressed in red flannel and ringing

a damned bell while the director of his son's preschool stood in the middle of Dudley Street convulsed in laughter.

She managed to finish crossing the street before the light changed and arrived at his corner, her gaze never swerving from him, her smile never waning. "Well, now, Mr. Russo," she greeted him. "It says on Michael's registration form that you're a police officer. We'll have to correct that information, won't we."

He expected to feel indignant. He'd already had to put up with some ribbing from Mahoney and Jesper, his backups, who'd cruised past him in a patrol car ten minutes ago. He'd endured a double take from Tom Bland, a P.I. who'd stopped by the squad room just as John had been leaving; Tom had asked John to leave a new laser-jet printer under his tree. But Molly's smile wasn't mocking. She seemed almost relieved that he was masquerading as Santa. He wondered how she would feel if he told her he had a gun tucked into the elastic waistband of his baggy red trousers.

"Mike doesn't know," he said. Mike was still young enough to believe that policemen helped pedestrians across the street and assisted drivers when their cars broke down, and maybe, on rare occasions, arrested bad guys. He didn't know that policemen sometimes had to do nasty, brutal things—like pretending to be Santa to solve a bank theft.

"What are you doing?" Molly asked, peering up at him. Even in the cold, with her body hidden inside a thick down parka, he could smell her gingery fragrance. Her ears were turning red. He wanted to cover them with his hands to warm them.

He reminded himself again that she was the director

of his son's preschool. "I'm on a case," he said succinctly.

"So this pot for collections…?"

"That's legitimate."

"The money's going to—" she angled her head to read the sign "—Higgins House?"

"It's a homeless shelter."

"I know." She dropped a dollar bill into the kettle. "Is this your case, then?" she asked, sounding a little funny when she said *case,* as if the word was alien to her. "To collect money for the homeless?"

A woman in a bulky fur coat entered the ATM vestibule, and John scrutinized her without losing track of Molly. He could have told her he was working and couldn't let her distract him with conversation, but he didn't want her to leave him. Now that he was reasonably sure his costume hadn't done his image too much harm in her eyes, he didn't mind having her around.

Didn't mind? Hell. He *liked* having her around. A lot.

"The police support Higgins House. We'd rather see street people someplace safe and warm at night, especially at this time of year. But for now, the charity is just a cover."

"A cover?"

He was able to turn back to Molly once the lady in the fur coat entered the bank proper. Molly's eyes were round with fascination. He was momentarily dazzled by the flecks of gold in them, like tiny dots of summer sunshine warming the December morning. "There have been a couple of ATM robberies," he explained.

"At this bank?" She gaped at the building. He

didn't think her eyes could grow any rounder, but they did. "The Children's Garden has all its accounts here!"

"Don't worry about it."

"But I was about to deposit the tuition checks in the ATM machine."

"Go ahead. Nothing's going to happen. I'm right here."

"But you said—a theft—"

"No violence. Someone's just withdrawing money illegally. Don't worry."

She eyed the bank warily, then pivoted back to him. "Well, I guess—"

"Hang on a second." A familiar choreography down the street caught his eye. An elderly man, a young man bumping into him and stopping to apologize, another young man coming up behind him. John had seen the moves before. He knew immediately what was going down.

He touched Molly's arm, maybe to keep her from speaking, maybe to reassure her...maybe just because she was close to him and he was about to abandon her and he didn't want her to think she'd done anything wrong. He handed her his bell and strode past her down the sidewalk, his gaze riveted on the second young man. As he closed the distance between himself and the punk, he accelerated his gait, not quite running but walking faster, until with a sudden burst of speed he lunged at the kid, slinging his arm around his shoulder and hurling him against the wall of the nearest building. "Where's the wallet?" he asked quietly.

"What are you talking about?" the young man protested.

Pinning the kid's arm behind his back and immobilizing him against the wall, John reached under the padded bulk of the Santa coat for his shield. "Police," he said, flashing the leather folder in front of the kid's nose. "Where's the wallet?"

"You don't got any right—"

John almost didn't hear the light tap of a wallet hitting the pavement by his feet. He wedged his toe under it and kicked it straight up, snatching it from the air with his free hand. Flipping it open, he read from the driver's license inserted into one of the plastic sleeves. "You dropped this," he said.

"I don't know where that came from!"

"It says you're sixty-eight years old," John continued, flipping the wallet open with his thumb. "And this photo—it's amazing. Somehow, the motor vehicle bureau put that gentleman's face on your license." He angled his head toward the older gentleman, who stood watching John and the punk in bewilderment. "This kid picked your pocket, Mr. Rosenblatt," John told him, reading his name off the driver's license in the wallet.

"Oh, my God!" Mr. Rosenblatt shook his head and pressed a hand to his chest in dismay. "Thank you! I don't know, I'm Jewish, but I think I'll have to convert. To think Santa Claus saved me from a pickpocket…"

John smiled faintly. Mahoney and Jesper ought to be in the vicinity—they were supposed to patrol the neighborhood all morning while John was undercover. Sure enough, he spotted their squad car down the block, cruising slowly toward him.

He waved them over, then shoved the pickpocket into the back seat of the cruiser. "His partner ran," he told the patrolmen after explaining the situation.

"But maybe if you torture him, he'll give his buddy up. Mirandize him first."

"Got it," Jesper said, winking. "First we read him his rights and then we torture him. Sounds like a plan."

John left Mr. Rosenblatt to give a statement to Jesper and Mahoney. After adjusting the plump cushion of his artificial belly beneath his bright red overcoat, he sauntered back to the corner of Newcombe, where Molly stood gawking at him.

Nearing Molly, he noticed that the color had drained from her cheeks, leaving them as pale as the winter sky. "Are you all right?" she asked in a whisper-thin voice.

"Sure."

"And that man?"

"Which one?"

"Both."

He grinned. "The perp is fine. The victim decided he believes in Santa."

She swallowed and lowered her gaze to the pavement. "I guess it's all in a day's work to you. But...it frightened me."

He shrugged, not sure what to say. Telling her not to be frightened wouldn't necessarily reassure her. Besides, some of the stuff he did *was* scary. A cop never knew until after the dust settled whether a situation had merited fear. While something was going down a cop simply couldn't permit fear to get anywhere close to him.

He took the bell from her and she shrank back a step, still pale, still staring. "Do things like that happen often?"

"Pickpocketing? Sure."

"No, I mean—chasing people down and throwing them around and having to deal with...with that kind of thing."

He wished he could put her mind at ease, but lying didn't work for him. "Things like that happen a lot," he said, gesturing behind him at the place where the incident had occurred. "As a detective, I don't usually have to deal with it. I'm usually not impersonating Santa on a downtown corner."

"I guess it was a good thing you were today," she said. "I'm sure that older man is very happy about it. But..."

He waited for her to go on. Her hair was so straight and soft that when she moved her head it slid back and forth like a silk fringe. She bit her lip and glanced up at him once more.

"But?" he prodded.

"I'd hate to think of how frightening your work must seem to Michael."

He remained silent, wondering if she was going to find a connection between his handling of the street punk and Mike's alleged aggression. These preschool teachers with their child-psychology backgrounds... They could probably make all sorts of connections, blame him for everything they thought was wrong with Mike. And maybe they'd be right.

"I should think," she went on, "that most children would be terribly disillusioned to find out that Santa was really just a cop in disguise."

"Just as disillusioned as if they found out Santa was their father," he observed, still braced for criticism.

"Does Michael know what you do?"

"He knows I'm a cop. I don't go into details."

She nodded. "I don't advocate dishonesty between

parents and children. It's just…he strikes me as emotionally fragile. I don't know what's going on with him, Mr. Russo—and it's none of my business. But I have the feeling it wouldn't take much to make him snap.''

Defensiveness rose inside John. He resisted it, forcing himself to consider what she was saying without letting his ego get in the way. The fact was, Mike *was* fragile. John ought to be pleased that his son's teacher had noticed.

He hated discussing his private life, but if it enabled Molly and her staff to help Mike, he ought to fill her in. ''Mike's mother walked out,'' he said, watching Molly closely, measuring her reaction, calculating the nuances of her expression. If he saw pity in her face, he'd pull Mike out of the school. He wouldn't want to have his son educated by a woman who pitied him. ''She left six months ago. It's been hard on him.''

''You're divorced?''

''Yes.''

''I see.'' No pity. Actually, the glimmer in her eyes might have been comprehension. ''Thank you for telling me. There are some other students at the school from broken families. It helps the staff to know these things.'' A faint smile crossed her lips. ''Well. I guess I'd better do what I came downtown to do. Back at the school, they're probably wondering what's taking me so long.''

He nodded and turned his gaze to the bank. The ATM sat idle, the vestibule empty.

She pulled a deposit envelope from her purse and started toward the bank. Once she reached the door, she twisted to look back at him. ''Be careful, John, okay? Don't let anything happen to you.''

Before he could reply, she was inside. He took a moment to digest her words, her concern. He could have told her that being careful was what he did best, and that if it was in his power, he wouldn't let anything happen to him. But he was too…what? Surprised? Flattered?

Touched. Touched that she'd called him John, touched that she was going to treat him as if he were someone whose well-being mattered to her. Someone she didn't want anything happening to.

It had been a long time since a woman had cared that way about him. A long, long time. He'd almost forgotten how nice it felt.

"MICHAEL NEEDS a time-out," Amy announced, nudging the sulking little boy into the front room.

Molly rose from her chair behind the desk and scrutinized the child. His hair was mussed, his lower lip curled in a profound pout. Tears had left glistening streaks on his skin. He glowered at her as if daring her—although what he was daring her to do, she couldn't guess.

Despite their dampness, his eyes were his father's, dark and defiant, seeing too much and revealing too little. Molly had spent the better part of the morning thinking about Michael's father's eyes, his low voice, his tentative smile. His steel-hard control. The utter incongruity of a man like him playing Santa, and the equal incongruity of Santa chasing down a pickpocket. The danger he'd put himself in. The way he'd referred to his divorce only in terms of his son's well-being, not his own.

"He and Dana both wanted to play with the same toy airplane," Amy reported. "Michael resorted to pushing and shoving. He grabbed the plane and swung at Dana with it. He missed, but..."

Molly gave Michael her sternest frown. "Is that true, Michael? You tried to hit Dana with the plane?"

Michael's lower lip protruded even farther, but he wouldn't apologize. "My plane," he said in a wobbly voice. "I play with the plane."

"School toys have to be shared," Molly reminded him. "And you aren't allowed to hit other children. You know that rule, Michael. Hitting isn't allowed."

"I play with the plane," he repeated. "I had it first."

"Go sit in the chair," Molly ordered him in a firm but gentle voice. The chair she'd pointed to was an adult-size piece of furniture, upholstered in a tweed fabric to match her desk chair and positioned in the corner of the entry, within sight of the desk. Sometimes children had to be removed from the activity of the main room to compose themselves, to calm down and chill out. In this case, Molly hoped that a few minutes by himself in the chair would give Michael a chance to reflect on what he'd done wrong.

She watched as Michael plodded to the chair and climbed up into it. With a nod to Amy, who departed from the office, she settled herself back at her desk. She pretended to work, reviewing accounts in the computer. But the sorry truth was, she'd been pretending rather than working ever since she'd returned to the school from her bank errand. All morning and well into the afternoon, she'd been restless, distracted, lost in memories of her brief encounter with John Russo. Calculating the school's monthly accounts hadn't been enough to contain her thoughts.

Now her thoughts journeyed to John's son, dwarfed

by the too big chair. His legs stuck out straight and his shoulders reached only the middle of the seat back. His gaze locked on to hers, still holding a challenge.

She resolutely swiveled her chair back to the computer and tapped at the keys. She could almost hear Michael's respiration; she could almost feel it, even though he was eight feet away from her. She was acutely conscious of him even though he didn't squirm, didn't speak, didn't do anything to call attention to himself. His mere presence was enough to distract her, just the way mere thoughts of his father distracted her.

She entered a few more numbers onto the computer spreadsheet, then yielded to Michael's silent summons and lifted her gaze to him. He was still sitting, one sneakered foot jiggling slightly, his hands gripping the arms of the chair. Tears cascaded down his cheeks, twin rivers of sorrow.

Molly recognized the thin line between caring for her students and losing her objectivity. She might be about to cross that line, but she couldn't just sit by while a little boy wept in silence.

"Do you need some lap time?" she asked.

He didn't say a word as she stood and circled the desk. The tears kept spilling down his face as she crossed the small room, eased his clenched fingers from the arms of the chair, lifted him and sat, pulling him down onto her lap. Only then did he let go, curling up against her and sobbing inconsolably.

This wasn't about a toy airplane. This was about a young, vulnerable child whose mother had walked out on him, whose father did stressful, dangerous work. It was about a little boy who had to let out some of the pain.

She closed her arms around his trembling body and rocked in the chair, letting him weep, letting him soak her sweater with his tears. She wondered when he'd last cried this hard, whether he'd been held like this. "Shh." she said. "Shh. It's all right." She wondered when someone had last convinced Michael Russo that it was all right—and whether, by claiming that it was, Molly was lying to him.

If she was, she hoped he would forgive her. Because right now, more than anything else, Michael needed to believe that it *was* all right, that when he ran out of tears his life would be a little bit better. If she could give him nothing else, she would give him her lap and her arms, her consoling murmurs and the hope he would need to keep going.

JOHN HOOKED HIS FINGER over the knot of his tie and tugged, loosening it enough so he wouldn't choke. A quick glance in the mirror above the sink revealed the face his Santa whiskers had hidden for most of the day. It also revealed a bemused smile. He'd caught the ATM thief—or, more accurately, the thieves. Given their ages, he almost thought they'd respond better to interrogation if he kept the Santa suit on.

But it was hung neatly on a wire hanger on one of the wall hooks in the squad's locker room. Interrogation or no, John was glad to be back in his civilian clothes.

He adjusted the straps of his holster on his shoulders, then left the locker room. Muriel, the squad's administrative assistant, grinned up at him from her desk. "They're in room two with their father," she told him. "Coffey says to handle this one delicately. You know who their father is, don't you?"

John moved to his own desk and picked up his note-pad. "Dennis Murphy?"

"The five-hundred-dollar-an-hour attorney."

"If that's what he pulls down, it's funny his kids have turned into bank robbers."

Muriel shook her head and laughed. "Go easy on them, Russo. They're petrified. And their father's a tough hombre."

"Right." He lifted his notepad and a pen and headed down the hall to the interrogation rooms. At room number two, he knocked on the door and then opened it.

Two pairs of worried hazel eyes peered up at him from two extremely worried seven-year-old faces, one male and one female. The Murphy twins were in deep doo-doo, and to their credit they knew it. John wasn't so sure about the mastermind of the heist: their baby-sitter, the fifteen-year-old son of the woman whose account was being illegally emptied via the ATM.

The mastermind and his mother were in another interrogation room with Lieutenant Coffey. John had won the honors with the Murphy twins and their tough-hombre lawyer father. The kids looked cherubic, but John wasn't fooled.

The hotshot lawyer strode briskly around the table and gave John's hand a bruising shake. "Dennis Murphy," he said. He was tall and fit, with a full head of dark blond hair and a direct stare. His suit looked unobtrusively expensive, but his tie, like John's, was loosened at the collar.

"Detective John Russo," John said, nodding toward the children. "I've already met Sean and Erin."

The twins shot each other a nervous look and then studied their hands intently.

"Would you care to fill me in?" Murphy asked. "I got a call at my office that the kids had been arrested."

"Brought in for questioning," John corrected him. "They've been accomplices in a series of ATM robberies."

Murphy narrowed his gaze on John for a moment, then turned to his children. "Start talking," he said.

"It was Todd's idea," Erin explained feebly.

Murphy frowned. "Todd?"

"The baby-sitter."

John smiled privately. Maybe he wouldn't have to interrogate the children; their father would do his job for him. "Todd who?" Murphy asked, making John wonder why a father wouldn't know the name of his children's after-school baby-sitter.

"He lives across the street from us," Sean volunteered. "Mom asked him to watch us."

"And he talked you into robbing a bank?"

"We didn't know that was what he was doing," said Erin. "I thought he was just giving me a shoulder ride."

John leaned against the door and folded his arms across his chest. The twins were speaking the truth. He'd observed them during his Santa stakeout—two tykes, cute as all get-out, walking down the street with a tall, indolent teenager in a lined denim jacket, baggy jeans, a mushroom hairdo and a diamond-chip earring, the vision of adolescent chic. Just before entering the bank, the teenager—Todd—had swooped Erin up onto his shoulders. Then the threesome had entered the ATM vestibule, and Todd had positioned himself so that Erin's navy blue jacket blocked the lens of the surveillance camera. Then Erin's brother Sean had pushed the buttons on the ATM, removed the cash and handed it to Todd.

"He told me what buttons to push," Sean said earnestly. "He said it was his money. I liked pushing the buttons. It was cool, Daddy, you know? Like on a spaceship or something. All these buttons."

"He wouldn't let me push the buttons," Erin complained.

"You got the shoulder ride," Sean countered.

"Where the hell was your mother?" Murphy asked, his voice a low growl.

"Out," Erin said.

"With her boyfriend," Sean added.

John took it all in without reacting. Murphy scowled and turned to John to explain. "My ex-wife has custody," he told John. "I had no idea this was going on. I mean—I know she's got a social life. I just didn't know she was leaving the kids in the care of a criminal punk."

"Todd's nice," Sean argued. "He let me push the buttons."

"Todd," John clarified, "was robbing money from his parents. That wasn't his money. It was theirs. He was withdrawing money from their account with his mother's ATM card." The card was currently marked as evidence. John had recovered it when he'd arrested the threesome. "Do you know how Todd got his mother's card?"

"Was that the little credit card?" Sean asked.

"The card you put in the machine before you pushed the buttons."

"He said it was his card."

"Did it have his name on it or his mother's?"

Sean studied his hands again. "I don't know."

"Did he tell you how he got the card?"

Sean shook his head. John directed his gaze to Erin, who shook her head, too.

"He stole it," John told them. "He stole it from his own mother."

"That wasn't very nice of him," Erin said quietly.

"And then he took his mother's money while you blocked the bank camera."

"I didn't know," Erin said, then glared accusingly at John. "And you know what? I think it's very mean of you to pretend you're Santa Claus. I think the real Santa Claus wouldn't like that at all. I think he'd be very mad at you."

Unable to come up with a defense, John laughed. "You're right. But I'd explain to Santa that as a police officer, I'm doing a good thing by making sure Todd stops robbing his mom. And I think Santa would forgive me."

Erin looked dubious. Sean eyed John curiously. "Is that a real gun?" he asked.

"Yes."

"Do you ride in a car with lights and sirens?"

"Not usually. I can put a light on the roof of my car, but mostly it's just a plain car."

"If I was a policeman," Sean said, "I'd want a siren."

"Look, what are we talking about here?" Dennis Murphy interrupted. "Where are we going with this?"

John had no intention of charging the Murphy twins with anything. All he wanted from them was enough information for him to get Todd qualified for juvie supervision, counseling, whatever it took to straighten him out before he ruined his life. If John was very lucky, the twins would have had the spit scared out of them so badly they'd never get into trouble again.

"I'm going to release your children, Mr. Murphy," he told the father. "I think we've got enough to get the baby-sitter into juvenile court and under supervision. He's a minor. If he can get back on track, he should be able to avoid jail. It's a first offense. It's a first offense for you guys, too," he added with a stern look toward the twins. "It had better be your last offense."

A smile of gratitude crossed Murphy's lips. "I appreciate how you've handled this, Detective. I think my kids stumbled into something they didn't understand. Which doesn't exonerate them, but I think it would be better dealt with at home."

"You might have a word with your ex-wife about who she's hiring to watch the kids," John suggested.

"Oh, I'll do that," Murphy muttered grimly. He removed a small leather folder from an inner pocket of his jacket and pulled out a business card. "Let me know if you need anything. I'll make sure the kids understand how serious this situation is."

John nodded and slipped Murphy's card into his shirt pocket.

"What was Erin talking about, that nonsense about Santa?"

John smiled. "Ask her." He opened the door and stepped out into the hall. It was a quarter past five, the windows already dark with the early approach of evening. He'd have to do his paperwork quickly so he could pick up Mike from preschool by six.

So, he thought, watching Murphy usher his children through the squad room and down the stairs, Erin thought the real Santa would be mad at him. Maybe she was right. Maybe Santa didn't like having detectives pretending to be him. Maybe Santa would be even less pleased than John to learn that, thanks to his successful bust of the pickpocket that morning, John was going to get stuck pretending to be Santa again.

The weeks leading up to Christmas were usually a period of increased street crime. People carried more money with them, and their minds were on shopping, parties, all the joys and stresses that accompanied the holiday season, rather than on their personal safety. Coffey had decided that John could help keep downtown Arlington safer during the holiday crush by going undercover as a street-corner Santa in various downtown neighborhoods over the next couple of weeks, watching for muggers, shoplifters and thieves.

John wasn't crazy about the idea, but helping people like Mr. Rosenblatt to hang on to their wallets was part of his job. If that was what he had to do, he'd do it.

He wasn't sure how he was going to get through the holiday crush himself. Molly Saunders had warned him that Mike was ready to snap, and John was hardly in the mood for Christmas this year. But maybe if he kept dressing up as Santa, a little of the season would rub off on him. Maybe if he donned the padding and the wig, the hat and the bright red suit, he'd get some idea of how to survive the next few weeks, how to make them good for his son.

CHAPTER FIVE

MOLLY AND HER TEACHERS took turns serving late duty, staying at the school until the last full-day students at the Children's Garden were picked up by a parent or guardian. Shannon was on late duty that evening, leaving Molly free to go. But she had chosen to remain at her desk until at least one of the children—Michael Russo—was picked up.

By six o'clock, the sky had grown almost as dark as midnight, and flurries dusted the air. Given the impending snowfall, she should have been eager to head for home while the roads were still clear and dry. But she wanted to make sure that Michael was fully recovered from his emotional outburst of that afternoon. She wanted to see him safely delivered into his father's hands.

Sure. As if the hope of seeing Michael's father had nothing to do with it. As if she had no interest whatsoever in John Russo, the Dudley Street Santa.

His arrival was announced with a gust of chilly air as he pushed open the door and stepped into the building. Molly glanced up from her papers, saw him—and felt the impact of his presence like a blow to the gut. Or maybe a blow to her soul.

She was in trouble. John Russo was too…attractive. Too sexy. Too dangerous. He was a man who didn't even need a gun to overpower people. He'd overpowered a pickpocket with his bare hands. All it took for him to overpower Molly was the mere hint of a smile.

He was dressed in regular clothes now, no padding, no baggy red pants and fluffy white wig. His thick, black hair shimmered with droplets of water where snowflakes had melted on it, and a burgundy scarf was slung carelessly around his neck inside the collar of an unzipped leather bomber jacket. Smelling the cold scent of winter on him reminded her of the colder scent of fear she'd inhaled that morning when she'd witnessed him chasing after that street thug. John Russo was not a peaceful man.

No wonder his son wasn't a peaceful child.

Instead of walking directly down the hall to get Michael, he paused by her desk, his eyes meeting hers above the sprawl of paperwork on her blotter. They were infinitely dark and unreadable.

"Hi," she said, smiling shyly.

Something glittered in the depths of his eyes: curiosity, interest, recognition. *Something.* His lips quirked into a slightly bigger smile. "Hi."

The air in the entry got warmer as he stood at her desk, peering down at her until she felt obliged to stand. He still towered over her, but not by quite as much.

She wished he would say something, but he didn't. He only stared at her, that enigmatic smile tweaking his mouth.

Unable to stand the silence, she spoke instead. "Did you catch the bank robber?"

"Yeah." Instead of looking pleased, he lost a few degrees of his smile. "Robbers," he corrected her. "Three of them."

"Three?" A lump of panic filled her throat and she

swallowed it back down. The thought of John apprehending *three* thieves all at once... He could have been hurt. He could have been killed. He could have been forced to use his gun.

"A fifteen-year-old ringleader and seven-year-old twins."

"No!" Relief that John hadn't faced a formidable opponent blended with dismay that children so young were engaging in criminal activity. "A fifteen-year-old I could believe, but *seven?*"

"The teenager conned them. They thought it was a game. They didn't know they were breaking the law." He shrugged, and what was left of his smile faded away. "Their parents are divorced. I think they got overlooked."

"It happens." She studied his face, suspecting that he was comparing those misguided twins to his own son. "In divorces, the parents need to give their children extra attention just so they don't get lost in the shuffle."

"Sometimes they can't." A muscle fluttered in his jaw. "Sometimes one of the parents disappears."

"Which doubles the burden on the parent who stays. But the burden is worth it, John. You know that, don't you?"

His mouth twitched, as if he wanted to smile again.

"So, does this mean you're all done with your Santa impersonation?"

He shook his head. "My boss wants me to wear the costume and catch some more pickpockets. It's the perfect stakeout disguise, given the season."

"You wear it well," she teased.

He permitted himself a brief smile. "The girl twin warned me that the real Santa wouldn't like it."

"I think she's mistaken. The real Santa would very much like you to catch pickpockets."

"Thanks for the vote of confidence." He glanced toward the hallway. "Is Mike back there?"

Molly sighed. If she told him about Michael's day, his good humor would evaporate completely. But it was her job to keep parents apprised of their children's behavior at school. "Michael had a bit of a rough time today."

John's focus narrowed on her. "What happened?"

"He..." She took a deep breath and reminded herself that her primary responsibility was as a professional. She had to tell him. "He got into a fight with a classmate over a toy plane. He tried to hit the child with the toy."

John absorbed that without comment.

"No one was hurt," she explained. "But it wasn't acceptable behavior. Michael has difficulty sharing."

"He's an only child."

"That doesn't mean he's exempted from learning how to share. It's a skill he needs to know."

"I'll talk to him."

"It takes more than talk," she cautioned. "It takes training and practice. This week in the Daddy School we'll be dealing with sharing and possessiveness and how fathers can help their children overcome their innate selfishness." When John didn't respond, she continued. "It would be great if you could come. You and Michael both."

"So he can learn how to share."

"So you can learn how to help him. He completely lost his composure today, John. He couldn't understand why the toy wasn't all his. When his teacher put him in time-out, he went on a crying jag."

John's jaw flexed but he said nothing.

"Afterward, he was so exhausted he fell asleep in my lap."

"He was in your lap?"

"Well...yes." Molly knew the risks of holding children. She'd heard about enough weird lawsuits and shocking charges to understand that a teacher had to be very careful about touching a student. But the Children's Garden was a preschool, and her students sometimes needed a hug. No threat of a lawsuit was going to keep her from hugging a child who needed it. If John wanted to arrest her for holding his son on her lap, let him try.

He searched her face, probing, digging around as if he had a search warrant for her thoughts. "Thank you," he finally said, his voice barely above a whisper.

She dared to press her luck. "Will you come to the Daddy School class this Saturday?"

He raked a hand through his hair. "Maybe," he said.

"I hope you do come. I think it would be good for Michael." *And for you,* she wanted to add. It would be good for the tall, reserved man who didn't want his son to get lost in the shuffle, the dark-eyed man who looked so wonderful when he smiled, but who didn't smile nearly enough. The quiet, private man who seemed to need so much but refused to ask for it.

HE DIDN'T WANT TO GO to a Daddy School class on Saturday. But then, there were lots of things he did that he didn't want to do. Like stand on the corner of Bank Street and Hauser Boulevard in a red flannel Santa suit looking for trouble.

Hauser Boulevard was downtown Arlington's major shopping area, and the retailers had dressed the neighborhood up to put people in the right frame of mind for spending money. Metal arches wrapped in artificial holly and strung with lights spanned the street every few yards, and most of the shops had Christmas trees in their front windows, or tinsel, or short, fat, Santa mannequins who looked a hell of a lot jollier than John felt.

Why shouldn't they be jollier? Unlike him, they didn't have to keep their eyes peeled for muggers, shoplifters and punks.

Somewhere in Arlington, crimes were being committed. John ought to be solving them. He was good at sifting through evidence, even better at noticing details in a crime scene that other cops overlooked. The trouble was, Coffey also thought John was good at standing on busy city corners and watching for minor malefaction.

In his next lifetime, John decided, he would *not* be so good at things. When they were kids, his sister Sarah, the prima donna of the family, once explained to him: "You know how come Linda and Nina have to do the laundry and I don't? Because the last time I did the laundry I screwed up. I put the fabric softener in the bleach dispenser and Mom threw a fit. She said I almost destroyed the washing machine. So now, when she needs a load done, she asks Nina or Linda to do it."

Not a bad strategy, screwing up. The trouble was, John was too damned responsible to screw up. He couldn't always do a good job, but he was incapable of deliberately doing a bad one. So if Coffey needed a figurative load of laundry done, he'd ask John, confident that John wouldn't put the fabric softener in the bleach dispenser.

Last night's snowfall had left less than an inch of snow on the ground, but all that was left along the curbs was a ridge of gray slush. The overcast sky promised more snow, but promises were broken all the time. John hadn't seen a single flake descend from the clouds, though he'd felt the icy bite of winter through the red wool flannel Santa suit and the thermal underwear he was wearing underneath.

He didn't want to go to Molly Saunders's Daddy School class. Not because he didn't think Mike would benefit from it. Not because he didn't think Mike needed work on his sharing skills and John needed work on his fathering skills. Not because he had anything more exciting planned for Saturday morning.

He didn't want to go because Molly turned him on.

Thoughts of Molly burned deep inside him like a pilot light, a flame capable of igniting a furnace if only he twisted the tap and released some fuel. Yet he couldn't do that, couldn't let the heat thaw him. He couldn't chance it. He had too much going on in his life, too many demands on him, too much emotional stuff. What little he had to give belonged to Mike.

Besides, he'd already learned from his failed marriage that he lacked whatever secret ingredient it took to make a woman happy. In bed, he could offer satisfaction. But not in a relationship.

What if Molly Saunders was interested in nothing more than satisfaction in bed?

For God's sake, she was the director of his son's preschool. She devoted herself to nurturing little kids. How could John think of her in sexual terms?

He knew damned well how. Those lips of hers, the

caramel-soft eyes, the sweet curves of her body. Her sassy, shiny hair. Her smile. Her confidence.

Last night, after he'd gotten Mike to sleep, he'd popped open a beer, sprawled out on the sofa in the den and tried to watch TV. But his mind kept wandering to Molly, to the way she'd smiled when she'd spotted him in his undercover getup, to her pallor when she'd watched him take down the pickpocket, to the way her gaze had locked on to his, made him want to pull her inside the oversize red jacket and feel her warmth against him. When he closed his eyes, he pictured her holding his son on her lap, letting him lose his temper and cry and fall asleep.

The way a mother would. The way Mike so badly needed to be held.

His feelings were all mixed up, a tangle of emotions like razor wire, too sharp to unravel without getting cut to shreds. He wanted Molly for his son, and he wanted her for himself. He wanted Mike to get her love. He wanted himself to get her passion.

He wanted things he had no right to want. And if he went to her Daddy School class on Saturday, it would only make him want her even more.

He exhaled a puff of white vapor through his fake beard. Two shoppers ambled down the street toward him, well-dressed, well-coifed middle-aged women laden with red-and-green holiday-decorated shopping bags. He remembered to ring his bell and utter a lackadaisical "Ho, ho, ho."

The woman with fewer bags rummaged in her purse as they neared him. "Higgins House," she said. "That's where all those street winos go in the winter, right?"

A strange impulse possessed John. He was always

honest, always straight, yet something shook the devil awake inside him. "I'm one of those winos, ma'am," he lied.

The woman fell back a step and clutched her hand to the silk scarf knotted at her throat. "Oh, I—I didn't mean—well, you look so clean."

"Yes, ma'am. They hosed me down before they put me out here."

She blushed, obviously mortified by her tactlessness. Her companion passed some of her packages over to the first woman. "Let me give you something, young man," she all but pleaded, pulling a bill from a leather wallet and shoving it into John's gloved hand. "That's just for you, for having the strength to redeem yourself. Merry Christmas!" With that, she hustled her friend away.

Chuckling, John smoothed out the bill. Fifty bucks. He folded the bill in half and slid it through the slot in the kettle's lid.

Lifting his gaze, he saw Molly.

She was emerging from a luncheonette, carrying a paper bag. Once again, she wasn't wearing a hat, and he thought of her ears turning pink from the cold, as pink as the tip of her nose.

He wondered what she was doing in this part of town, so far from the preschool. But when she smiled at him, he stopped wondering. He didn't care.

"Was that a bribe?" she asked, looking at the kettle.

Her smile was contagious—or maybe he was just happy to see her, because he found himself smiling, too. "I think it was more of a payoff."

"What's the difference?"

"A bribe is before the fact. You give a cop a bribe

if you want him to do something for you. A payoff is after the fact, after he's done something for you."

"I see. And what did you do for those two ladies?"

"I refrained from calling them idiots."

"Such integrity." Molly hugged the bulging bag to her. In her thick down parka she looked shapeless. But he'd seen her out of her jacket. He knew where she had curves, where she was slim. "I'm getting an education. Yesterday I got to see you catch a pickpocket, and today I got to see you do the right thing with a bribe. I mean a payoff." Her smile shimmered.

He caught a whiff of a peppery aroma rising from her bag. "Lunch?" he asked.

"Clam chowder. Cara said this place—" she waved toward the deli "—has the best clam chowder in Arlington. I volunteered to buy some for the staff. I got two quarts. I hope it's enough."

"It's going to get cold," he noted, then gave himself a mental kick. Reminding her it could get cold was as good as inviting her to leave.

Fortunately, she didn't accept the invitation. "I was planning to zap it in the microwave when we're ready to eat it. Lunchtime isn't for another hour."

He considered the evidence with a small degree of professional detachment. Molly had driven all the way across town to buy two quarts of clam chowder that wasn't going to be consumed for an hour. The director of a preschool was running a lamebrain errand—and that story about the deli's having the best clam chowder didn't wash, either. The best clam chowder in Arlington came from Moise's Fish House on the West Side. Everybody knew that.

Molly had come to the shopping district for some

other reason. He was curious, but he couldn't question her like he would a criminal.

"How's Mike?" he asked.

"He's having a good day."

"No tears?"

"No problems." She angled her head, studying John intently. "What does he say at home, John? Does he talk about school? I know this is only his second week at the Children's Garden, and he doesn't seem upset about being there, but at home…is he stressed out? Does he tell you about his day?"

"He seems happy," John said.

"He doesn't mention any problems? Anyone he doesn't like?"

"No." But now she had his suspicions revved up. "Who doesn't he like?"

"No one in particular that Amy and I have noticed. I wanted to know if you were seeing anything at home that we aren't seeing at school."

John thought for a minute. If he told her he wasn't seeing anything at home, she might think he was ignoring his son. "I think he'd be happier if you let the kids eat cookies."

She grinned. He practically heard the whoosh of heat flaring inside him as the pilot light ignited.

He didn't want this. Not now. Not with her.

"I'd better get back to work," he said, giving his bell a perfunctory swing.

"I'd better get back, too. I'll see you later," she said, still wearing that radiant grin, still glowing warm enough to thaw the polar ice caps. Cripes. He didn't want to want her warmth and her smile, he didn't want to be able to visualize her shape inside her parka and imagine how she would feel.

If it were only sex he wanted, he knew enough places to find it, and those places were not the Children's Garden Preschool. But when he looked at Molly, smiling at him even as she backed away toward Bank Street, he understood that sex wasn't all he wanted. And that scared the hell out of him.

BY FRIDAY, he'd figured out that Molly sightings weren't merely a coincidence. She was following him.

Well, not exactly following him, but finding him in his various Santa posts around the city. By the end of Monday, he'd stopped an attempted mugging and nabbed a drug dealer doing a brisk retail trade in loose joints in the alley between a stationery store and a video rental place. With those two collars he had pretty much doomed himself to more Santa duty on the streets of Arlington. He got a day off from the red suit and fake beard on Tuesday, when he had to testify in court on an attempted homicide. It turned out not to be much of a reprieve, though. The defense attorney was a sharp-witted woman in a gray suit, with a machine-gun mouth and blond hair. Oddly enough, she had the same last name as Molly. She'd looked a little like Molly, too, except for the fair coloring. She'd done her damnedest to slash John's testimony to ribbons.

John was used to being dissected alive by defense attorneys. Nothing Gail Saunders did rattled him much. He just recited his testimony and tried to guess whether such a sharpshooting lawyer could be related to the woman who had held his son on her lap when he'd been crying.

He would have asked Molly Tuesday evening when he went to the school to pick up Mike, but she wasn't there. One of the other teachers was standing guard by the front door, dismissing the kids. John hadn't met her before—she was in charge of the Tiny Tots group, she told him—and she'd made him show her two pieces of identification. "One of the children in the Pre-K class is the object of a difficult custody battle," she'd explained once John had shown her his police badge and driver's license. "I'm sure as an officer of the law, you know how messy those can be. The non-custodial parent has made some threats, so we have to be very careful to whom we release the children."

If John had had more energy, he would have told her she ought to be more careful whom she talked to about the students' personal business. But he'd been wiped out from his long day on the witness stand and vaguely disappointed that Molly wasn't behind the front desk when he'd arrived, as well as irritated to think that the following day he was going to have to put on the Santa outfit and stake out Arlington's busy streets once more.

Despite the warnings of young Erin Murphy, John thought Santa probably wouldn't mind his impersonation. The saint of Christmas would probably be very happy with the crimes John was shutting down on the busy winter streets of Arlington. In four days of undercover Santa work, he'd accumulated a handful of collars—drug deals, shoplifting, muggings, one misdemeanor assault and an attempted car theft.

But he was bored. He was grossly underutilized and underchallenged, and if Coffey didn't let him get back to his real work soon, he was going to be a lot closer to snapping than he'd ever been before.

The only thing was, Molly kept showing up. No matter which end of Hauser Boulevard he was on, whether he was in the shopping district or the banking district, she found him. Central Avenue, Newcombe...she found him.

By Friday, he realized she was actually looking for him.

"Hi," she said, emerging from an office supply store with a carton of printer paper. "How's the Santa business today?"

"Same as yesterday," he said with a smile. The truth was, he'd been looking for her, waiting for her to show up, wondering what excuse she'd have for him today. He'd spent the morning searching the crowds for crooks and punks, but also for a petite hatless woman with luminous eyes and a smile that never failed to ignite him.

"Well, now I can refill my printer," she said, gesturing with the carton. "We're down to colored construction paper, and—"

"Are you stalking me?" he asked. It was a rude question, a crude one. But he had to know. He was tired of trying to guess what she was up to, and until he knew for sure, he wasn't going to be able to figure out how to control his reaction to her. This much heat was a dangerous thing. John didn't know how to deal with it. Maybe she could explain it for him, the way her teachers at the Children's Garden explained the alphabet or the rules of sharing to their students.

"Stalking you?" She hesitated, then tossed back her head and laughed. "Yes, I think I am."

He closed his eyes. For a moment, he couldn't feel the blustery air, the frizz of his fake beard, the weight of his wig at the nape of his neck. All he felt was *her*, the gutsy, joyful force of her.

"You aren't going to arrest me, are you?" she asked, then laughed again.

"No." The word came out low, almost choked, and he coughed to cover his embarrassment. He wasn't used to a woman pursuing him—at least not a woman like Molly. Sherry had pursued him, true, but she'd been different. She'd been the kind of woman who went after what she wanted when she wanted it and then, if she discovered it was no longer what she wanted, she discarded it. She'd pursued John until she had him, and then she'd left him to pursue someone else, even though leaving him meant leaving Mike, as well.

He couldn't imagine Molly abandoning a child.

"It's just that you look so funny in your Santa Claus outfit," she explained. "I know if I see you in it, it'll have me smiling for the rest of the day. And there's always some errand that has to be run at the school, so..." Her smile faltered slightly. Her eyes grew more intense, the brown darker, the gold speckles brighter. "Maybe you aren't going to arrest me. You're going to have me committed."

"You're not crazy," he said, unsure what to add. He was sort of insulted—she thought he looked *funny* in his Santa disguise?—but mostly he was flattered. He'd never before been accused of making someone smile all day.

"I'm being a pest," she murmured. "I'm sorry."

He caught her chin before she could lower it and tilted her face up so he could gaze into her eyes. He wished he weren't wearing gloves and he could place his fingers against the smooth skin of her jaw. It would feel like velvet, he was sure. "Don't apologize."

She didn't speak. Neither did he. He couldn't imagine how she could stare at him in his goofball camouflage without smiling right now—if not erupting in hoots and guffaws. She was right: he looked like a dweeb dressed up as Santa.

She looked...she looked like the most honest, natural woman he'd ever met.

"Will I see you tomorrow?" she asked, her voice barely above a whisper.

Tomorrow? She'd see him tonight when he stopped by the school to pick up Mike if she stuck around the school late enough. Tomorrow wasn't a school day, though. It was Saturday.

"The Daddy School," she said in answer to his unvoiced question.

If she'd been asking him for a date tomorrow, he'd have had to say no. Only because he knew dating her would be a mistake. He wasn't right for a woman like her. He wasn't warm the way she was. He wasn't open and affectionate. He was a man who occasionally started his day with a murder-suicide, and when he was done scrubbing the blood off his psyche, he didn't have much left to give a woman.

But she wasn't asking him for a date. She was asking him to come to her school and learn how to develop Mike's sharing skills.

Maybe he was standing too close to her. Maybe the curve of her cheek against his gloved hand, and the dazzling faith that shone deep in her eyes, sapped him of the ability to think clearly. Because even as he cautioned himself that he shouldn't let her warmth reach too deep inside him, even as he comprehended that he had to keep his distance from her in every way he could, he heard himself say, "Sure, I'll be there."

CHAPTER SIX

"IN A WORD," Gail announced, "you're crazy."

"Thanks for the unsolicited advice," Molly replied. "And you obviously can't count. That was *two* words."

Gail shoved a limp lock of wheat-colored hair from her forehead and slumped in her chair. She and Molly were seated at the table in the small eat-in kitchen of Molly's condominium. Molly had invited Gail over for dinner so they could discuss what to send their parents for Christmas. But a long time ago they'd stopped debating whether their parents would prefer a year of weekly housecleaning service—Gail's suggestion—or a wide-screen television set—Molly's idea. Over a supper of broiled salmon steaks and salad, they'd somehow drifted from the subject of Christmas gifts to the subject of police officers. One police officer in particular.

"I'm telling you, the man was like ice on the witness stand. I can't believe you could be blushing over him. He was cold enough to give a polar bear frostbite."

"Well, that's his job, isn't it?" Molly countered, not daring to voice her fear that her sister could be right, that John Russo could actually be as cold as Gail claimed. He wasn't effusive. He didn't wear his heart on his sleeve. But she had sensed heat inside him.

She'd seen flickers of flame in his eyes, glimmers of warmth in his too rare smile.

Gail's antipathy toward John had nothing to do with him in particular. She hated all cops. That he had been a prosecution witness, testifying against her client, only made her resentment specific to the occasion. "Did you break him?" Molly asked, not sure what answer she hoped for. "Did you destroy him on the stand?"

Gail pursed her lips and shook her head. "It wasn't for lack of trying," she muttered. "I'm still going to get my guy off. A lot of their evidence is circumstantial. The fact that your boy Russo didn't crack under pressure doesn't mean I didn't make headway."

Molly suppressed a smile. She was glad John hadn't cracked—and she felt disloyal for being glad.

"So, what exactly is going on with you and Detective Russo?" Gail asked.

"Nothing."

Gail took a sip of chardonnay, lowered her glass and shook her head again, this time in disbelief. "Every time you think about him, your face turns red."

"It does not," Molly argued. Her cheeks instantly betrayed her, growing warm with a blush. "Anyway, I can't help it if he's gorgeous. You saw him yourself. Tell me you didn't think he was gorgeous."

Gail snorted. "He's a cop. Enough said."

"Absolutely. Enough said. Let's talk about that deluxe TV for Mom and Dad."

Gail refused to take the hint. "Let me tell you about cops, Molly. Forget about the homicide case I'm defending, where your buddy testified for the prosecution. Let me tell you what happened with a case I took on today. A kid is walking down Central Avenue after school, okay? He's drinking a beer. A cop yanks him aside and asks to see some proof that he's legally old enough to drink. The kid is only seventeen, so of course he can't show any proof of age. So the cop, without a warrant, reaches into the kid's pocket and discovers that the kid is carrying a piece. And now they're trying to lock the kid up on a weapons charge.''

''Forgive me if I say this client of yours doesn't exactly sound like a candidate for 'Most Likely to Succeed.' ''

''That's irrelevant. In my opinion, the boy *can* succeed. He's got to clean up his act, get some counseling and stop the underage drinking.''

''And his gun?''

''I don't like guns any more than you do,'' Gail said. ''But the cop had no right to search for it. He didn't have a warrant. Instead of helping the kid to work out a drinking problem, the cop is trying to put the kid in jail.''

''I'm sorry,'' Molly said, ''but I'd rather see that kid in jail than shooting some innocent person.''

''The point,'' Gail lectured, ''is that cops think they're above the law. They have the power of the badge, and they think that exempts them from the Bill of Rights. You know it's true, Molly. It happens all the time. And your pal Russo is no better or worse than the rest of them.''

''Not all cops are bad,'' Molly argued, amazed to hear herself defend police officers to her sister. ''I saw John Russo stop a pickpocket from stealing an elderly gentleman's wallet. And he straightened out some kids, too. Seven-year-old bank robbers.''

"Seven years old?" That shut Gail up.

"And he didn't send them to jail."

"Seven years old?" Gail took a hard slug of wine. "Geez. What's the world coming to?"

"I don't know. But I do know that as a cop, Russo did something good for those kids."

"Seven years old," Gail muttered under her breath. She shook her head. "At seven years old, your biggest crime was stealing my Barbie doll."

"I didn't steal her. I just borrowed her," Molly said with a smile. "And I forgot to return her for a long time."

"Yeah, like years." Gail leaned back in her chair and sighed. "I will concede that on occasion, a cop might do something right. Even a blind squirrel finds a nut sometimes. But there's something about that uniform that alters most cops, like Superman, only in reverse."

"Russo doesn't wear a uniform," said Molly, trying to will the heat out of her cheeks. "Unless a Santa suit counts as a uniform."

Gail chuckled. "A Santa suit? Well, it doesn't matter what he's wearing. He's got a shield and a gun. That's all he needs. It's very nice that Russo helped Jamie McCoy gain permanent custody of his daughter and saved an old man from a pickpocket—and kept two primary school kids out of jail. But the bottom line is, he's a cop. He's one of *them*."

Molly reached across the table and patted Gail's hand. When they were children, the fact that Gail was three years older than Molly counted for something, but not anymore. They were equals now, and Molly was as likely to comfort her sister and give her advice as to be on the receiving end. "I know you've got a good reason to hate cops. But that was a long time ago, Gail. Ten years.''

"Ten-and-a-half," Gail corrected her with a wry smile. "But it's not just that." Her jaw tensed, throwing the tendons in her neck into relief. Shadows darkened her eyes. "I work in the public defender's office. I see what cops do every day. I see how they abuse their power."

"John Russo doesn't abuse his power."

"How do you know that?"

Molly bit her lip. She *didn't* know that. She didn't know what he did with his gun when she wasn't around. She didn't know whether he searched suspects without warrants or, for that matter, whether he took advantage of innocent young college students with broken taillights. There was so much she didn't know about him.

But she knew his eyes were sad. She knew he loved his son. She knew he was trying to cope with a difficult situation, doing his best and worrying that his best wasn't anywhere near good enough.

She also knew she was spending too much time thinking about his brooding gaze, his capacity for love and a whole bunch of other things about him. Like his height, and the breadth of his shoulders, barely visible inside his Santa tunic, and the length of his legs. And the depth and darkness of his hair. And the way his lips fought against the smiling reflex—and on a few blessed occasions lost the battle.

"You're blushing again." Gail pursed her lips in obvious disapproval. "He hasn't kissed you or anything, has he?"

"No. I'm sure he has no interest in me, anyway." Molly stood and cleared the plates from the table, tired of having to face her sister and her own troubling thoughts. "I'm just the lady who runs the day care center where he sends his son." *It doesn't matter that he touched me. It doesn't matter that he cupped his hand around my cheek and gazed into my eyes and sparked a few unfamiliar fantasies to life.* "He probably doesn't think much of me at all." *He thinks I'm a stalker.* "And he didn't even want to come to the Daddy School tomorrow. He agreed to come only because we're going to deal with how to help children to become better sharers. His son doesn't share well." *John Russo thinks I'm a twit, Gail. Don't worry. Your little sister is safe from the Big Bad Cop.*

"Better that kids learn to be sharers than bank robbers," Gail murmured, obviously mystified. "Seven years old? It's hard to believe. Were they armed?"

"I don't know."

"I wonder if my office got a call on it. They were probably some poor kids trying to find the money to pay their families' heating bills."

Molly chuckled. "How romantic, two noble little second-graders saving the world by scamming an ATM."

"An ATM?" Gail crossed to the counter beside the sink and lowered the dishwasher door. Molly started rinsing the plates, then handed each plate to Gail to place in the dishwasher rack. They knew each other's moves perfectly; they had the timing down pat. "Maybe these kids are computer whizzes. Geniuses—or is it genii? Maybe they robbed the bank out of boredom. They need a good gifted children program."

Molly's chuckle expanded into a full laugh. "Have

some more wine, Gail. I like what it does for your imagination.''

"No more wine for me. I've got to drive home. So, what are we going to do about Mom and Dad?'' she asked, clicking the dishwasher door shut and pivoting to face her sister. "The TV is a nice idea, except they'll complain about it.''

"They'll complain about the housekeeping, too.''

"But they'll love it.''

"Like they'll love the TV.''

Gail grinned and gave Molly a hug. "Gotta go. We'll work this out later.'' Her smile waned as she drew back and studied Molly. "Keep your guard up around Russo, okay? I know Clint Eastwood was sexy in all those Dirty Harry movies. But his regard for the Constitution was less than zero.''

As if Molly were going to lie awake all night while she thought about the Constitution. As if Molly had ever dreamed about Clint Eastwood the way she was dreaming about John Russo.

As if she ought to be dreaming about the father of one of her students. As if there was a chance in hell that such a dream could possibly come true.

MOLLY SEPARATED the fathers from their children Saturday morning. John watched Mike, the other children and a teacher vanish up the stairs to the playroom on the second floor of the Children's Garden. Seven fathers remained downstairs with Molly, searching the partitioned rooms for adult-size chairs.

She barely smiled at him, which was fine. They'd both taken a chance yesterday, Molly by admitting she'd been searching for him downtown each day and John by touching her. They'd both risked something, and while John couldn't speak for Molly, he knew he couldn't afford such risks.

Half of him believed he was attracted to her only because, six months after Sherry had walked out on him—and more than a year after their marriage really entered its death throes—he was just plain hungry for a woman. But the other half of him kept dwelling on the thought that if all he wanted was a woman, he could find one easily enough.

But he didn't want just any woman. He wanted a woman who could comfort and teach his son, a woman who could verbalize her concerns and express her feelings instead of fleeing to Las Vegas and leaving her family behind. He wanted a woman who could warm a room with her smile.

Molly's smile that morning was meant for all the fathers, not just for him. Even so, it thawed the permafrost in his soul. It made him feel as if he were taking steps, doing something for his son, moving in the right direction.

"The tables will hold you," she assured the men in the room, leading them into the Pre-Kindergarten section and gesturing for them to make themselves comfortable on the small furniture. John wasn't the only man who looked awkward surrounded by pint-size chairs, knee-high cupboards and low tables. He felt like Gulliver in the land of the Lilliputians, and he bet the other fathers did, too.

Molly appeared totally at home in the enclosed space. Dressed in a textured beige sweater, blue jeans and loafers, she looked like a college sophomore, young and idealistic and brimming with energy. But she was a woman, someone who'd admitted to following him around town all week. Someone with eyes that danced with light, with curves that did wicked things to his libido.

"Today's class is about sharing," she said, perching herself on one of the tables and surveying the men, some of whom sat gingerly on a table facing hers while others, like John, took seats on the carpeted floor. Her gaze skidded past him, as if she were afraid to meet his stare. He was disappointed and relieved at the same time. He didn't know if his face gave anything away, but he sure as heck didn't want her to pause long enough to read lust in his expression. Or doubt. Or panic.

"Gordon, I know we talked a bit about this last week," she said, addressing one of the men balanced precariously on the broad Formica-topped table near John. "You mentioned that ever since your baby was born, Melissa has had a lot of trouble sharing."

Gordon nodded. "She has all these toys she hasn't played with since she was a year old. But the minute her brother reaches for them, she snatches them away and insists that they're hers and he can't have them."

"Baby toys?" Molly asked.

He nodded again. "She's three and a half years old. She outgrew those toys ages ago. Stacking rings, squeaky toys, push toys—she's way past those things now. But the instant she sees Justin go for one of them, they're hers, hers, hers. I just don't know what to do. They *are* hers—or at least they *were*. But she ought to be sharing them."

"Ideas?" Molly asked, her gaze scanning the other fathers.

"I'd say you've got to be firm," suggested a stocky man in a plaid flannel shirt. "Just tell her she hasn't got a choice."

"Yeah, but then it's forced," another man argued. "It doesn't come from inside her. I want my kid to be generous from his heart, you know? You can't impose generosity on a kid."

Molly turned to John, silently inviting him to offer a theory. He didn't trust himself to come up with any good ideas, though. With a small shrug, he declined her invitation.

Turning away, Molly addressed the group as a whole. "Here's what I think is happening. It has nothing to do with the toys but everything to do with sharing. Melissa is envious of the time and attention her brother is getting. She can't come right out and admit that she's jealous of him, so she exercises what little power she has—over her playthings."

"In other words, it's sibling rivalry playing itself out," Gordon summed up.

Molly smiled. "One thing children have a great deal of trouble sharing is attention. We notice this quite often during class time. If a teacher is working with one child, another will come over and demand her attention, even if the first child *needs* the teacher right then and the second child doesn't."

"Okay, so that's the diagnosis," Gordon allowed. "But I still don't know how to get Melissa to let her brother play with her old push toys."

"You have to give Melissa what she's really asking for—not her push toys, but parental attention. She's feeling a little neglected, Gordon. Lots of times, when a child is having trouble sharing, it's a cry for attention. In fact—" she circled the group again with her gaze "—when children have problems sharing things, it's nearly always a symptom of something else. They feel overlooked, or they want attention. Sibling rivalry is often an issue.''

''My son's an only child,'' the stocky man in denim observed. ''No sibling rivalry, but he still won't share.''

John shifted on the hard floor, interested to hear how Molly would analyze the man's situation, which reflected his own. ''One thing about only children,'' she said, ''is that they don't really get into a sharing habit. At school they have to share, but every toy at home belongs to them alone. The adults in their lives aren't competing for the Lego or the *Goodnight Moon* book. Only children should invite playmates to their house as often as possible. This enables the child to develop the sharing habit. We need to teach all our children, whether or not they have siblings, that the ability and willingness to share is a life skill that will make things go better for them. We teach certain values in school, and one of those values is that our own world is a better place if we can make it a better place for others. In a way, generosity is a very selfish practice.'' She smiled, and several of the fathers smiled with her.

''Another issue that leads to sharing problems is control,'' she continued, shooting a brief but knowing glance John's way. ''If a child feels he has no control over the major events in his life, he'll try to control his possessions.'' Her gaze returned to John and stayed there.

''So what do you do?'' he heard himself ask. ''How do you fix that?''

He hadn't meant to participate in the discussion. He was there to listen and learn, not to mouth off about his own problems. That he would expose himself to these men, all of them strangers, puzzled him. What was it about Molly that had prompted him to speak up?

Her smile. Her eyes. The way she elicited trust.

"Naturally you can't give a child complete control over his life," she said, her voice gentle to soften the harsh truth. "There are things *we* can't control in *our* lives. Part of growing up means learning to accept that some things are beyond our control. Kids learn every day that they can't control much of anything in their lives.

"One thing you can do to give a child a sense of control is to establish that certain things are exclusively his. For instance, his shoes. Children don't share shoes. Or a special glass that he always gets to drink his milk from. Or curtains for his bedroom. Let your child pick out the curtains. Hang a bulletin board in your child's room and let that be all his to decorate. Even if he shares a bedroom with a sibling," she added, including the other fathers, "let him or her have that bulletin board. And one or two toys that are that child's and no one else's. Not even visiting friends can play with those very special toys. Not unless the child permits it.

"Giving your child the chance to control a few things will make him feel less powerless in the grand scheme of things. Having complete ownership over a particular teddy bear is not going to bring an absent parent back, or earn him respect among his peers, or any of a million other things he might want. But it will give him a modicum of control over his life."

She continued, elaborating, offering other ideas, luring other comments from the fathers. John leaned back against the divider wall and absorbed her wisdom.

What she said made sense. Even if he'd told her nothing about his life and Mike's, it would have made sense. He hated to admit that coming to the Daddy School was a good idea, but it was.

The discussion was still going strong when a toddler stampede down the stairs alerted the Daddy School participants that two hours had passed. Children spilled into the room, charged through the open gate into the Pre-Kindergarten area and leaped into their fathers' arms, yammering about what they'd done upstairs. There had apparently been a huge pillow fight, with balloons and beach balls and all manner of bulky but harmless weaponry. The children were exhilarated, breathless and giggling.

"It's a mess up there," the teacher said apologetically to Molly. "We got a little of it cleaned up, but the time got away from us."

"That's all right." Molly stood and smiled at the teacher. "You did a great job keeping them occupied up there. I'll finish the cleanup." She waved and shouted a farewell to several of the fathers as they wrestled their youngsters into thick winter jackets and woolen caps.

Like the other kids, Mike babbled about the Great Pillow War. "We got big pillows!" he exclaimed. "With stuff like in the foam pit. Everybody hit everybody! It was great!"

"I'm sure it was," John murmured, his gaze chasing Molly as she bent to help one child with a zipper, stood and conferred with a father, then spun around to acknowledge another child, who was tugging on the back of her sweater. "Is it very messy upstairs?"

"No mess," Mike swore, which meant it must be a major disaster.

It wasn't John's disaster, of course. But it didn't seem fair for Molly to get stuck cleaning it up all by herself.

Damn it—fair had nothing to do with his inclination to help her straighten things out in the aftermath of the pillow fight. The truth was, he didn't want to leave the Children's Garden yet.

He didn't want to leave Molly yet.

He moved against the tide of departing fathers and children, like a fish swimming upstream to spawn. At last he reached Molly, who was waving farewell to the Daddy School students. "Mike and I will help you tidy the upstairs room," he volunteered.

She peered up at him, her smile fading slightly. "You don't have to do that."

"I didn't say I had to." He shrugged, refusing to let her discerning eyes daunt him.

She studied his face for a long moment, as if reading an involved message in it, a message he would have preferred her not to interpret. Then she lowered her gaze to Mike. "Do you want to help your dad and me clean up?"

"Yeah!" Mike bellowed, breaking from his father's clasp and clambering back up the stairs.

Molly eyed John with amusement. "He doesn't do that for me," John muttered. "He never wants to help clean up at home."

"Then I'll take this—" she gestured toward him "—as a personal compliment." Laughing, she pursued Mike up the stairs.

John headed after them. At the top of the stairs he assessed the room. It wasn't too awful, but it needed work. Some furniture was overturned, and balloons and soft, squishy balls were strewn about the center of the room. Tufts and scraps of foam rubber littered the floor.

"Michael," Molly instructed him, "what I want you to do is gather up the little pieces of foam and add them to the foam pit, okay? Your father and I will handle the heavier stuff."

Mike romped across the room, gathering fistfuls of foam, dropping half of what he picked up en route to the foam pit. He seemed to be having a grand time, which bemused John. The kid never cleaned up his messes at home, not without being nagged and scolded. Even then, John sometimes didn't have the strength to force the issue. He just couldn't bear to get into a battle of wills with Mike after a day spent tussling with suspects in the interrogation rooms or on the streets.

He wondered how Molly managed to motivate Mike. She'd barely even asked him to pick up the foam, and he was off and running. Maybe, like his father, Mike had developed a soft spot for the teacher.

John glimpsed her righting chairs in the kitchen area. The fluorescent ceiling fixture caused her hair to shimmer as if someone had threaded filaments of pure light through the dense brown locks. Her cheeks were pink, not the vivid shade he'd seen when she'd been outdoors in the wintry air, but a tawny pink, the color of health and high spirits. The color a woman might blush during a peak moment of sex.

Shoving aside that notion, he scooped up the assorted balls and tossed them into a tall mesh-sided bin. Then he helped Molly put the rest of the furniture back in order. Once that was done, they added their efforts to Mike's, gathering up the last of the tattered foam and returning it to the foam pit. While John worked, a million thoughts crowded his mind, things he'd like to say to her, things that couldn't be said. Things about her eyes and her smile and the magic she seemed able to work on his son. Things about control, about the lack of it. Things about how smart she was, scary-smart, smart enough to make him feel like an idiot when it came to Mike.

"Oh, gee, it's late," she said, checking the wall clock, which indicated it was twelve thirty. "I shouldn't have kept you. I appreciate the help."

"No problem." He plucked a few stray shreds of foam from the floor and handed them to Mike, who dashed over to the foam pit and hurled them in.

"Michael must be starving. You'd better go get him some lunch."

"How about you?" John asked, deciding he was in a brave—or maybe a foolish—mood. "Do you want to join us for lunch?"

She opened her mouth and then shut it, obviously taken aback. Okay, so he was a fool. He'd over-stepped. She was going to say no.

"Actually, I brought some cheese, crackers and fruit to eat here," she explained. "I was going to give the kids a snack, but I got so caught up in the class, I forgot. I don't feel like taking all that food home. We could have a picnic here if you'd like."

As soon as she spoke, she looked apprehensive. In fact, she looked pretty much the way he felt—as if she feared her question marked her as a fool.

They could be fools together, and then their fool-ishness wouldn't matter. "Hey, Mike," he called to his son, who was wiggling between the ropes to climb into the foam pit. "You want to have a picnic here with Ms. Saunders?"

"A picnic!" Mike climbed out of the pit and raced over to where Molly and John were standing. "A picnic! I want a picnic!"

"I guess the answer is yes," he said, turning back to Molly.

She smiled up at him. Her smile convinced him that saying yes might not have been such a foolish move, after all. Something about the warmth of her smile, the generous curve of her mouth and the mesmerizing glow in her eyes made it impossible for him not to smile back.

CHAPTER SEVEN

MOLLY WASN'T SURPRISED when Michael fell asleep. Afternoon naps were a typical part of a two-year-old's daily routine—and even if they weren't, she knew Michael would have run out of steam sooner or later, given that he'd been functioning at turbo-speed for so long. His idea of cleaning up the play area had entailed a great deal of running in circles, jumping up and down, throwing foam scraps around the room and bellowing gleefully. When Molly had unpacked the food she'd brought, he'd been too keyed up to sit still while he ate. He'd gobbled some cheese, squirmed in his chair, eaten a bit more and charged around the room shrieking and giggling. To have the entire second floor of the Children's Garden practically to himself—without having to share *anything* with other children—was too exciting to accept calmly.

But eventually he'd tired himself out. He'd been explaining, in adorably garbled English, how cheese came from cheese cows who made it in their bellies and it came out instead of milk, when all of a sudden, in midsentence, he'd curled up on the floor with his little butt in the air and his thumb in his mouth, let out a weary sigh and closed his eyes. And that was that.

While he'd been awake, Molly and John hadn't eaten much. They'd been too distracted by the child, and too busy trying to get him to settle down and have his lunch. But once he'd come to an abrupt halt and John had carried the sleeping boy to a carpeted area out of the bright light for his nap, the adults could relax.

Relaxing obviously wasn't something that came naturally to John Russo. He arranged his body on the floor in the kitchen play area, propping his back against the toy refrigerator and extending his legs under the table. Molly brought the tray of cheese, the bowl of green apple wedges and the box of wheat crackers down onto the floor and sat facing him, cross-legged, with the food between them. "There," she said with a smile. "Now it's a real picnic."

He almost smiled back. "What do you do during the week when a kid crashes like Mike just did?"

"We have nap time worked into the schedule," she said. "In his group, everyone sleeps. In the Pre-K group, some of the kids have outgrown the need for a nap, but they still have a rest time. Kids need their rest."

She bit into a wedge of apple and inched closer to John. She told herself she wanted to reduce the distance between him and herself so they could keep their voices down and avoid rousing Michael. But the way Michael was sleeping, they probably could have screamed louder than cheerleaders after a touchdown without waking the child. The bottom line was, she wanted to be closer to John, even though the buffer of space might be the only thing saving her from her wayward desire.

It wasn't fair that John should be so handsome. Feature for feature, he wasn't exactly a hunk. His face was narrow, his chin too angular, his nose too long.

And his eyes—too guarded, too inscrutable. He wasn't bulked up like a bodybuilder. And in his flannel shirt, black denim jeans and boring leather chukka boots, he wasn't going to be mistaken for a fashion trendsetter.

Yet when had Molly ever given a hoot about style? She had no time for fashion trends. She couldn't care less if buff bodies were considered hot. John was lanky and loose-limbed, and he was plenty hot enough as far as she was concerned. If a magazine hired him to pose for a centerfold, she would be the first in line to buy a copy.

She mustn't allow herself to think of him in those terms. Even without Gail's frantic warnings about cops in general and John's coldness in particular, Molly knew better than to nurture a crush on the father of a student at her school. She had no business wanting to sit closer to him, contemplating the power of his gaze, the soul-deep force of his rare smile. She had no business trying to picture him sprawled naked in the pages of a beefcake magazine. Even if the vision her mind conjured up was phenomenal.

That they were surrounded by miniature chairs, a make-believe sink, a pink toy vacuum cleaner, plastic cups, pots and pans and empty egg cartons and oatmeal cylinders helped her to regain her perspective. What with the bright lighting and the high ceiling, the ambiance was about as unromantic as Molly could imagine.

Just as well. She shouldn't be thinking about ambiance—or about romance. Right now she had an opportunity to learn more about the Russo family. The more she knew, the more she could help Michael. She ought to put this time to good use.

If only John weren't looking at her that way, with

his head back and his lids lowered. If only his legs weren't so long, his shoulders so broad. If only he didn't have the sexiest damned mouth she'd ever seen.

"Did you find the Daddy School class helpful?" she asked.

"Yeah."

Well, there was a real conversational gambit. He nibbled on a handful of crackers and continued to gaze at her, saying nothing.

"Michael hasn't had any more outbursts this week," she reported. "Amy says he's really working hard to keep himself together."

John pressed his lips into a grim line. "I wish he didn't have to work hard at it."

"All young children do," she reassured him. "Even children who haven't been through everything Michael's been through." *Some adults have to work at it, too,* she almost added. Just because John had figured out a way to lock everything tight inside him didn't mean such self-containment was normal or particularly healthy. If he and Michael could figure out a way to average each other out, they'd both be a lot better off.

John regarded her curiously. "Is he the most screwed-up kid here?"

"Oh, no. Not by a long shot." She grinned. "Which isn't to say he's the most well-adjusted kid, either. But at least he knows where his home is, and he knows his dad is going to be there for him every day. We've got all sorts of unusual family situations represented in the school. We've got a sister and brother who are being raised by their grandparents because their parents are in jail. One of Michael's friends is being raised by his gay father and his lover. We've got a little girl whose parents are in a vicious custody battle. The mother has custody, and the father keeps threatening to snatch the girl and run. Compared to that, Michael's family life is pretty stable.''

"But that girl...both her parents want her," John observed.

The amazing thing about him was that the harder he tried to rid his voice of emotion, the more emotion she felt churning just below his cool surface. His tone was level, his words laconic—but his eyes radiated a pain so fierce she could almost feel it inside her.

Did he still love his ex-wife? she wondered. Or did he despise the woman who had thrown his son's life into turmoil? Was there anyone else in the picture? Another woman poised to take his wife's place? Someone who might love Michael as much as John did?

She dried her fingers on a napkin and propped her chin on her hands, her elbows planted on her knees. "You know," she said gently, "the more you tell me about what's going on with him, the more we'll be able to do for him here at school."

John's eyes flashed with suspicion, which was slowly replaced by acceptance. He nudged the plate of cheese away, bent one leg and rested his arm across his knee. "What do you need to know?"

She scrambled for a reply. She hadn't expected him to capitulate so easily. "Whatever you feel comfortable telling me."

A curt laugh escaped him. "I don't feel comfortable telling you anything," he conceded.

"Well—"

"But for Mike's sake..." He raked his hand through his hair, his vision focused on some distant point as he collected his thoughts. "I married his mother because she was pregnant. It was the right thing to do, and I thought we could make it work. But she wasn't happy."

Molly waited for more. Apparently John believed he'd told her everything she needed to know. When his silence extended beyond a full minute, she said, "So your wife just walked out?"

"She found someone else."

Now it was Molly's turn to collect her thoughts. She could sort of imagine walking out on a man like John Russo, a man so taciturn, so self-protective, a man who carried a gun. But she couldn't imagine leaving him for someone more intriguing or attractive. She couldn't imagine that a more intriguing, attractive man existed.

Maybe John's ex-wife had found someone easier. That was an explanation Molly could believe. John was not an easy man.

"Nowadays," she remarked, observing the shadows shifting in his eyes and the hint of tension in his jaw, "when a woman gets pregnant by accident, the guy is as likely to run away as to marry her."

"Or the woman gets an abortion," he said. She was surprised; she'd thought it but wouldn't have dared to speak the word. "That wasn't right for us, so we got married." He shrugged.

"You strike me as a very responsible man," she murmured, hoping she didn't sound pompous or patronizing.

He chuckled, a low, husky sound in his throat. "Responsible. That's me."

She smiled uncertainly. "Share the joke?"

He studied her, his eyes dark enough to contain a

world full of night. "I've got six brothers and sisters," he told her. "Some pull more weight than others. One of my brothers is disabled. One had a drug problem for a while. A couple of them were on their way to big things and couldn't take care of the small stuff." He shrugged again. "I was one of the responsible ones."

"Michael is lucky you're his father."

"I'm responsible for him, too." He half smiled, signaling that he meant the statement in more than one way.

She was dying to ask him more about his family, about how a clan with so many children moving in so many directions could produce a man as solid and focused as John. But her curiosity troubled her. She deliberately shut it down, retreating to safer ground. "My sister said you testified against a client of hers on Tuesday."

"Was that your sister?" He nodded. "I wondered."

"That's my sister. She's an attorney in the Public Defender's office."

He nodded again.

"She said you were Mr. Cool on the stand."

He grinned. "Her guy is guilty."

"She thinks otherwise."

"She's wrong."

He was as opinionated as Gail. Molly wasn't about to recite her sister's arguments about how the police were always overstepping their bounds, trampling all over the Constitution to make an arrest.

She was tempted to ask more about his job, but that would only remind her of Gail's view of cops. Molly would think about his gun, and she'd think about the good he did—and the violence, however legitimate, he employed to gain that end.

Nor did she want to discuss Michael with him, even though Michael was allegedly the reason she was asking all these nosy questions. Her true interest was John. The kind of father he was, the kind of man.

"So you're responsible on the stand and you're responsible with your son and you're responsible with your brothers and sisters," she summed up. "What do you do when you're not being responsible?"

The question seemed to stump him. "If you're asking whether I grab my revolver and shoot out streetlights, no, I don't," he said.

She wished he hadn't mentioned his gun. But now that he had, it reminded her of how tightly strung he was. No one should have to be that responsible all the time. "I meant," she said, smiling in spite of his stern expression, "what do you do to unwind? What do you do when you want to let go?"

He contemplated the question for a long moment. "I don't."

"You don't let go?"

"I've got a kid. I've got a job."

"You've got responsibilities, I know. But you need to let go sometimes, John, or you'll burn out."

His frown told her he wasn't thrilled with her advice. He glanced away, studying the music area across the room from the play kitchen. His brow creased and his mouth twisted in a scowl. He wrestled with his thoughts until his temper subsided; when he looked back at her, he appeared to be in complete control, which was really rather unfortunate. He needed to lose control, not cling to it so vehemently.

"What do you suggest?" he asked, his voice taut and hard, as if the words hurt him coming out.

"How about the foam pit?" she asked, angling her head toward the end of the room.

His frown returned, this time not angry as much as bewildered. "What?"

"The foam pit. Dive in and jump around. It'll do wonders for you."

"I don't want wonders," he muttered.

But she was already on her feet, beckoning for him to join her. If she could convince him to remove his shoes and flail around in the pit, he would realize its therapeutic value. Maybe he'd feel so much better afterward, he would have to admit the value of cutting loose and he'd find some more appropriate way to blow off his tension.

He stood slowly, watching her with obvious skepticism. Feeling his gaze on her, she strolled to the foam pit, yanked off her sneakers, shoved down the rope-mesh fence and climbed in. Her feet sank into the loose flooring of foam. Arms akimbo, she grinned, daring him to join her.

He stared at her. Obviously the mere idea of entering the foam pit unnerved him.

Molly took a shaky step, her feet sinking deeper into the foam rubber. It was like walking on a trampoline. She dropped to her knees and sighed with pleasure. The cushioning softness of the foam seemed to cradle her.

Peering up, she saw John take a hesitant step toward the pit, another step—and then he halted. His mouth shaped a taut, dubious frown.

"Are you scared?" she challenged him. Short of dragging him into the pit—a physical impossibility—

she figured the only way she could get him in was to goad him.

Without a word, he bent over and tugged the leather laces of his boots. Once they were untied, he wrenched them off his feet and straightened up. His eyes remained hauntingly dark, so dark Molly could practically believe he *was* scared. Not scared of being swallowed by the pit but scared of letting loose and having fun.

Grimly, as if braced for the most unpleasant experience of his life, he swung one leg over the top of the mesh, then the other. He stood towering over her, glowering down at her. "Now what?"

"Now have fun," she suggested bluntly, swallowing her amusement at his dour expression.

He was clearly at a loss. Having fun did not come naturally to him. He needed help.

She filled her hands with bits of foam rubber and flung them up at his nose. Most of them missed his face, but they struck the real target she was aiming at: his composure.

His frown intensified, cutting a sharp crease across the bridge of his nose and tightening the corners of his mouth. But Molly sensed laughter behind his harsh demeanor, laughter that needed only the slightest bit of coaxing to come out.

She rose to her feet, swaying slightly, and hurled two more fistfuls of foam at him. This time a plush foam ball smacked him in the chin.

Suddenly she was John Russo's target as he gathered up handfuls of foam rubber and strafed her with them, right hand, then left, then right again, both equally accurate. All of his foam missiles hit her. The laughter she'd been hoping for burst out of him, dark and devilish, as he pelted her with a barrage of foam.

Giggling, she staggered backward, lost her footing and fell. He descended to his knees, sweeping armfuls of foam off the floor of the pit and attempting to bury her with them.

She let out a tiny shriek, not loud enough to wake Michael, and scrambled away. He grabbed her ankle and dragged her back toward him through the lush carpet of foam. She bubbled with laughter, squirming and resisting, then twisting onto her side and hurling chunks of foam at him. Whatever she tossed at him he swatted away or tossed right back.

He was smiling. Really smiling. Smiling so broadly his eyes shimmered with fire and his cheeks creased with dimples, and all the pain and worry of his burdens seemed to have melted from him. Laughter rose from his throat, low and delicious. Flecks of foam rubber lodged in his hair.

She reared back to throw another handful of foam at him, but he caught her wrist in his hand and blocked her throw. She couldn't breathe, she was laughing so hard...or maybe what made her breathless was the firm clasp of his fingers around her arm, the nearness of him as he pressed her back down into the resilient floor of the pit.

He didn't let go of her wrist. He just hovered above her, his eyes blinding her with their dark beauty, his smile changing, becoming less bright, more thoughtful.

She was still panting. So was he. The air seemed electric between them, and she knew something dangerous would happen if she didn't prevent it. She was going to have to slide her wrist from his grip and congratulate him on having cut loose for a few minutes. She was going to have to take control.

But this was all about ceding control, wasn't it? It was all about tossing off one's responsibility for a few precious minutes.

And he was still above her, his face so close to hers, his black hair falling around his face.

She reached up and plucked a shred of foam from a silky lock above his brow. He seemed to hold his breath, and his smile vanished. *Enough*, she warned herself—she'd taken enough of a chance touching his hair, letting him touch her arm, lying on her back practically beneath him as he leaned over her. She couldn't let this continue.

Yet she couldn't seem to stop herself. There was another bit of foam snagged in his hair just above his ear, and when she reached for it her fingertips brushed against his earlobe. She didn't exactly see him flinch, but she felt it. She sensed it in his nearly inaudible sigh, in the altered angle of his jaw, the motion of his fingers against the skin of her inner wrist. Not a trace of his smile remained.

Molly wasn't smiling, either. Somehow, this had become deadly serious.

Bowing, he touched his mouth to hers.

She should have known this was coming. She should have known as soon as she'd invited him into the pit, as soon as she'd thrown the first bits of foam at him, as soon as she'd tried to crawl away and he'd hauled her back. She should have known.

She *had* known, and she could have brought the game to a halt. But she'd wanted his kiss too much.

His lips covered hers, cautious and relentless all at once. He exercised restraint, yet his hunger seared her.

His fingers moved against the bare skin of her arm and then glided down, interlacing with her fingers. The pressure of his palm against hers unleashed a rush of heat inside her.

Her mind told her this was a kiss and nothing more. But her heart told her it was infinitely more. It was John Russo, a man who had been hurt but who refused to use his hurt as an excuse to behave badly. A man she hadn't stopped thinking of since the first time she'd seen him, armed and dangerous and talking about his son as if he weren't even aware of how armed and dangerous he was. A man whose kiss could make her want to laugh and weep. He was a man who laughed too rarely—and probably never wept at all.

Need, hot and throbbing, surged through her as he moved his lips on hers, light yet demanding, devouring with gentle nips. She longed for him to claim her mouth, to open her and take her. She yearned for him to sink down onto her, settling between her legs so she could feel the full potency of him. She ached for him in a way she'd never known before, heedless of all the messy complications that could arise if she didn't regain her control very soon.

Not too soon, though, she prayed, and her prayer was answered when he lowered himself, arranging his body over hers, and skimmed his tongue along the edge of her teeth. She sighed, alarmed at how grateful she was, and opened her mouth.

He groaned. It was a quiet, feral sound, born somewhere deep in his soul. She wondered whether he considered kissing her an irresponsible act, and if he did, whether he cared. Maybe kissing her was just as meaningful—or meaningless—to him as jumping into the foam pit had been. For all she knew, he might think of this as just one more way to abandon responsibility.

Even that notion didn't make her want to stop. Not when his weight was warm upon her, his kiss deepening, his tongue tangled with hers. Not when he tightened his grip on her hand and plunged his other hand into her hair, curling his fingers to hold her head steady so he could kiss her more thoroughly. Not when he pressed between her thighs and groaned again, his heat hard against hers.

He wanted her, maybe as much as she wanted him. As he withdrew and then thrust his tongue again, as he rocked her body with his, as he slid his chest against her until the tips of her breasts grew almost painfully tight, she wondered if he was as lost as she was. This was a man who lived his life within narrow boundaries, who'd once made a mistake with a woman and was trying, all these years later, to make up for that mistake. How much could he really let go?

Not as much as she could.

She had been imagining this moment, dreaming about it, for too many days, too many nights. Now that the reality of it had arrived, her heart was bounding ahead, striving toward the next moment. One kiss and she was wishing for things that couldn't be, that shouldn't be.

He was a cop, the father of a student. He was a man under enormous pressure, a man who wouldn't know how to forgive himself for doing the wrong thing.

She tried to say his name, but her voice emerged in a tremulous moan. He freed her lips, breaking the kiss—but then denied her the ability to speak by brushing his mouth against the curve at the base of her throat. All she could do was moan again.

He lifted his head. She opened her eyes and they slowly came into focus. Damn, but he was beautiful to look at. Even more beautiful now, when he was aroused.

"John?" She could barely speak. Her voice was ragged, her breath shallow. Her neck tingled where his lips had branded it.

He flexed his fingers against hers seductively. She had never before considered the flesh between her fingers an erogenous zone. A warm shudder rippled through her, making her want to arch against him.

It took all her willpower to hold herself still. "We really shouldn't be doing this," she murmured, sounding strange to herself, her voice faint, lacking conviction.

He released her hand and propped himself on his arms. She peered up into his shadowed face. The smile that had illuminated his eyes was gone, replaced by layers of caution. He held her gaze for a moment, then averted his eyes and pushed himself off her, leaning back on his haunches. "I'm sorry," he said, addressing the rope railing of the foam pit.

"No." It didn't matter that kissing her student's father was wrong. She didn't want him to be sorry about it. *She* certainly wasn't sorry.

He shoved himself to his feet. After a moment's hesitation, he extended his hand to help her up. She sat without his assistance, then took his proffered hand and let him haul her to her feet. If she felt wobbly this time, it had nothing to do with the yielding foam beneath them.

He released her as soon as she got her balance and ran his hand across his face as if to rub away the effects of the kiss. He continued to avoid her gaze, glancing over at his slumbering son and then back at the pit, at the long indentation where their bodies had rearranged the foam. "Don't take it out on Mike, okay?" he said.

"Take *what* out on him?" *The fact that I'm suffering from incurable lust for you? The fact that I regret having stopped you, and I'm as frustrated as hell, and you can't even bear to look me in the eye?*

He overcame his aversion to her, although it appeared to cost him. Sliding his hand under her chin, he angled her face until her eyes met his. He stared at her, as if willing her to understand so he wouldn't have to spell anything out. Her will was as stubborn as his, though. She refused to nod. If he had something to say, he'd have to say it.

He did. "I was out of line."

"Out of line? What is this, an etiquette class?" She laughed, more from anxiety than because she actually thought John's statement was funny.

"No, Molly. Not etiquette." At least he had the courage to continue staring into her eyes, allowing her to see him. She couldn't read much in his face besides discomfort and regret, but that was enough.

Sighing, she ordered herself to gather what little poise she had left. He felt bad about what had just happened. He felt guilty. He had cut loose and let go and been irresponsible, and he wasn't about to forgive himself or let her grant him absolution. "Don't be so hard on yourself, John. The only way you could have been out of line would be if..." She drifted off, aware of what she was on the verge of confessing.

"If what?"

She wasn't going to let him intimidate her. She was

going to prove to him that losing control wasn't a sin. "If I said no. Which I didn't."

A hint of the light she'd seen in his eyes returned, and he lifted his hand again, this time to cup her cheek. As soon as she felt his palm against her skin he dropped his hand, then turned away, swinging one leg and then the other over the rope wall of the pit. He held the rope low for Molly to climb out, and offered his hand. She refused to take it.

As soon as they were both out of the pit, he crossed to his boots and laced them on. He didn't speak and she wasn't surprised. What else could he say? He wanted her, and he didn't want to want her. And if his current mood remained, if he ever wanted her again, he would do nothing about it.

For the sake of his son? she wondered. Or for his own sake?

Still without speaking, he walked over to the corner where Michael was lying, hunkered down and nudged the boy's shoulder. Michael made a whimpering sound and rolled over. "Time to go, Mike," he murmured.

"Okay," Michael said sleepily.

John waited until Michael was sitting, then straightened up. "Do you want some help with the food?" he asked, motioning with his head toward their forgotten picnic.

No, Molly didn't want any help with the food. The only help she wanted was in breaking down the wall John seemed so determined to keep in place around him. Perhaps she'd slipped through a crevice for a brief interlude, but she had no doubt that the minute he left the Children's Garden he would be hard at work plastering that crack, making it waterproof and rock-tough once more.

For those few precious moments in the pit, she actually might have reached him. But now he was gone again, withdrawing, taking his child and pulling back. Being responsible.

Maybe she ought to be grateful. But she wasn't.

CHAPTER EIGHT

"His lawyer called me again," Abigail's mother was telling Molly. "I don't even know where *he* is. The lawyer won't tell me. I told his lawyer to call my lawyer, but he never listens. The whole thing is making me nuts."

Molly hoped she looked as interested as she ought to be. What Elsie Pelham was saying was important. Molly needed to know about the custody arrangements of her school's pupils—and she needed to know the home environments her students were coming from. But two days after John had kissed her, she was still dazed and distracted, struggling to keep her focus on the present. Her memory of those few passionate moments in the foam pit kept dimming her mind like a dense winter fog.

She'd been all but useless on Sunday when she and Allison Winslow had driven down to Stamford to look at bridal gowns and dresses for the attendants. Allison had oohed and ahhed over sophisticated white silk sheaths and fairy-tale confections of satin and lace, and like a dolt Molly had just nodded and mumbled, "That one's nice." She just couldn't get excited about bridal dresses when she was suffering from emotional arrhythmia, her heartbeat becoming syncopated whenever she thought about John—which was most of the time.

"I know the only reason his lawyer is calling me instead of my lawyer is to frighten me," Elsie Pelham prattled on. "It's a kind of harassment."

"I understand that it upsets you," Molly interjected. "I hope you're not projecting your concerns onto Abigail."

"She doesn't even ask about her father. But it's hard, you know? Every time the phone rings, my blood pressure rises through the ceiling. I'm really trying not to drag her into it, but it's hard."

"We'll do whatever we can to give her a stable environment here," Molly assured her. "You ought to talk to your lawyer. As you say, this other attorney is harassing you. Maybe there's some legal way you can make him stop."

"I mean, because I don't even know where my ex is. The court gave me custody, and if that jerk cared, he could've stuck around in town so he could see Abbie on the weekends. Instead he just took off, and now his lawyer is in my face."

Molly smiled gently. "I can't give you legal advice, Elsie. All I can give you is child care advice. And you know what I'll tell you there—you've got to make Abbie feel secure and loved and try to keep her as far as possible from the strife between you and your former husband."

"I know, I know." Elsie Pelham sighed. "Thanks. I'll give my lawyer a call. Even though the minute he picks up his phone the meter starts running. That's the real reason they're doing this, you know—to cost me money. My ex is exacting revenge for the settlement. He resents every penny I got—and believe me, there weren't too many pennies in that settlement. And now it's all going to my lawyer."

Molly nodded again. She truly felt bad for what Elsie was going through. Some lawyers were in it for nothing but the money. And the people who wound up suffering the most in ugly divorces like this were the children. "I'll tell Shannon to pay extra close attention to Abbie," she promised. "If we see any signs of stress, we'll let you know."

"She's my baby," Elsie said, buttoning her wool coat and thrusting her hands into her gloves. "I want her to have a good Christmas."

"Of course." Still nodding, Molly shaped a compassionate smile for Elsie and waved her out the front door. She couldn't solve the woman's problems for her, but she could pledge that as long as Abigail Pelham was at the Children's Garden she would be all right.

It was a pledge she honored with all the children at the school, no matter who they were or where they came from or what was going on in their parents' lives. That included Michael Russo.

And there she was, thinking about John again.

The door swung open, letting in a gust of chilly air. Like the embodiment of her thoughts, Michael skipped past her desk and into the front hall, singing "The Wheels on the Bus" but garbling the words. She grinned at the way he mangled the verse about the wipers—he called them "Wet Wipes"—and turned expectantly toward the door, both hoping and fearing that John would enter.

Her hopes and fears were realized. John stepped across the threshold, his hair windblown, his bomber jacket zipped against the cold, his hands in his pockets and his gaze resolutely on his son.

"Hello," she said. He might want to avoid looking

at her, but *she* wasn't going to be a coward about it. He was here, and the least he could do was acknowledge her existence.

He turned toward her reluctantly. The dark beauty of his eyes stunned her. His expression conveyed so much—only she couldn't interpret it. She knew there was a message in his eyes, in the enigmatic curve of his lips, the rugged angle of his chin. If only he was as eloquent with his words as he was with his gaze.

"Hi," he said.

Now what? If Saturday's kiss hadn't happened, Molly could have asked him how Michael's weekend was. But Saturday's kiss *had* happened, and the daily morning drop-off ritual was no longer a simple thing.

As difficult as John was to read, she got the impression that he was uncomfortable, regretting the time he'd spent with her on Saturday, regretting the kiss. He probably would prefer to pretend it never happened. But ignoring the truth wasn't one of Molly's talents.

"How are you?" she asked cautiously.

He studied her at her desk, his eyes narrowing on her upturned face. His smile grew more mysterious but it didn't disappear. "Loaded question," he said, then glanced down the hall at Michael. "Are you having trouble with your boots, Mike?" he asked.

"No, I can do it," Michael shouted back. Molly heard the thud of a boot hitting the carpeted floor, followed by Michael's cheerful, off-key warble, "The Wet Wipes on the bus go *swish, swish, swish!*"

John chuckled. Turning back to Molly, he fell silent, as if embarrassed that she should see him enjoying his son's dreadful singing. "I've got to go," he said abruptly, pivoting on his heel.

She wanted to grab hold of him and force him to talk about what had happened Saturday. She and John had shared something significant, and she didn't want to forget about it.

But she couldn't force him to accept what he would rather deny. She couldn't force him to want her today the way he'd seemed to want her Saturday. He might have lost control then, but he wasn't going to lose control now.

She considered this a sad thing, and not just for selfish reasons. For a few precious minutes in the foam pit, John had laughed and played. He'd been carefree, not a police officer or a single father, but a man having fun.

He wasn't carefree anymore. And that was a loss to him as much as to her.

"WHERE'S YOUR SANTA SUIT?" Dennis Murphy asked.

John wondered what the hotshot lawyer was doing in the detectives' squad room. Was Murphy here on a client's behalf or did he have personal business with John?

Maybe last week's situation with his children and the ATM had backfired in some way, requiring further police action. Or perhaps Murphy had just stopped by to razz John about his Santa Claus disguise. What with the holiday hubbub in the station house lobby, where crews were setting up a huge spruce on one side of the entry and an enormous electric menorah on the other, Murphy's comment might be his way of commenting on the holiday spirit.

What John had to say about the holiday spirit wasn't printable, so he kept his mouth shut.

He was already in an unsettled mood when he'd arrived at headquarters that morning and discovered the tree lying tethered on a flatbed truck outside the station house. He didn't like the way Molly could get to him with such a seemingly innocent question as "How are you?" That was the normal courtesy acquaintances used, wasn't it? "Hello. How are you?"

Except that Molly was no mere acquaintance, and nothing that happened between them could be considered a normal courtesy. Not after Saturday.

He shouldn't have kissed her. He shouldn't have let her reach inside and take hold of his soul the way she had. He had no time for an affair with her, no energy. The whole thing had *failure* written all over it.

As if seeing her wasn't enough to remind him of everything that was screwed up in his life, he'd arrived at work and seen the tree. Like the reproachful wag of a finger in front of his face, it reminded him that he was going to have to get a Christmas tree for Mike. Last year, Sherry had argued that standing a huge, messy fir tree in the living room would be more trouble than it was worth, given that Mike was too young to understand Christmas. She, after all, would be the one stuck watering the tree, decorating it and vacuuming the needles from the carpet every day. If she didn't want a tree and Mike didn't care, why get one?

But that was last year. This year, Mike knew damned well what Christmas was all about—if not the religious significance, then certainly the part about Santa leaving a sleigh-load of toys under a tree.

John felt inadequate and overwhelmed. Not only did he have to get a tree, but he had to buy ornaments and tinsel and all that Christmas stuff, plus gifts for Mike. He had no idea what Mike needed or wanted other than a second toy airplane. The kid was too young for a bike or baseball gear. Did they make basketball hoops for two-year-olds? John had no idea.

Molly would know.

Thinking of her brought on a memory of her standing behind her desk at the preschool, peering up at him with her caramel eyes and saying, "How are you?" He'd known he couldn't answer, "Fine." She'd wanted a *real* answer, one he wasn't able to provide—one he could hardly begin to put into words.

Dennis Murphy was approaching his desk. He had to stop obsessing about Molly and act friendly, like a proper officer of the law.

Murphy drew to a halt at John's desk and glanced at his civilian apparel. "So you're not impersonating Santa anymore?"

John gazed up at him over his typewriter. The department had a few word processors, but they were used by the secretaries, not by cops. Preparing their reports was something Arlington's finest did the old-fashioned way.

He shook his head. "Sorry to disappoint your daughter, but I'll be out on the streets as Santa this afternoon."

"I hate to think my kids are old enough to learn Saint Nick is a fraud, but I don't hold you accountable. You did those two a tremendous favor," Murphy said earnestly. He adjusted the blazer of his thousand-dollar suit and smiled. "I've got a client upstairs, called in for questioning about a bit of financial legerdemain he might or might not have witnessed. I thought, on my way upstairs I could stop by and say hello." He smiled. Even his teeth looked well-groomed. "Actually, to express my gratitude."

John shrugged. He hadn't considered his actions on behalf of the Murphy twins anything out of the ordinary.

"Thanks to their little walk on the wild side," said Murphy, "their mother is paying closer attention to the baby-sitters she hires. This is a good thing."

John nodded.

"You handled the entire incident with great sensitivity."

Translation: *I owe you big for not opening juvie files and traumatizing my kids.*

John studied Dennis Murphy. Like John, Murphy was a single father, but he wasn't the custodial parent dealing with the day-to-day stuff. If anyone should have John's sympathy, it was Murphy's ex-wife, struggling to find a decent baby-sitter for her children. Mike had been through a few sitters himself: Norma, whom he'd loved, and Harriet Simka, whom he'd hated. John knew just how difficult it was to find the perfect caregiver.

"I guess I'd better get myself upstairs and make sure my client doesn't shoot his fool mouth off," Murphy said, flashing another smile. John held his own smile in place until Murphy had vanished into the stairwell. Then, expressing his mood with a quiet curse, he ran through the last of his voice mail messages and headed for the locker room to change into his Santa Claus costume. He wished he could put on a jolly spirit along with the padding and the beard. Saying "Ho, ho, ho" convincingly was going to be impossible when all he could think of was Molly, Molly, Molly.

SHE WONDERED HOW LONG she could put off any sort of meeting with him. He obviously felt uncomfortable with her, and his discomfort made her uncomfortable. She wasn't going to be able to avoid him forever—but that didn't mean she couldn't try.

Monday afternoon it was easy enough; she simply asked Cara to remain at the desk for the hour when parents came to retrieve their children. "I'll be upstairs straightening up the second floor if you need me," she explained.

"I can handle her," Cara said sunnily. Molly didn't doubt it. With her beauty and her sweet disposition, Cara could handle a grizzly bear coming off a hunger strike. Elsie Pelham and her messy divorce would be a snap.

Going upstairs and sweeping the scattered sand from the floor around the sand table was a snap, too—at least compared to coming face-to-face with John Russo again. Sooner or later she'd have to confront him. But she had a decent chance of delaying the inevitable for another day. Tomorrow morning she could arrange to be busy in the supply room while the children were coming in, and she had a dental checkup scheduled for four o'clock that afternoon, so she'd be out of the school by the time parents came to start picking up their children.

But if she made a habit of staying away from the front desk, she would be unavailable for other parents who liked to talk to her and hear about how their children were progressing. And even if she could elude John for the entire week, he might show up Saturday at her Daddy School class.

Not likely, she thought with a snort.

It wasn't like her to hide from situations—or from

people. She hated lying or laying low. It simply wasn't her style.

Damn it, she wasn't going to act as if she were afraid of John Russo. Maybe he was afraid of her, but for heaven's sake what could she possibly do to him, besides remind him that one time in his too restricted life he'd cut loose and had fun and kissed Molly?

Her dentist found no cavities on Tuesday, so Molly had no reason to return to the dental clinic Wednesday. She took her station at the front desk in the morning, but when she heard Michael enter, she gravitated toward the supply room, where she remained for a safe ten minutes. If John had wanted to talk to her, he could have marched right past her desk and into the supply room the way he had the first day he'd come to the Children's Garden. But if he'd entered the building at all, he left it without making his presence known.

She managed to keep him away from the forefront of her mind most of the day. The school was busy and noisy. Swirls of snow descended from the sky and dusted the backyard play area, forcing teachers to cancel their usual outdoor activities. Cooped up inside, the children grew rowdy and restless. The staff needed Molly's help in keeping everyone occupied and out of trouble. She organized the Pre-K class to script and stage a puppet show for the younger students. She opened and mopped up several quarts of finger paint for the older toddlers, put together a potty-training clinic for the young toddlers and led circle games for the tiny tots until her hands were sore from clapping and her voice was faded from singing.

"I've got to leave," Cara said at five-thirty. "I promised to take my sister to the mall for Christmas shopping tonight."

"Go ahead," Molly told her. "Let me know if they've got any good sales." She watched her assistant zip up her parka, lift the hood over her hair and set out into the snow. Only about an inch had accumulated. The roads wouldn't be bad.

Even with the roads cleared, though, Molly was anxious to leave. She didn't want to be around when John showed up.

Unable to abandon her post by the front door, she straightened out her desk, turned off her computer and rehearsed what she hoped was a nonthreatening smile. When Elsie Pelham came in, Abigail was so full of exuberant chatter about the snow that her mother didn't have a chance to vent about her custody battle. Other mothers and fathers came and went. Each time the front door opened, Molly's heart lurched a little, then settled back into its rhythm when she saw that the person entering wasn't John.

She waved off Keisha and her father, then checked her watch. Six-fifteen. No sign of John.

Shannon emerged down the hall with Michael. "Everyone else is gone," Shannon reported. "Do you want to stay with him till his dad comes or should I?"

"I'll stay," Molly said. She might as well see John and get it over with. It wouldn't be so bad, since they'd have Michael between them. They'd be so busy wrestling him into his boots and jacket and mittens, they wouldn't have time to talk to each other. She wouldn't have a chance to gaze into his eyes. She wouldn't have the chance to decipher his smile—if he was smiling, which wasn't likely.

Six-twenty. Michael sat on the floor of the hall, engaged in a fight to the death with his boots. He'd gotten one boot halfway onto his left foot before giving up and attempting to wriggle the other boot onto his right. Molly peeked past the front door into the parking lot but saw no approaching headlights.

"Let me help you with those boots," she suggested.

"My daddy's here?"

"Not yet."

"My daddy's a police."

"I know that," she said, kneeling on the floor next to Michael and easing the boot over his heel.

"He's at the policeman place."

"I'm sure he is. He'll be here soon."

"We can go there."

"I don't know about that," said Molly. "If we go there while he's on his way here, we'll miss him."

"He's at the policeman place," Michael insisted.

"I tell you what. I'll give the policeman place a call and see if he's still there."

Michael followed her into the office area, his boots clomping loudly with each step. Little boys had a way of walking to maximize noise, and Michael proved himself to be an expert at it. He looked so much like his father, yet in behavior he was the opposite—loud, rambunctious, uninhibited and easily given to laughter or tears.

While Molly looked up John's business phone number in Michael's file, Michael experimented with jumping in his boots. They made a clumsy galumphing noise, which obviously pleased him. He jumped again and squealed.

"Quiet," Molly whispered as the phone was answered on the other end, a weary-sounding woman identifying Arlington Police headquarters. "Can I have John Russo's line, please?"

She heard a click, then five rings, and then John's

voice on a tape, saying he was away from his desk and she could either leave a message after the beep or remain on the line. She remained on the line.

After a minute, the woman who'd originally answered the call said, "Arlington Police Headquarters. This call is being recorded. Can I help you?"

Molly identified herself. "I'm trying to find out if Detective Russo has left for the day. I have his son here at my preschool, and it's now—" she checked her watch and scowled "—a half hour past pickup time."

"Hang on a second," the woman said. Judging from the muffled sound, Molly assumed she'd covered the mouthpiece with her hand before shouting, "Hey, Steve, you know John Russo's car?" There was a pause, and then, "Is it still in the lot?" Another pause, and the woman spoke back into the phone. "His car is in the lot, so I guess he's still here. He must just be away from his desk."

"Can you give him a message?" Molly asked, following Michael's clomping dance around the office with her gaze. "Tell him to stay put. I'll drive his son to the police station."

"Okay. I'll leave a message."

"Thanks." Molly hung up the phone and smiled at Michael. "You were right. Your daddy's at the policeman place. Let's go."

THE SNOW WAS WET, and the ground was warm enough to keep it from sticking. The roads glistened, but they weren't dangerously slick. Molly clicked on her windshield wipers, and Michael burst into his version of "The Wheels on the Bus" once more, crooning gleefully about Wet Wipes going swish.

"Do you like snow?" she asked, glimpsing him in her rearview mirror. The school kept spare child booster seats on hand, and she'd strapped him into the middle rear seat of her Saturn.

"I like snow," he told her. "It's big and cold and you can make snowmen."

"Well, this snow looks pretty slushy. I don't know if you'll be able to make a snowman with it."

"I can make a snowball."

"I bet you could do that." She turned the corner. Rush hour was winding down, but there was still a fair amount of downtown traffic. Headlights reflected off the streets and glared into her eyes.

Why hadn't John picked up Michael? He always picked his son up on time. If he was running late today, why hadn't he at least called to let Molly know? Did he really hate her that much?

Who cared if he did? He knew the school rules, and he would be the first to describe himself as responsible to a fault. Something must have happened, some involved case. Maybe he was locked inside an interrogation room, breaking down a suspect, making the poor guy sweat and squirm. Maybe the suspect was about to spill the beans, and John didn't want to halt the interrogation when he was so close to a breakthrough. Maybe he was flashing his gun under the guy's nose, flashing his badge, rattling the keys to a jail cell. Maybe he was throwing around his weight as a police officer, intimidating someone, abusing his power.

And maybe she shouldn't listen to Gail so much.

They reached the police station, parked in one of the spaces marked for visitors, and entered the sprawling lobby. A seven-foot-tall spruce stood on one side of the room. Michael let out a cheer and raced over to it, suddenly agile in his boots. "A tree, a tree! A Christmas tree!"

Molly smiled and let him dance around the tree for a minute. It was dressed in flashing colored lights and ribbon-wrapped foam balls. Across the vaulted lobby stood a huge menorah topped with nine flame-shaped red lightbulbs, none of them yet lit.

"Come on, Michael," she said when it seemed he wasn't going to leave the tree without urging. "Let's go find your daddy."

"A Christmas tree," he explained to her, slipping his small, mittened hand into hers and letting her lead him away. "Santa Claus leaves presents under the tree. He comes down the chimbley."

"Chimney," she corrected him. "That's right."

"Where's the chimbley here? They got a chimbley in the policeman place?"

"Sure they do."

"And a fireplace? Gotta have a fireplace. Santa comes down the chimbley to the fireplace."

"I don't know if they have one of those," Molly said, leading Michael over to a broad counter behind which officers and dispatchers swarmed. "But Santa knows how to get into buildings even if they don't have fireplaces. He's very clever."

Michael nodded in agreement. "He's smart. He gives children toys."

Molly suppressed a laugh as she crossed the lobby to the counter and caught the eye of a uniformed woman on the other side. "Excuse me. Where can we find John Russo? He's a detective here."

"Russo? Up one flight of stairs and turn left."

Molly thanked her. Still holding Michael's hand,

she headed for the stairs. A slow anger began to simmer inside her. John should have called the school. He should have been as responsible today as he always was. He shouldn't have neglected his child, even though Michael was too excited about this new adventure—driving in the school director's car to the police station at night, seeing snow, seeing a Christmas tree—to care much about his father's oversight. Molly cared. And her anger built.

They reached the landing and she turned left, entering a small squad room with six desks occupying the cramped space and a glass-walled office overlooking it. No one was in the squad room. She ventured in, thinking that if she could figure out which desk was John's, she could leave him a scathing note about his carelessness toward his son. Before she could locate the desk, the door to the glassed-walled office opened and a man emerged. He was of average height, his chin softened by age. "Can I help you?" he asked, peering at her through thick eyeglasses.

"I'm looking for John Russo. I'm Molly Saunders, the director of the preschool where his son Michael is a student."

The man looked troubled. "Didn't they call you? Someone was supposed to call you."

Molly's anger was doused by a shower of icy fear, colder than the snow falling outside. "No one called me."

"He—uh..." The man glanced toward Michael, then wove among the desks to Molly's side so he could speak in a softer voice. "I'm Lieutenant Coffey," he said. "John ran into a bit of trouble today. He's at Arlington Memorial Hospital."

"Oh, my God." The words emerged in a quiet rush,

and she instinctively tightened her grip on Michael's hand. She responded to the lieutenant's words not as a teacher but as John's friend, someone who cared about him and his child. "Is he all right? What happened?"

"Well..." He sighed. "He brought down a perp. Unfortunately the perp had a knife."

"Oh, my God," she said again, only this time she scarcely had the breath to pronounce the words.

"He was taken directly to Arlington Memorial, but he told one of the uniforms at the scene to make sure someone called his son's preschool. But with one thing and another..." Lieutenant Coffey sighed again and lowered his eyes. "I guess it slipped past us. I'm sorry." He glanced down at Michael.

Michael's wide, dark eyes focused on Lieutenant Coffey and then on Molly. He looked worried. He couldn't have understood everything the man had said, but he understood enough to know something terrible was going on. "I want Daddy," he said in a tremulous voice.

"I know you do." Molly staggered through her thoughts, trying to construct a plan of action. If she took Michael to the hospital, he would be with his father. But what if his father had been gravely injured? What if he was right this minute in intensive care, plugged in to tubes and monitors, fighting for his life?

The perp had a knife. The lieutenant's voice echoed inside her skull, making her tremble, filling her mind with horrifying possibilities. *The perp had a knife.*

She couldn't take Michael home with her, even though she would like to. It would be too presumptuous. John had withdrawn from any personal relationship with her. She couldn't just take over as a surrogate parent in this crisis.

If he was in desperate shape, his relatives would have been called. He had all those brothers and sisters—some of them might be pacing the hospital's waiting room right now. She could take Michael and let one of his aunts or uncles look after him for the night.

Her heart pounded. Her eyes burned with fear. But she couldn't let Michael know how frightened she was for his father. She had to make sure he was safely in the care of someone who loved him first. After she did that, she could worry about John.

She sent a silent prayer heavenward, then gave Michael's hand a gentle squeeze. "Let's go," she said. "Let's go find your daddy, okay?"

He smiled up at her with so much trust, it was all she could do not to burst into tears. "Okay," he said. "Let's go see Daddy."

CHAPTER NINE

WHEN THE NOVOCAIN finally wore off, John's right arm was going to hurt like hell. But right now, he wasn't feeling any pain.

What he *was* feeling was a heady mix of exhaustion and exhilaration, a strange emotional high that came from the realization that he had outwitted death.

From the moment he'd set down his bell and kettle to check out the mysterious shadows he'd seen dancing in the alleyway between a high-end card shop and a jeweler on Hauser Boulevard, he'd sensed that he wasn't going to have a pleasant time of it. A good cop trusted his intuition. Just as an allergic person might feel an itch in the presence of dust or cats, a cop felt an itch in the presence of bad news. By the time John saw the knife, he was itching all over.

It was a kid, a street punk, dressed straight out of the Generation-X fashion manual. The woman wasn't much older, but she was better groomed—probably an office worker out to do some Christmas shopping on her lunch hour. The knife had a six-inch blade that could have stripped the pelt off a bear, and it was pressed to the woman's throat. The kid was asking her to do something obscene to him when John drew his revolver out from under his Santa tunic and said, "Police. Drop it."

The kid didn't drop the knife, although he did drop

the woman, shoving her against the grimy brick wall and bolting around the rear of the card shop and back out the other side onto Hauser. John took off after him.

On the sidewalk, the punk tried to lose himself in the milling crowds of holiday shoppers. John tucked his revolver back into the elastic waistband of his slacks; there were too many innocent people in the vicinity to risk taking a shot. The kid still had his knife, though. He gripped it in his fist and plowed through the throngs, which had the good sense to part before him like the Red Sea, leaving a path for John as well. Anyone wise enough not to block the path of a creep with a hunting knife was also wise enough not to block the path of a really angry cop charging down the sidewalk in a Santa Claus costume.

As he ran, John considered the punk's knife, but only in the most reflexive way. There was a chance of injury—serious injury—and he factored it into the equation. He wasn't one of those crackpots who acted as if they were immortal or who measured their manhood by how many stupid chances they took. But he had witnessed a felony—assault with a deadly weapon—and it was his job to bring the bastard down.

Pedestrians screamed and gasped as he sprinted past them, but he tuned them out, hoping they'd stay out of his way. He would likely run over anyone who crossed his path at the wrong time, but if he slowed down, he'd lose the punk. Instead he ran faster, harder, closing in on the kid until he was near enough to attempt a flying tackle. Feeling the exertion in his thighs, he leaped forward, snagged one of the kid's ankles and landed him.

John saw the sharp glint of silver in the punk's hand as they tangled and rolled along the slushy pavement.

He didn't feel the first cut, but he heard the rip of his sleeve as the blade gashed through the red flannel. They wrestled some more, and he noticed large circles of red spreading into the slush. But even then, he felt nothing more than anger that this thug, this useless piece of human excrement who had hauled a woman into an alley and threatened her life, dared to resist him.

He used his hand to deflect the second slash of the knife, but the blade sliced through his glove, stinging wickedly. More blood leaked onto the sidewalk. John's blood.

Fueled by rage, indignation and that fierce sense of justice that kept good cops from going bad or giving up, he slugged the punk in the jaw, snapping his head back. Stunned by the blow, the kid deflated, his eyes getting wilder but his body losing power. Before he could regain his breath, John had him on his stomach, the knife tumbling from his fingers as John cuffed his hands behind him.

Only after John had rolled the kid onto his back again, with his manacled hands under him and John's knees planted firmly on his chest, did John turn off his reflexes and turn on his brain. Struggling to catch his breath, he reached under his tunic for his radio. When he pulled it out and lifted it to his face to call for assistance, he realized that his glove was soaked with blood and his fingers were tingling.

If he tried to stand, he would probably collapse. So he just stayed where he was, sitting on the creep while he called for backup. He remained on the chilly sidewalk, watching his blood leak in dark stains through the cherry red fabric of the Santa suit, and waited for help.

He might have faded to black once or twice on the ride over to Arlington Memorial, but all in all, his injuries weren't critical. No major arteries had been punctured, no tendons severed. Eighteen stitches closed the wound in his forearm, and a flock of butterfly clips currently held the skin of his palm together.

He was alive. He'd nailed a punk who didn't deserve the space he took up in the world. He'd saved a woman from an assault. He'd gotten cut. He was bloody but unbowed. He had survived.

Definitely a high.

The doctor molded wads of bandage into the curve of his palm, arched his fingers around the packing and then wrapped about a mile of gauze around it. "If you use this hand, it's not going to heal," he said. "I'm binding it this way so you won't be able to move it and reopen the cut."

"Uh-huh." John's tongue felt as dry and rough-textured as the bandage. He needed a drink. As soon as he picked up Mike and got home, he was going to pour himself a generous portion of something strong.

"I know you're right-handed, so this isn't going to be easy for you," the doctor commiserated. "But it's a tricky wound. Hands can take forever to heal if you don't keep them motionless."

"Uh-huh."

"What's your name?" the doctor asked evenly, measuring off a strip of adhesive tape and snipping it with a scissors.

John frowned. "John Russo. One of the uniforms took care of the paperwork—"

The doctor cut him off with a laugh. "I just want to make sure I'm not losing you. You have a glassy look in your eyes, Detective. It isn't too late to go into shock."

"I'm not in shock."

"Good. If you were, I'd admit you for observation."

"Come on, Doc. It's a scratch." He eyed his arm wrapped in a white bandage and then his immobilized hand. "Two scratches," he amended.

"And some bruised ribs," the doctor reminded him. As best John could figure, the perp had kicked him in the chest a couple of times while they'd been rolling around on the sidewalk. The punk had been wearing thick-soled Doc Martens. John had a few Technicolor welts on the left side of his chest, but they didn't hurt, either. Not yet.

His shoulders ached, but he suspected that was from sitting on an examining table with no back support. He and the doctor were enclosed in a small corner of the emergency room, a nook blocked off from the ER waiting area by a pale green curtain. The Santa tunic had been cut off him by an earnest intern who hadn't looked old enough to shave. Seeing the costume reduced to rags brought a wry smile to John's lips. Maybe, finally, he wouldn't have to play undercover Santa Claus anymore.

"What time is it?" he asked. "I've got to pick up my kid."

"You're not going anywhere until I release you," the doctor reminded him. "Wasn't someone from your squad supposed to bring some clothes to the hospital for you?" He eyed John's blood-spattered Santa trousers and shook his head.

"They're probably outside in the waiting room."

Nodding, the doctor smoothed the last strip of tape

around John's hand. "I'll see if they've arrived. Don't you dare move while I'm gone. I mean it, Detective. You stand up too quickly and you're going to keel over and smack your head on the floor. The last thing you need right now is a concussion."

"Uh-huh." He secretly tested his thumb to make sure the doctor hadn't taped it too tight. He wasn't planning to play the "Minute Waltz" on the piano anytime in the foreseeable future, but he had to have *some* movement in his fingers. If he couldn't do the most basic things—button his jeans, grip the steering wheel of his car—he'd be no use to himself or Mike.

The doctor set his tools neatly on a wheeled tray, then shot John a warning look and pulled back the green curtain.

"Daddy!" Mike shrieked from the waiting area, and a blur of energy flew toward John, barely slowing enough for him to make out the yellow rubber boots, the blue-and-green parka, the mittens flapping loosely from a cord strung through the jacket sleeves. Then he saw Mike's face. His tousled hair, his shining eyes, his dazzling smile.

John couldn't imagine a more welcome sight. And then he *could* imagine one, because it materialized before him: Mike hurtling joyously at him, Molly behind him, loitering near the curtain, cautious but hopeful, her eyes damp and her smile fraught with worry.

Had she been crying? For him?

If she'd shed any tears, it had probably been because she'd been stuck taking care of Mike for an extra hour, and Mike in top form could reduce anyone to tears. That was a safer explanation than the alternative: that she cared enough to cry over John.

Whether or not she cared, she obviously didn't feel

An Important Message from the Editors of Harlequin®

Dear Reader,

Because you've chosen to read one of our fine romance novels, we'd like to say "thank you!" And, as a <u>special</u> way to thank you, we've selected <u>four more</u> of the books you love so well, <u>plus</u> a beautiful cherub magnet, to send you absolutely **FREE!**

Please enjoy them with our compliments...

Candy Lee

Editor

P.S. And because we <u>value</u> our customers, we've attached something extra inside...

Peel off seal and place inside...

EDITOR'S FREE GIFT SEAL — THANK YOU

How to validate your
Editor's FREE GIFT "Thank You"

1. Peel off gift seal from front cover. Place it in space provided at right. This automatically entitles you to receive four free books and a beautiful cherub refrigerator magnet.

2. Send back this card and you'll get brand-new Harlequin Superromance® novels. These books have a cover price of $3.99 each, but they are yours to keep absolutely free.

3. There's no catch. You're under no obligation to buy anything. We charge nothing—ZERO—for your first shipment. And you don't have to make any minimum number of purchases—not even one!

4. The fact is thousands of readers enjoy receiving books by mail from the Harlequin Reader Service®. They like the convenience of home delivery...they like getting the best new novels BEFORE they're available in stores... and they love our discount prices!

5. We hope that after receiving your free books you'll want to remain a subscriber. But the choice is yours— to continue or cancel, any time at all! So why not take us up on our invitation, with no risk of any kind. You'll be glad you did!

6. Don't forget to detach your FREE BOOKMARK. And remember...just for validating your Editor's Free Gift Offer, we'll send you FIVE MORE gifts, *ABSOLUTELY FREE!*

GET A FREE CHERUB MAGNET...

This charming refrigerator magnet looks like a little cherub, and it's a perfect size for holding notes and recipes. Best of all it's yours ABSOLUTELY FREE when you accept our NO-RISK offer!

HARLEQUIN®

P L
F R E
S
H

YES!
I have plac
You" seal in the spac
send me 4 free book
magnet. I understand
to purchase any bool
back and on the opp

Name

Address

City

State

Than

With our
compliments

The Editors

Harlequin Reader Service® — Here's How It Works:

BUSINESS REPLY MAIL

FIRST-CLASS MAIL   PERMIT NO. 717   BUFFALO, NY

POSTAGE WILL BE PAID BY ADDRESSEE

HARLEQUIN READER SERVICE
3010 WALDEN AVE
PO BOX 1867
BUFFALO NY 14240-9952

NO POSTAGE
NECESSARY
IF MAILED
IN THE
UNITED STATES

comfortable enough to enter his little curtained compartment. She held his gaze for an immeasurable moment, then lowered her eyes to his naked chest, wincing when she spotted the bruises. She lifted her gaze back to his face.

"You're all right." It was half a question, half a sigh. Her voice wavered.

"Yeah."

Mike was skipping and twirling around the foot of the table, trying to figure out a way to scramble into his father's lap. "We were at the policeman place," he reported, bustling with excitement and self-importance. "We saw a tree. They have a very, very, very big tree. *This* big!" He extended his arms as wide as he could. "Is Santa Claus gonna leave toys for the policeman people?"

"I think he's going to leave toys that the policemen give to needy children in town," John explained. The Arlington Fire Department ran the city's Toys-For-Tots program, but the police force usually collected donations for the firefighters.

"Look at this!" Mike touched the bulky bandages covering John's hand. "Your hand looks so big! It's funny, Daddy!"

"It's all gauze and tape," John told Mike, ruffling his hair with his left hand. He wanted to cup his hand around the back of Mike's head and cling to him. He was beginning to come down from the high, and as he descended the truth caught up with him. If the punk had nicked a vein, he might have bled to death. He might have died on Hauser Boulevard on a cold, wet sidewalk in front of holiday shoppers. He might have died and never had the chance to see or touch or talk to his son again.

But if he wrapped his arms around Mike, the good arm and the bad, and hugged as hard as he wanted to, until he popped the sutures the doctor had tacked into his arm, until his muscles ached and his bruised ribs cracked and he squeezed tears from his own eyes, he would only frighten Mike. The boy didn't understand what John had just been through. He couldn't begin to understand. At his age, he shouldn't have to understand such awful things.

Mike's hair felt downy beneath his fingers, still baby soft. John traced the curve of Mike's skull down to the hollow at the nape of his neck. So precious, he thought. His little boy. His little boy might have lost his daddy the way he'd already lost his mommy.

But he hadn't. Fate had been kind to Mike this time. To Mike and John both.

He raised his eyes to Molly, who still hovered near the curtains, watching him. He wondered what she saw in his face, what his eyes might be giving away. "I'm okay," he murmured, needing reassurance as much as she did.

"I know." Her gaze journeyed to Mike, who wriggled out from under his father's hand and was bouncing around the curtained nook again. "What happens now?"

"Someone from my squad was supposed to bring me my clothes." He glanced down at his bare chest. Those bruises *were* nasty. No wonder she kept gaping at them.

"There are a lot of officers out there," she said. "At least six of them."

He eyed the clock hanging on the wall behind the table. "They probably ended their shifts and came over. When one of us gets hurt, we do that."

"That's nice." Her voice sounded rusty. "Do you want me to see if one of them has your clothes?"

What he wanted was for her to stay right where she was, in his line of vision. Actually, no—he wanted her to come closer so he could hug her the way he couldn't hug Mike. He wanted to absorb her strength. He wanted her soft, warm curves to remind him that he was alive.

Mike found the blood pressure cuff dangling from a wall rack and tore the Velcro with a loud rasp, jolting John and clearing his mind. He glanced at his son, then back at Molly. As he continued his descent from euphoria, he realized he was cold. Cold and tired.

"The doctor is getting my clothing," he said.

"Even with clothes, John, you can't drive home like that." She gestured toward his right hand.

"Shh." He peered toward the curtain, wondering if the doctor had overheard her. "If they think I can't drive home, they'll make me spend the night here."

"Maybe you *should* stay the night. Just in case."

"No." Arlington Memorial was a fine facility, but John had heard enough stories about people who went into hospitals to have a nose job and wound up paralyzed for life, people who had the wrong leg amputated or the wrong kidney removed, people who had gone in for routine tests, picked up bacterial infections and died. Besides, if he had to spend the night at Arlington Memorial, who would take care of Mike?

Molly's earnest gaze gave him his answer. Of course she would take care of Mike if necessary.

But John was too selfish to want her to take care of his son. What he wanted was for her to take care of *him*.

Cripes, where had that thought come from? Maybe

he was in shock, after all—or else he was still tripping on adrenaline. He shouldn't want Molly doing anything for him. She'd already done too much, taking care of Mike for the past hour and then bringing him here.

"What I was thinking," she said quietly, "was that maybe I could take you and Michael home. A police officer could drive your car to your house, right? You shouldn't be driving tonight. The roads are still a little slippery, and you..." Her gaze wandered to his chest again, to his lap where his right hand rested, to the thick bandage taped around his forearm. "You shouldn't drive."

"Okay." He told himself he was agreeing to let her transport him and Mike because she was right, he shouldn't get behind the wheel. But there was that selfish yearning again, that giddy defiance. He'd been stabbed. In his condition, stitched and patched and dazed, he didn't have to be responsible. If he absolutely had to, he could let someone else take charge for a few minutes.

Especially someone like Molly, who would do the right thing. She would make sure Mike's needs were met. She might even fix that stiff drink for John. Hell, he couldn't take more than a drink from her right now, anyway. He was sore. His hand was useless, and less than an hour ago his blood pressure had plummeted low enough to freak out the ER nurse. Any woman who got personal with him in the condition he was in would only wind up disappointed.

And he must be delirious, thinking about Molly in that context.

The doctor reappeared with Bud Schaefer, John's frequent partner. Carrying the apparel John had worn to the station house that morning, Bud was a welcome sight. "Hey, Russo, how's it going?" Bud said almost shyly. It was bad form for fellow officers to reveal anything too intimate to each other, like fear or concern. Seeing a colleague hurt was one of the hardest things a cop had to endure.

"I've felt better," John responded, attempting a smile. His head had started to throb.

Bud turned his gaze to Mike, who was still playing with the Velcro fastening of the blood pressure cuff. "Hey, Tiger, remember me?"

Mike raced over. "You're a policeman guy."

"That's right. I work with your dad."

"That means you're a policeman guy."

"Well, I'm going to help your dad get into some real clothes. So maybe you might want to go back out to the waiting room." He eyed Molly, searching for assistance.

"Michael, come with me," she said, extending a hand and a warm grin. "Let's go look at the nurse's computer again. Would you like that?"

"Will she make the colors change on the screen?"

"Maybe she'll do that again if you ask her nicely."

Mike skipped over to Molly, took her hand and dragged her past the curtain, out of the room.

Bud directed his inquiring gaze to John. "Who's the lady?" he asked as he shook the wrinkles out of John's shirt and held it up, positioning it so John could slide his left arm into the sleeve.

John hated being assisted into his own shirt, but he didn't have much choice. Swallowing his anger—none of this was Bud's fault, after all—he thrust his good arm into the left sleeve. "She runs Mike's preschool."

"Yeah?" Bud's tone left no doubt that he sensed

that more than just preschool was going on between Molly and John. "She's cute."

"Yeah."

"Very cute. On a scale of one to ten, I'd give her an eight at the very least. Nine if she was taller."

John said nothing. He didn't like the idea of Bud—or anyone—assigning Molly a score, but if he said so, Bud might guess that John had special feelings for her. Instead, he concentrated on easing his injured arm into the other sleeve. "Could you drive my car home for me?" he asked. "She's going to take me and Mike home. She's got a kid seat in her car." As if that was why John wanted to ride with her instead of Bud.

"Yeah, sure." He reached into a pocket of the slacks he'd brought for John and pulled out the key ring. John identified the car key and Bud manipulated it off the ring. They collaborated to get him out of his Santa pants and into his slacks. Closing the fly turned out to be not too hard—he wasn't too clumsy with his left hand—but buttoning his shirt was a bitch. He wound up sitting helpless while Bud did the buttons for him.

"How are you going to do this on your own?" Bud asked.

"Unbuttoning it won't be so hard. After I get the shirt off, I'll stick to pullovers."

"You taking tomorrow off?"

"I'll see how I feel."

Bud tied the laces on John's boots. It was humiliating to be so dependent on someone for such elementary tasks. He wondered if Mike ever felt this way when John helped him in and out of his boots. "Do us all a favor and don't come in," Bud said, kindly keeping his gaze on John's feet. "You'll be useless, and you'll have all the secretaries fussing over you and ignoring the rest of us."

John grunted. If he couldn't even tie his own shoes, he sure as hell wasn't going to be worth much tomorrow. But it wasn't Bud's privilege to decide for him. Nor was it Coffey's, or the doctor's, or anyone else's. It was John's decision alone.

He had to write up a report on today's arrest. Someone had to take the victim's statement, if that hadn't already been done by someone else. And she'd have to do a visual ID of the perp—but someone had probably taken care of that, too. Anything he couldn't do over the phone tomorrow could wait a day, he supposed. Or one of those fussing secretaries could drive over to his house with a laptop and get him through the paperwork.

He didn't want a department secretary at his house. He didn't want anyone...except Molly. Molly, whose eyes had filled with tears for him.

He gave himself a quick inspection and found himself fully attired. Moving his head made it ache. His chest ached, too, on the bruised side. At least his arm and hand were still numb from the anesthetic. But once that wore off...

Bottom line: he was a wreck, barely held together by surgical thread. The high was gone and John was crashing.

He smiled weakly. "I'm going to try to stand now."

"I'll catch you if you fall." Bud took a half step backward, giving John room to set his feet on the floor.

He wobbled. Cymbals crashed inside his skull and the muscles along his spine threatened to contract. His knees felt spongy, and if there had been anything in his stomach, it would have come back up. The room tilted slightly and he closed his eyes.

He wasn't going to fall. Not when the only person around to catch him was Bud. If falling was his fate, he wanted only one person to pick him up. She was way too small to lift him, but what she lacked in physical mass she made up in inner strength. He had no doubt she could catch him if he tumbled.

"Go get Molly," he said.

HIS HOUSE WAS EXACTLY what she would have expected if she'd ever thought about it: a neat, nicely proportioned ranch, not too big and not too small, sitting at the center of a well-tended half-acre lot. The snow had stopped, leaving a thin veneer of white blanketing the front yard and driveway. "Let me open the garage," he said, twisting in the passenger seat to reach the door latch with his left hand.

She touched his shoulder to stop him. Through the leather of his jacket she felt bone and muscle, strength and stubbornness. He went still beneath her touch but didn't turn back to her. "First of all," she said, "you shouldn't be yanking on garage doors. Second, if I park in there, where will your friend park your car?"

Slowly he relaxed under her hand, shaking his head and smiling wanly. "If you pull in—" he waved toward the garage door "—I won't have as far to walk."

"Okay. I'll drive in and drop you off, then pull back out and park on the street." She let go of him, only to extend her hand for him to pass her his keys. He was obviously reluctant to cede them, but he must have realized he couldn't hoist the hinged door up on its tracks with only one functioning arm.

"Dana says you push a button and his garage opens," Michael reported from the rear seat. "Like magic."

"That's called an automatic garage door opener," Molly said, closing her fingers around John's key ring and yanking on the parking brake. "I'll be right back."

The cold air slapped her cheeks as she climbed out of the car. She needed its bracing effect to clear her mind after the shock of seeing him sitting on the examining table in the emergency room.

She'd been horrified by the bandages, of course. The officers pacing the waiting area had told her about the knife. In fact, they'd described its size with relish, until she'd pointed to Michael and they'd realized that the gruesome details of John's injuries would frighten him—to say nothing of scaring the heck out of her. Knowing the size of the knife, she could guess at the severity of the wounds beneath the gauze.

But more than John's injuries had affected her. She'd been stunned by the sight of his chest, lean and streamlined and utterly male. Her gaze had taken in the narrow indentation of his navel, and his nipples, and the arch of his collarbones, and his broad, bony shoulders, and his biceps, not bulging with brawn but firm and sinewy, hinting at his strength without bragging about it.

She'd seen his shaggy hair, his jaw shadowed by a day's growth of beard. She'd seen the odd shimmer in his eyes. And then she'd seen the bruises discoloring one side of his rib cage. She'd stared at the bandages again. And then his eyes. And then his naked chest.

Myriad responses had buffeted her. She'd been so afraid for him, and so relieved. She'd been appalled by his wounds and sympathetic about his pain. But underlying those rational reactions, like a soft, pulsing bass riff almost drowned out by the high notes, she'd been aroused by his profoundly male beauty.

But he hadn't accepted her offer of a lift home because he wanted to be ogled. If anything, he wanted to be assisted into a comfortable chair and left alone. He wanted her to take care of Michael so he could rest. That was the only reason she was at his house.

She heaved the garage door open, got back into the car and coasted into the garage. Before John contorted himself to reach for the door latch, she was out of the car again, racing around to his side and opening his door for him. He shot her a look of resignation combined with annoyance. She knew he resented his helplessness, but there wasn't much she could do about it other than what she was doing.

Michael tumbled out of the car as soon as she released him from his child seat. "Is it dinner? I'm hungry, Daddy," he announced, as if this were a night like any other.

Molly unlocked the door connecting the garage to the house and stepped aside. Michael slipped his hand into his father's as they went in.

After moving her car back out to the street, she returned to the garage and entered the house. John and Michael were in the kitchen. It was cleaner than she would have expected a male-dominated kitchen to be, but devoid of decorator touches. The curtains were plain, the refrigerator without magnets, the days of the wall calendar marked with an angular scrawl. Michael was seated on the linoleum floor, struggling to remove his boots. John leaned against a counter, his face pale and his mouth taut.

"Sit," Molly commanded, figuring he would probably prefer to be ordered about than to be babied. "I'll help you with those boots in a second, Michael," she added, unfastening her jacket and shrugging out of it. She glared at John, who hadn't moved. "Sit," she repeated. "There." She pulled a chair away from the table and pointed to it, then turned her back on him and draped her jacket over another chair.

By the time she knelt down next to Michael, he'd triumphed over his boots. He tossed them into a corner and frolicked off, shouting, "I'm starving! I'm gonna play now."

Without Michael to focus on, she had no choice but to look at John. He had freed his left arm from his jacket and was gingerly easing his right arm through the sleeve. He tossed the jacket onto the seat of the chair where she'd draped her parka, then lifted his gaze to her. His cheeks looked hollow, their contours emphasized by his five-o'clock shadow. His eyes seemed haunted.

"Did the doctor give you any painkillers?" she asked.

"Yeah." He reached into the pocket of his jacket and pulled out a small bottle of pills. He read the label, then set the bottle on the table. "There's a bottle of Scotch in the cabinet above the fridge," he said. "Glasses are on the shelf above the toaster."

She caught herself before lecturing on the dangers of mixing liquor with prescription drugs. He hadn't taken one of the doctor's painkillers—and he *had* read the label with its numerous warning stickers. He was a cop; surely he knew what he was doing.

Gail would give her a long, vehement reprimand for placing that much faith in him. But Gail wasn't here now, and Molly's only purpose was to make this evening work out for John and his son.

She dragged a chair over to the refrigerator, climbed onto it and opened the cabinet. Pulling down the bottle of Scotch, she told herself that just because she was puttering around in his kitchen didn't mean she was making herself at home in his house. Her friend Allison would feel more comfortable in this situation. She was a nurse, used to seeing that patients' needs were met.

Molly brought the chair back to the table and then located a glass on the shelf he'd indicated. She presented him with the glass, and the fingers of his left hand brushed hers as he took it from her. He set the glass on the table, twisted the cap off the bottle and poured out an inch of the gold-hued liquor. She stuffed her hand into the pocket of her jeans, as if that would erase the feel of his callused fingertips whispering against her skin.

"Would you like me to fix something for dinner?" she asked brightly. "Or I could run out and pick up some fast food if you'd rather."

"I'm not hungry," he said, then took a sip. "If you could throw together a sandwich for Mike, that would be great."

She surveyed the contents of the refrigerator, found bread and American cheese and pulled them out. Then she eyed John reproachfully. "I don't care if you're hungry or not. You have to eat, too."

He sent her what began as a scathing look but softened into a grudging smile. "You're going to make me?"

She smiled back. "You bet I am. Where do you keep soup?"

"Do you boss the kids around, too?"

"Where's the soup?" she persisted, planting her hands on her hips and giving him her sternest frown.

He shrugged in defeat, then took a sip of his drink. "Left of the sink," he said. "*Do* you boss the kids around?"

She swung open the cabinet, pulled down a can of tomato soup and proceeded to locate a pot on her own. "Yes, I boss the kids around. I boss everybody around. I'm trying to train Michael to say 'Yes, Boss' whenever he addresses me. I'd also like to train him to salute, or maybe to bow in my presence, but we haven't gotten that far yet."

John surprised her by laughing. She was glad she'd managed to defuse his tension and distract him from his pain. She was also glad she'd gotten her mind off that vision of him sitting on the ER table, shirtless and unbearably sexy despite his wounds.

She worked at the stove, stirring milk into the soup, then preparing cheese sandwiches to be grilled in a frying pan. Every now and then she heard the dull thud of John's glass meeting the table as he lowered it. It was a friendly sound, the sound of a husband keeping his wife company while she fixed supper.

Stupid thought, she chided herself.

"Why do you call him Michael?" he asked abruptly.

She turned from the stove and frowned. "As opposed to...?"

"Mike."

She smiled and pivoted back to her cooking. "If he asked me to call him Mike, I would. He's never asked."

John said nothing. She stole a glimpse of him as

she searched the cabinets for bowls and plates. He appeared to be in deep thought. When she carried the bowls to the table, he glanced up at her. "That's nice," he said. "Respecting him that way. Not presuming."

She didn't respect Michael's choices to be nice. Respecting children was the foundation on which the school rested. But she was glad John thought it was nice, anyway.

"My family still calls me Johnny," he admitted. "They used to call me Johnny-Come-Lately."

"Really?" She treasured this revelation. John exposed so little of himself, and she savored every small scrap of information. "Why?"

He shrugged again, then winced and repositioned his right arm on his lap. "I was always the last to speak up. If everyone else was shouting, I'd just sit back and listen until they were all done. Then maybe I'd say something—if I had something to say. I was always late with my comments."

"Listening is better than talking, sometimes," she said.

"They thought I was slow. Not *slow,*" he amended, tapping his finger against his temple to indicate that he meant mentally slow. "But slow on the draw. Late to react."

"No," she argued. She'd seen him react with terrifying speed to the pickpocket on Dudley Street. She assumed that he'd reacted with equal speed today when he'd taken on an armed hoodlum. She pictured him chasing down a man with a big, horrible knife in his hand. She pictured him knocking the man over, fighting off his slashing attacks.... The very idea made her shudder.

"Did you draw?" she asked quietly, bracing herself to accept whatever answer he gave.

He frowned. His gaze traced hers to his right hand, resting motionless on the table. He raised his eyes back to hers. "You mean, did I draw my weapon on him?"

She nodded and swallowed her anxiety. The thought that he'd clutched a gun in his hand, his finger on the trigger, the power of life and death in his grasp...

She couldn't stand to think of him shooting at anyone. But he'd been deflecting the lunges of a hunting knife. He *should* have shot the thug.

She hated herself for even thinking such a thing.

"No," John said. "The sidewalk was too crowded."

"He could have killed you."

John's gaze merged with hers. The opaque darkness of his irises let nothing out, or in. "Yes," he said laconically. "He could have killed me."

The scent of burning cheese summoned her back to the stove—which was just as well, since looking at him, seeing the torment in his eyes and hearing the detachment in his voice was too disturbing. She couldn't stand to think of him risking his life as he had that afternoon. Nor could she stand to think that he could have protected himself and defeated his enemy only by risking other lives. What an agonizing equation to live by.

"Michael?" she hollered, busying herself with the sandwiches. "Could you please come to the kitchen? Dinner's ready."

Michael raced into the kitchen, skating across the smooth floor tiles in his socks. "You gonna eat with us?'' he asked Molly. "Daddy, is she gonna eat with us?"

"Yes," he said so firmly she turned off the stove and pulled another bowl and plate from the cabinet. It seemed easier than arguing with him.

Once the food was on the table and Michael was strapped into his booster seat, he asked John, "How's your boo-boo?"

"It's okay," John said stoically.

"Did you get hurt?"

"Not much."

"Who hurt you?"

Molly could practically feel the waves of tension emanating from John. He didn't want to have this discussion. "Some guy," he answered vaguely.

"Why?"

"Why what?"

"Why did some guy hurt you?"

John shifted in his seat and downed a spoonful of soup. "I don't know," he said. "Someone from the Public Defender's office will find a reason, I'm sure." He must have noticed Molly stiffening as she thought of her sister defending thugs just like the one who'd gone at John with a knife. But he didn't retract the statement.

Disloyal though it was, she couldn't blame him.

Michael beamed at Molly. "Musta been a bad guy."

"Musta been," she said weakly. Her mind was churning. She wanted to defend her sister. She wanted to point out that, while John hadn't fired at the bad guy, another cop might have shot him, just to prove he had the law on his side. Another cop might have killed him without a moment's regret just because being a cop automatically made him the good guy and gave him that right.

Right now, though, her sympathies lay with John. John, who listened before he spoke, who thought before he acted. John, who forced himself to consume his soup even though he wasn't hungry. John, who was sore and battered and had every right to resent bad guys and the lawyers who defended them—and the sisters of those lawyers.

Maybe she was a traitor. But tonight she'd seen John's pain. She'd perceived his fear. She'd comprehended his strength.

Tonight she was on his side.

CHAPTER TEN

BY THE TIME they'd finished their supper, it was already nearly eight-thirty—Michael's bedtime. Molly offered to stay long enough to get Michael settled for the night, and John accepted the offer.

"Daddy don't like to give me a bath," Michael related as Molly helped him into the tub.

"*Doesn't* like to," she corrected him. "Why not?"

"I make it wet everywhere." He proceeded to demonstrate, splashing the water with his hands and sending a spray over the side of the tub, where it landed half on the floor and half on Molly.

"Stop!" Snaring his slippery wet wrists, she reached behind her for a towel, blotted the dampness from her sweater and dried the floor. "If you want to play, you've got to keep the water in the tub." She found a plastic cup by the sink and handed it to Michael. "You can fill this with water and empty it out back into the tub."

"I dump it!" Michael boasted, then poured a cupful of water over his head and shrieked with delight.

"As long as you keep the water in the tub." She lifted his washcloth and swirled it around under the water. "Look. It's a fish!"

"No, it's not," he said, staring at her as if he considered her an idiot.

"It's a washcloth fish. Whoosh!" She pulled it through the water and around his knees.

He giggled. "I catch the fish!"

But the fish eluded him long enough to swipe the bar of soap, and when he did finally catch the fish, it managed to wriggle around, spreading suds across his belly and under his chin, where grime striped the creases. The fish floated through his fingers, swam down his back, plunged under the water and then rose again to saturate his hair for a quick shampoo.

By the time Michael was toweled off and in his pajamas, his teeth brushed, his time on the potty profitably spent and his hair combed, Molly's sweater was almost dry. "Bedtime," she announced.

"No, no, no! I get a book," he insisted, darting down the hall ahead of her and into his bedroom.

She followed as far as his open door, trying hard to ignore the room across the hall. That was probably John's bedroom, a sight she would be better off avoiding. As it was, she was going to spend her night dreaming about his bare chest, his strong arms, the bruises staining the arch of his rib cage, the flat stretch of his abdomen. She didn't want a vision of his bed encroaching on her dreams, too. She didn't want to know how big it was, what color the linens were, how many pillows he used.

Michael emerged from his room carrying a Curious George book. "He has a man in a big yellow hat," he informed her, trotting back down the hall. "Daddy reads it to me."

"Daddy is resting," Molly said. She hadn't seen John since he'd taken his half-consumed glass of Scotch and, at her insistence, retired to the den. She hoped he'd fallen asleep—sleep was essential for healing. "I'll read the book to you, Michael."

But the boy was way ahead of her, prancing toward the den and shouting, "No, no, no! Daddy read the book."

She chased him into the den, hoping to catch him before he woke his father. She was too late, though. If John had been asleep before, he wasn't now.

He lay sprawled out on the sofa, his tall body barely fitting across the cushions. As Molly entered the room, he was laboriously pushing himself up into a seated position. His movements were wooden and cautious, and his left hand shook slightly under his weight. His hair was mussed, his eyes gradually coming into focus.

"I'm sorry," she said, entering the room hesitantly. "I tried to stop him from waking you."

"That's all right." His voice was low and hoarse, and his gaze lingered on her for a brief moment before shifting to his son. "Did Molly give you a bath?"

Michael nodded, then commanded, "You read me this book."

John took the book and patted the cushion beside him. Michael scrambled onto the couch and snuggled up next to John. He cast a superior look toward Molly, then turned back to his father and pulled John's uninjured left arm around his shoulders. John started to read.

Molly tiptoed to a chair and sat. Perhaps this was a moment the Russo men might have preferred to share without her, but they hadn't asked her to leave, so she stayed. She listened as John read about the man in the yellow hat finding Curious George in the jungle and bringing him home to live in the city. He read about how George got into trouble while the man was out of the house. Michael laughed, pointed to the pictures and offered a running critique: "That's bad, to smoke a pipe. It makes you cough," and "The firemens have silly hats."

By the time John reached the last page, Michael seemed to have melted into his side. The child was warm and malleable, half asleep. "Okay, Mike. Bedtime," said John, closing the book.

Michael shut his eyes, mumbled something and sank into slumber. One of the great talents of two-year-olds was their ability to fall asleep anytime, anywhere, without any warning.

"I can carry him," Molly said, springing to her feet.

"That's all right." John tossed the book onto the coffee table, nudged Michael onto his lap, then tightened his left arm around the child's limp body and balanced it against his shoulder. He stood, swaying on weak legs and embracing Michael even more tightly.

Molly clamped her mouth shut so she wouldn't argue with him about whether or not he had the strength to carry his son. Obviously carrying Michael was something he needed to do. If the risk of swooning and dropping the kid couldn't stop him, Molly's nagging certainly wouldn't.

She followed him out of the den and down the hall, just in case John stumbled. At the doorway to Michael's room she halted while John tucked his son into bed. She heard the rustle of sheets, the flap of a blanket and John's voice murmuring, "Here's your bear. Go to sleep now. Daddy loves you."

She moved down the hall to the living room, allowing John a bit of privacy. Pacing to the window, she eased back the drapes and peered out at the snow-dusted front yard. She didn't turn until she heard

John's footsteps, soft against the maroon carpet. Her eyes met John's for less than a second before she steered them toward the fireplace mantel, which held a set of brass candlesticks and an empty crystal vase.

"If everything's okay, I guess I'll head for home," she said, wondering why the prospect of leaving made her so melancholy.

John's silence lured her gaze back to him. He raked his left hand through his mussed hair. His bandaged right hand hung awkwardly at his side.

"You'll be all right, won't you?" she asked, then wondered what sort of response she hoped for. Even if he wouldn't be all right, she couldn't stay. This was his home. She didn't belong here.

He said nothing. His eyes, so sleepy just a few minutes ago, were lucid now, burning. Above his unshaven jaw his cheeks had regained a touch of color, the sickly pallor waning. Of course he would be all right. He didn't need her to stay.

So why didn't he tell her to leave? Why didn't he thank her and walk her to the door? Why did he keep staring at her as if waiting for her to say something more?

"Did someone bring your car back from the police station?" She cringed inwardly, wondering why she was stalling.

He nodded. "While you were giving Mike a bath."

Hearing his voice was something of a relief. She just wished he'd say what had to be said: *Good night. Goodbye. Thanks for your help.*

But his mention of the bath reminded her of something. "Michael needs a bath toy," she told him. "If he had something to play with in the tub, he wouldn't be so busy splashing water out of it."

"A bath toy."

She must have been insane to bring it up. She was supposed to be easing herself out the door, saying the goodbyes John seemed reluctant to utter. She was supposed to be detaching herself from the Russos, not including herself in their lives any more than absolutely necessary.

"A plastic boat, maybe," she went on, unable to stop herself. "Or a duck, or a frog. Something that would keep him occupied while he's soaking in the tub."

John's gaze seemed to pin her in place. He looked earnest and bemused, more desperate for help than he'd been when he'd walked out of the hospital a couple of hours ago.

"They're sold in toy stores," she continued, wishing he wouldn't look at her like that, wishing she had the willpower to leave. "A bath toy would make a good, inexpensive Christmas present, and I'm sure he'd love it."

"Okay."

That brought the bath toy discussion to a conclusion. Molly could go now. She could march into the kitchen for her jacket, then march out the front door. She could say goodbye...if only he didn't keep staring at her that way.

"I'll get my jacket," she said bluntly, an anxious attempt to save herself from her own overheated thoughts.

"I'll get it." He pivoted and walked out of the living room. His steps were slow but certain. He wasn't going to stagger and wind up in a dizzy heap on the floor, but he lacked the purposeful grace he usually displayed, the sense that he couldn't be deterred or distracted, that he was in charge of his own world.

It seemed important to him that he get her jacket, one small gesture of courtesy for his guest. Molly wouldn't deprive him of that. She waited where she was until he returned with the parka. He held it up as if to help her into it, but with only one hand functioning he couldn't hold it for her to slide her arms through the sleeves. She smiled gently, took it from him and put it on.

"Thank you," he said.

"No problem. Are you sure you're going to be all right?"

He smiled wistfully, lifted his heavily bandaged right hand and brushed his thumb across her lower lip. The bandages smelled sterile, bitter with antiseptic, but he was close enough that she could also smell the heady aroma of Scotch on his breath and the faint tang of his aftershave. It took all her self-control not to flick her tongue over her lips where he'd touched them, not to reach up and pull his face down to hers.

She couldn't. She wouldn't.

"I'd better go," she said.

He sighed, let his hand fall and took a step back. "The roads might be messy," he warned. "Take it slow."

She knew how to drive on slippery winter roads; she didn't need his admonition, at least not when it came to her journey home. But there were other hazards tonight, hazards much more dangerous than the rare icy patch on the road. Gazing into his eyes, remembering the feel of his lips on hers, picturing his lean, virile chest...

There were plenty of hazards, all right. She ought

to be grateful that John was cautioning her—and himself—to take it slow.

She ought to be, but she wasn't.

HE WOKE UP feeling like crud. His arm was on fire
and the drum solo being played inside his skull was
loud enough to drown out a concert. None of that
bothered him as much as Molly's absence.

She'd fit in too well last night. Having her around
had seemed too natural. When he'd tucked Mike into
bed, he'd had to stop himself from waving Molly into
the room and asking her if she wanted to give the kid
a kiss good-night.

From the moment a couple of EMTs had strapped
him onto a gurney for the ambulance ride to the hospital, the only useful thing he'd done with his right
hand was touch Molly's mouth. And touching it hadn't
been what he'd truly wanted to do. He'd wanted to
kiss her, wanted it in a crazy way.

Just thinking about the velvet texture of her lips
made him hard. Which was an embarrassing state to
be in when his son was standing at the foot of his bed,
gaping at him. "I go to school," Mike said.

John twisted to look at his alarm clock. The digits
9-4-3 glowed bright red at him.

He swore under his breath, then forced himself to
sit. Another curse filled his mouth as pain burned like
a laser through every nerve between his elbow and his
fingertips. Even his upper arm and shoulder were sore.
And his ribs. They flared with a feverish ache every
time he inhaled. Maybe the doctors had read his
X rays wrong. Ribs that were only bruised couldn't
possibly hurt this bad, could they?

"I go to school now," Mike said.

John forced himself to tune out the pain—and that other ache, the one in his groin, caused by a kind, tough, wise woman loaded with more sex appeal than he could handle in his weakened state. He shoved back the covers, eased his legs over the side of the bed and reached for the faded terry cloth robe he'd tossed on the nearest chair last night. Before Mike was born, he used to sleep naked, but he'd learned, from incidents like this morning, that Mike didn't always respect a closed bedroom door. For discretion's sake, he'd gotten into the habit of sleeping in a T-shirt and boxers, and keeping his robe close at hand.

"You taking me to school?" Mike asked.

John tied the robe's sash around his waist, blinked to clear his foggy vision and studied the small boy gazing up at him. Mike wasn't going anywhere dressed the way he was, in his football pj's with the built-in slippers. And he wasn't going anywhere that would require driving. John's hand was on fire. The mere thought of sliding the key into the ignition was enough to nauseate him.

"No school today," he said.

"No school?"

"We're both taking a day off."

Mike mulled that over, then grinned and skipped around the room. "Molly comes here! Molly's gonna come!"

If that were true, John might well have joined Mike in a little revelry. "No Molly," he said grimly. "Just you and me."

It took him forever to fix a pot of coffee left-handed, but he didn't trust himself to call Coffey before he'd gotten some caffeine into his system. While the coffee brewed, he trudged into his bathroom, took one look at himself in the mirror above the sink and discovered a few curses he hadn't realized he knew. His jaw was dark with stubble, his eyes pocketed in shadow, his brow pinched. If he'd looked even half as bad last night, Molly ought to be grateful he hadn't tried to kiss her.

Hell. Even if he'd looked his absolute best, she'd have been grateful. With a failed marriage behind him, a scrappy kid underfoot and a career that required the occasional ambulance ride to a hospital emergency room, he was no one's idea of Mr. Right.

He brushed his teeth left-handed, which felt weird, and took a leak left-handed, which felt even weirder. Returning to the kitchen, he downed a pain pill, filled a mug with coffee, heaped a bowl with Cheerios for Mike and lifted him into his booster seat. Then he dialed headquarters to report that he was taking a sick day.

Coffey was appropriately sympathetic. He assured John that Bud Schaefer would bring the assault victim in for a lineup, but that the collar would belong to John. He asked if John felt strong enough to be able to dictate his statement to one of the secretaries if she went to his house. John said yes. He wasn't in the mood to give a statement, but he also wasn't in the mood to refuse his boss's request.

He wasn't in the mood to keep track of a giddy young boy, either. Driving Mike to the Children's Garden himself wasn't possible, given the way he felt, but he couldn't ask someone else to drive Mike for him. He hated having to beg for favors.

So he spent the day in the den with Mike, watching through bleary eyes as the kid firebombed make-believe airports, drop-kicked Duplo blocks, drew a crayon self-portrait on the front page of the *Arlington Gazette's* Metro section and watched the video of *Mary Poppins* John's mother had given him for his birthday.

John popped painkillers and sipped ginger ale and every now and then dozed off. He gave his statement to the department secretary, who showed up with a laptop, and he fielded a call from the doctor who had stitched him up. The doctor wanted to have a look at John's wounds tomorrow. John said sure, hung up, and listened to Mike mangle "Supercalifragilistic" at the top of his lungs.

It was for situations like this that a man needed a wife—not for himself but for his son. If Molly hadn't accompanied him home from the hospital last night, he wouldn't have been able to fix a real dinner for Mike, not even a snack as trivial as soup and a grilled-cheese sandwich, and he would have had to put Mike to bed without a bath. John wouldn't have made it without Molly yesterday. He could barely make it without her today.

Odd how, when he thought about a wife, he didn't think about Sherry. If she'd been around yesterday, she would have seen the knife assault as just one more bit of proof that cops existed in a world she wanted no part of. She had always resented the special demands of his job. "Why can't you work nine to five like a normal person?" she used to complain. "Why don't they pay you more? Why can't you get a real job?"

Because a cop was what he was, he would tell her. A cop saw the world a certain way, just as an artist did, or a fisherman, or a priest. It was a calling, something you did because it was the only way to make sense of your life. People didn't become cops for the money or the hours. They didn't do it because they thought it would make their wives or husbands happy. They did it because they had to, because not to do it would be a kind of death.

It was something civilians couldn't understand. He doubted Molly would understand it. Her sister, that cool blond lawyer who made a living defending scum like the guy who'd sliced open John's arm, sure didn't.

By the time he put Mike down for the night—skipping bath time—John decided the day qualified as one of the longest of his life. The night felt even longer. He lay in bed, ignoring the pain in his arm for the deeper discomfort of his thoughts about Molly. Those who didn't feel the calling never understood those who did. They might respect a cop, but they couldn't really understand him.

One thing he didn't need was Molly's respect. He wasn't even sure he wanted her understanding. He wanted her passion, but he would probably have to settle for her knowledge of children and bath toys.

He had no right to ask for more from her than her expertise. If he did ask, she would have every reason to say no.

ELSIE PELHAM WAS ranting about the latest indignity her ex-husband's lawyer was inflicting on her when Molly noticed a familiar-looking man with salt-and-pepper hair and a neatly trimmed mustache come into the Children's Garden Friday morning. Next to him, chattering at full volume, was Michael.

Molly held up a finger to silence Elsie and turned to the man.

"Bud Schaefer," he identified himself, extending

an envelope to her. "We met at the hospital the other day."

She nodded, remembering. He was one of the officers in the emergency room waiting area—the one with John's clothes. She opened the envelope and slid out a sheet of lined paper. In a barely legible scribble, it said, "Bud Schaefer has my permission to pick up Mike. John Russo."

"He's not too good writing with his left hand," Bud explained.

Molly smiled, amazed that John could remember to send a written note about releasing his son to someone other than himself. He certainly had enough else on his mind right now. And with his injured right hand, he could have telephoned to let her know he authorized his friend to fetch Michael at the end of the day. Ordinarily she wanted written permission, but John's circumstances weren't ordinary.

"How is he?"

"Miserable," Bud reported cheerfully. "He's got a doctor's appointment today. They'll let him know how he's doing."

"He's going to drive to the doctor's office?"

Bud shrugged. "I'd drive him, but we've got our hands full with all those street punks he collared last week during his Santa gig. Besides—" he grinned "—none of us wants to get stuck wearing the Santa costume, so we're all keeping as busy as we can on other projects, if you know what I mean."

Molly knew what he meant: John was a nobler cop than the rest of them. He was willing to take the toughest jobs. She would have assumed that the toughest jobs for a cop involved raiding crack houses or hunting down mass murderers. Evidently the *really* tough jobs included dressing up in a silly Santa Claus costume.

"Does he—do you think he'd mind if I called? Just to see how he's doing," she explained, smiling blandly. She didn't want this friendly police officer to know how concerned she was about John, how deeply she admired him...how much she cared.

"I wouldn't advise it," he said, casting a quick look down the hall at Mike, who was engaged in a one-on-one with his left boot on the floor next to his cubby. He turned back to Molly. "He's been sleeping a lot. And when he's not asleep, he's grouchy as heck."

Molly nodded, trying not to let her disappointment show. How selfish of her to place her own longing to talk to John ahead of his need to be left alone. She thanked Bud for bringing Michael to school, waved him off and gave herself a stern mental lecture about not letting thoughts of John preoccupy her all day. At night, alone in her bed, she could think about him. But not today, with Cara out sick with bronchitis, a school full of rambunctious children and Elsie Pelham resuming her rant about her protracted custody battle.

And really, she told herself, why did she want to bother him with a phone call, anyway? If he wanted her to know how he was doing, he would call her. He had more important things on his mind than putting her mind at ease. She pictured him storming around his house, growling and snarling, and decided that she probably didn't want to talk to him, after all.

He hadn't been growling and snarling when she'd been at his house. The way he'd gazed at her and touched her...

He had obviously been too delirious to know what he was doing then. Now he was recovering, and his first task as he fought his way back to health was to reconstruct all his defenses. She had better things to do than try to breach them.

When Bud Schaefer returned to the school at five-thirty to pick Michael up, Molly politely asked him to pass along her good wishes to John. She waited until all the children were gone, then locked up the school and drove home. Yesterday's snow had melted, leaving nothing but ugly mounds of slush along the curbs. The festive holiday lights and decorations hanging in the shop windows along Dudley Road depressed her. They made her think of street-corner Santas, which in turn made her think of one particular Santa.

She wasn't going to think about John anymore. She wasn't going to think about the brush of his thumb against her lips. She'd helped out a school parent, period. She would have done as much for Abbie Pelham's mom, or Dana's, or Keisha's. Instead, she'd done it for Michael's dad, and now it was time to forget about it.

Or so she resolved as she headed off to her weekly Daddy School class Saturday morning. She was calm and composed, fully prepared to lead a discussion on ways to counteract the overwhelming materialism of the holiday season, how to shop for toys that would hold the children's interest for more than ten minutes on Christmas morning and how to counteract the barrage of commercials the kids saw on TV.

The last thing she expected was for John Russo to show up.

CHAPTER ELEVEN

"I GOT MIKE A TREE," he said.

Most of the other fathers had left; the two that remained were huddled with their young daughters near the front door, negotiating the details of a play date. John loitered in the Pre-K classroom with Michael, who was seated on the floor near the gate, working up a sweat trying to get his feet into his boots.

John looked markedly better than he'd looked Wednesday evening. He was clean-shaven, his hair relatively neat, his right hand wrapped in less bulky bandages. His eyes were still shadowed, his face a bit drawn, but his complexion had regained a healthy undertone and his lips were no longer pinched with pain.

He had on black jeans, a slate gray V-neck sweater with a white T-shirt underneath. The colorless outfit ought to have seemed drab, or even funereal, but on him it looked vivid, a bit dangerous and rather sexy.

Oh, yes, he was sexy. Molly didn't want to be viewing him that way, but she couldn't help herself. After not seeing him for several days, she only had to glance at him and her mind was abducted by memories of his naked torso, of his thumb caressing her mouth.

"A tree?" she asked, her voice steadier than her overheated nerves.

"White pine. Yesterday when Bud brought Mike home, I asked him to help us get it." He lifted his injured hand and pulled a face. "I'm useless by myself."

"You're not useless," Molly corrected him, thinking of all the things he could do with one hand and then thinking she'd better stop thinking about it. She distracted herself by contemplating her own failure to get a tree.

In Decembers past, she and Gail used to spend the holiday with their parents, but this year their parents had decided to take a Christmas cruise with friends. Gail had arranged with a few friends from law school to rent a cabin in Killington, Vermont, where they could greet Christmas on skis. Molly had declined Gail's offer to join them, because she'd already received an invitation from Allison to celebrate the holiday with her, Jamie and the baby. Allison had mentioned that she and Jamie had invited several other friends to their house for the holiday, including—ominously—Jamie's dear friend Steve, a classmate of his at Dartmouth and an extremely eligible bachelor.

Molly wasn't eager to let Allison and Jamie play matchmaker with their respective best friends, but she was even less eager to spend Christmas by herself.

In any case, she had seen no need to invest in a tree when she wasn't going to be home on Christmas Eve. To create a holiday mood in her condo, she'd decorated the living room with sprigs of holly and hung a wreath on the front door, and she'd placed cinnamon-scented red candles in her pewter candlesticks on the fireplace mantel. But the place didn't seem festive enough—and spending the holiday in the company of Jamie's dear friend from Dartmouth wasn't going to fix that.

John had a tree. He and Michael would have the

holiday spirit in their home. Molly was glad for them, but a part of her felt wistful, wishing she could share their holiday in some way. She warned herself that she shouldn't waste her wishes on the impossible.

"I don't have any decorations," John said, breaking into her thoughts.

"No decorations? You just said you got a tree."

"I have nothing to put on it. No ornaments."

"Don't you have any left over from last year?"

"I didn't have a tree last year."

She nodded, her mind churning. Last year Michael would have been a little over a year old, old enough to appreciate a tree. Maybe John hadn't wanted one—or maybe his wife hadn't. Last year at this time, she might have already been making plans to leave. It might have been the most wretched holiday John and his son had ever endured.

Then again, John's failure to get a tree last year might be no more significant than Molly's failure to get a tree this year.

"I was thinking," he said almost shyly. "Mike and I could take you out for lunch, and you could help us buy ornaments."

She knew John wasn't asking her on a date. But the way he gazed at her, his eyes so dark and enigmatic, said that this was more than just a casual invitation.

"A bribe," she guessed, then grinned to calm her overactive nerves. "It's a payoff if you buy me lunch *after* we shop for the decorations. But if you feed me *before,* it's a bribe."

He smiled, one of his rare, soul-deep smiles, like the one he'd given her when he'd declared war in the foam pit. It was a smile that simultaneously soothed and aroused her.

"I'm bribable," she said. "Would you like me to drive or can you manage it?"

They wound up driving both cars to Molly's condominium development, where she parked hers by her town house and then joined the Russos in theirs. John insisted that he was able to drive just fine, but once she was settled into the front passenger seat, she noticed his slight grimace as he attempted to wield the gear stick with just his fingertips.

In his car seat in back, Michael was exuberant. "We got a tree!" he declared. "A big, big tree! All the way to the ceiling. Daddy had to cut it."

"You cut your own tree?" Molly asked John, her amazement laced with disapproval. Going to a tree farm and chopping down a tree was fun, but not a suitable activity for a man who three days ago was rushed to a hospital suffering from knife wounds.

He shook his head. "I trimmed six inches off the top with a pair of scissors. Bud helped."

"I guess that's all right. But you really shouldn't overdo it, John. You've got to give your arm a chance to heal."

He shot her a rebellious glance, then turned forward again, working the steering wheel with his left hand. "I'm healing."

"Have you been to the doctor?"

"Yeah. He says I'm healing."

His tone left no doubt that he wanted her to drop the subject. Honoring the unspoken request, she twisted in her seat and asked Michael, "Does your house smell different now?"

"It smells like a tree," he reported. "A big, big tree."

The parking lot at the mall was packed with cars.

With less than two weeks until Christmas, hordes had descended upon the place to get their holiday shopping done. John navigated up and down the rows of cars for five full minutes until he located an empty space. Before he unstrapped Michael and let him out of the car, he pulled a foldable stroller from the trunk and snapped it open, using his right elbow and his knee to spread and lock the hinges. Molly was impressed by his agility, and by his foresight. Last week Michael had fallen asleep right after lunch. If he fell asleep today, the stroller would come in handy.

"I wanna push it," Michael demanded, grasping the chrome handles and zigzagging madly across the asphalt.

John raced after him as swiftly as he'd chased the pickpocket on Dudley. Even injured, he ran with a purposeful grace, his movements clean and efficient, his long legs devouring the space between himself and his runaway son. He was probably a fine athlete, she thought. So strong and limber, he was probably an exquisite lover, too.

Hazardous thought. She hastily brushed it aside.

John caught up to Michael before he wandered into the path of a moving car. Instead of commandeering the stroller, though, he shared it, gripping one side of the handle and letting Michael push the other, so they could steer in tandem toward the mall entrance.

Molly followed in their wake. The cold wind blew away Michael's voice before it reached her, but she knew he was talking to his father. He craned his neck to peer up at John, and his mouth moved incessantly. His little legs pumped alongside his father's, taking twice as many steps to cover the same distance.

How could a woman have walked out on them?

Molly wondered, touched by the rapport between John and his son. Of course, John's wife might have had valid reasons for leaving him. For all Molly knew, John might have been selfish as a husband. Maybe he brought his work to bed with him—and given the work he did, that couldn't have been particularly romantic. Or maybe he and his ex-wife simply fell out of love. Maybe the other man, the one John's wife had left with, was irresistible.

Or just possibly, the woman had been blind to what she had: a good man, a loving man, a man who took his responsibilities almost too seriously. An extraordinary man—and a wonderful son.

Reaching the mall entrance, John pulled Michael to a halt and waited for Molly to reach them so they could enter together. "I'm hungry," Michael announced. "We have lunch now."

"First get in the stroller," John said. "Then we'll get lunch."

"No get in the stroller! No, no, no!"

"I'm not letting you walk," John told him. The mall was mobbed with people. Molly didn't blame him for wanting Michael strapped safely into the stroller where he wouldn't be able to wander off.

"No stroller! I don't want the stroller!" Michael threw back his head and howled.

Not bothering to argue, John hoisted Michael up into his left arm and lowered him into the stroller. When Michael squirmed and tried to escape, John brought his right hand into play, pinning Michael in the seat while he strapped the belt around his belly. Molly saw pain crease John's brow as he used his injured hand. She wanted to help, but his forbidding glower held her at bay. This was between him and his flailing, shrieking son. She had no business intervening.

She held the stroller steady while John snapped the belt shut. Michael was out of breath from resisting his father and wailing, but John appeared unfazed, although his right fingers twitched from the strain. "I hate you!" Michael bellowed. "Bad, bad Daddy! I hate you!"

John's expression grew stony. Avoiding Molly's gaze, he eased the stroller's handle from her and pushed it into the crowds, heading toward the food court.

Just as she'd wanted to help him during his tussle with Michael, she wanted to help him now, reassuring him that his son didn't really hate him, that young children had limited vocabularies with which to express their anger. But John clearly wasn't in the mood to be reassured. He propelled the stroller through the crowds, as grim as a marine on the Bataan Death March, ignoring the glittery decorations and the cloying Christmas music being piped through the atrium.

By the time they reached the food court, Michael had subsided. He slouched in the canvas seat of the stroller, his cheeks tearstained and his lower lip curled in a magnificent pout. John steered the stroller to an empty table and set the brake. He flexed his fingers gingerly, then massaged the back of his right hand with his left. "What do you want to eat?" he asked Molly, his tone dry and measured.

She shrugged. Observing the war of wills between father and son had made her lose her appetite. Even though she knew Michael's behavior was perfectly normal for his age, she hurt for John—and hurt even more because he was so obviously determined not to accept any sympathy.

She surveyed the eateries surrounding the food court: sandwiches, salads, burritos, gourmet cookies, stir-fry, bagels, frozen yogurt, hot dogs, burgers and pizza. "A bagel, I guess. And a diet cola."

He nodded, hunkered down next to Michael and asked the same question. "A cookie," Michael said in a tear-choked voice. "I wanna cookie. Choc-chip."

"A hamburger and a cookie."

"No hamburger! No! I don't want it!" Michael revved up to wail again. "No hamburger! Daddy, no!"

Ignoring him, John straightened up. "I'll be right back," he promised as if he thought Molly expected him to disappear forever, leaving her with the tantrum-throwing child. Pivoting, he vanished into the milling crowd.

She lowered herself onto a bright green wooden chair beside Michael's stroller and stared at him until he stopped bellowing. It took him a good few minutes to compose himself. "Feeling better?" she asked pleasantly.

He sulked. He had probably forgotten what had upset him. Molly diagnosed his mood as prenap fretfulness. Most toddlers behaved terribly when they were tired.

"I want a cookie," he grumbled.

"You said you were hungry. A cookie won't satisfy your hunger as well as something nutritious would. But look—there's your daddy. He got you a cookie."

Michael perked up. Apparently all was forgiven. "A cookie? A big cookie?"

"Enormous," Molly observed, rising to take the

overloaded tray John was trying to balance between his left hand and the bandaged back of his right wrist. She lowered it to the table, then watched as John unwrapped a small hamburger and handed it to Michael.

Without a peep, he wolfed down the burger, guzzled his milk and pounced on his cookie. At the table above him, John and Molly ate their lunches more decorously. John seemed fatigued, either from battling Michael or pushing himself physically so soon after his stabbing. Most likely from both.

If anything, Michael was even more fatigued. His chewing slowed until he was just sucking on the cookie and struggling to keep his eyes open. "He's going to be asleep in five minutes," Molly predicted.

John glanced at the stroller. A smile flickered across his lips as he reached down, pulled the half-consumed cookie from his son's senseless fingers and used a napkin to wipe a smear of chocolate from the boy's lip. "Less than five minutes," he said as Michael began to snore.

John wrapped the remaining half of the cookie in a napkin and tucked it into the tote hanging from the back of the stroller. Then he leaned back in his chair and took a sip of his soda. His gaze settled on Molly, his lids slightly lowered as he observed her over the rim of his paper cup.

Despite the hundreds of shoppers swirling around them, munching on snacks and lugging bags of merchandise, Molly felt as if she and John were all alone in the mall. Despite the constant drone of voices and the omnipresent Christmas music, she could practically hear him swallow, hear him breathe. She almost resented Michael for conking out and leaving her all alone with a man who seemed far too capable of holding her imagination hostage, infiltrating her senses and making her forget everything she ought to remember.

She scrambled for something safe to talk about. "Are you going to see any of your sisters and brothers for the holiday?" It was a nosy question, but at least it distracted her from the sexual undertow she felt in his presence.

"Probably not. We got together for Thanksgiving."

"You mentioned that one of your brothers is disabled."

John nodded.

One thing she'd learned was that he never volunteered information. If she wanted to know something, she would have to ask. "What kind of disability does he have?"

"He's...slow."

"Ah." Her professional curiosity was whetted. Last year she'd had a girl with Down's syndrome at the school, and she'd really enjoyed working with her. "How is he doing? Can he live independently? Is he educable?"

"He lives in a supervised group home about a mile from my parents. He bags groceries at a supermarket. He's okay. He's a good kid." John laughed and shook his head. "He's three years older than me. I just always think of him as a kid brother."

"I'll bet you were very protective of him when you were growing up," she said.

John considered, then shrugged. "Nobody dared to give him a hard time when I was around, if that's what you mean."

"That's exactly what I mean." John's habit of taking responsibility for everyone must have developed when he was quite young. In his huge family, she assumed that he would have been the one most sensitive to his brother's needs. He would have made sure his brother was all right before he went off to play ball or hang out with his friends. That was the way John was, and she adored him for it.

She didn't want to adore him. But she'd never met a man like him before, a man so determined to do the right thing. She didn't care what Gail said about cops, their craving for power and their abuse of it. What power John had came not from his gun and his badge but from his ethics. He had earned that power, and she...

Well, *adored* was all she'd admit to.

"How about the rest of your siblings?" she asked, longing to know more about him, as much as he would tell her.

He smiled crookedly. "How about them?"

"What are they like? Are any of them cops like you?"

"No." He drained his soda and relaxed in his chair, patiently allowing her to finish her bagel. "Sarah's a singer and voice teacher in Boston. Jimmy was a high school baseball star. He coaches at a high school in New Jersey. Danny works at the supermarket in Pawtucket, Linda's a Realtor in Connecticut, and then there's me, and then Nina, who's got four kids and doesn't have time for much else. And then Bobby."

Molly was practically giddy from this unexpected outpouring of information. "What does Bobby do?"

John smiled wistfully. "He works for the postal service and tries to stay clean. He's had some problems."

"Drugs?"

"Yeah. When he was younger."

"I'll bet you took care of him, too."

John dismissed her guess with another shrug. "I kept him out of jail, got him into a program. He did the rest."

His modesty only made her adore him more. She could picture him exhorting his brother into treatment, forcing him to stay until he was clean and cheering him on every step of the way. She could just as easily picture him taking on any bully who dared to taunt his brother Danny.

Her own family was tiny compared to John's. And the one time her sister had needed protection, Molly hadn't been able to do anything for her. Afterward, she'd listened to Gail and comforted her and promised not to tell their parents what had happened. But she hadn't been able to protect her.

If John had been Gail's brother, he would have protected her. Molly was certain of it.

"I don't think my parents could have handled seven children," she said, deciding she adored John's parents, too.

"I can barely handle one," he admitted with a grin.

She crumpled her napkin and gestured toward the child in question. Michael seemed quite manageable at the moment, snoozing contentedly in his stroller, dreaming, no doubt, of cookies and Christmas trees. "We'd better do some shopping while he's asleep," she suggested.

With a nod, John gathered their trash onto the tray and carried it to the nearest waste bin. By the time he returned, Molly had released the brake on the stroller. "Where to first?" she asked. "Christmas tree ornaments?"

"A bath toy," John answered. "Santa's going to bring Mike one this year."

BY SIX O'CLOCK, a one hundred percent healthy person would have been ready to dive into bed and sleep for a year, and John was functioning at only about sixty-five percent. But somehow, Molly's presence had managed to invigorate him enough to keep him going all afternoon, doing what had to be done to make this holiday come out right for Mike.

John couldn't have managed without her. Her brisk efficiency and knowledge had enabled him to buy a Santa-size sackful of Christmas gifts for Mike and get them locked into the trunk of his car before Mike woke up. Under her guidance, John had purchased a plastic tugboat and barge for the tub; a zippered sweater—"He's too young for buttons, but he can handle a zipper all by himself," she had explained; several pads of blank white paper and a bucket of crayons; a couple of Dr. Seuss books; a set of Waffle Blocks; a dog hand puppet; a lightweight foam ball and a flexible basketball hoop that could be hooked over the back of a chair or a door; and, instead of a plain toy airplane, a kit of interlocking plastic pieces that could be built into the shape of a plane, a robot or a computer.

Once the gifts were stashed and Mike began to emerge from his nap, they'd retraced their steps through the mall, this time shopping for items John didn't have to sneak past the boy: strands of tiny silver-white lights, garlands of tinsel, nonbreakable tree ornaments with satiny finishes and, at Molly's insistence, a large package of multicolored pipe cleaners. "Michael can make some ornaments of his own with these," she'd said, tossing the package into John's shopping cart.

John had asked Molly to come back to his

house—to help Mike with the pipe cleaners, he'd suggested, though that wasn't his main reason for inviting her. Whether or not she'd sensed that he was inviting her as much for himself as for Mike, she had accepted. And sure enough, they'd spent what remained of the afternoon doing things for the tree he and Bud had set up by the fireplace in the living room—stringing lights, draping tinsel and hanging the satin bulbs.

By late afternoon, exhaustion had threatened to claim him. Rather than leave, Molly had ordered him to relax in the den. Then she and Mike had worked with the pipe cleaners, bending green ones into wreath shapes, red ones into bows and yellow ones into bells. Actually, the ones Mike made were unrecognizable, but he identified them for John so he'd know that the lumpy red-and-white twist was a candy cane and the blue wad of fuzz-coated wire was an M&M's candy.

It didn't really matter what they were supposed to be. Hung from the spiky green branches of the tree, they looked great.

John wasn't used to feeling sentimental about the holiday. In his childhood, Christmas always meant his mother did a lot of baking, special cookies and cakes she made at no other time of the year. But the tree the Russos used was artificial, and gifts were kept to a minimum—and were invariably chosen for practicality's sake because the family was always on a tight budget. When John and his siblings got older, they each gave one present to one sibling, determined by lot. One year Jimmy gave John a pack of baseball cards. Another year he'd gotten a pot holder from his younger sister, Nina. He'd always wanted to be picked by Danny, because his mother helped Danny choose a nice gift for whoever he'd drawn. No one ever got a pot holder from Danny.

As best John could remember, his favorite thing about the holiday was having a week off from school and playing in the snow on those rare occasions when Pawtucket was blessed with a white Christmas. But Mike would have a different memory of the holiday.

All because of Molly.

He stood across the living room from her and Mike, pretending to admire the tree but in fact watching her. Mike was squeezing one of his pipe cleaner ornaments so tightly that whatever shape it used to be, it was a different shape now. "I put it here," he announced, tugging at one of the few branches he could reach, a couple of feet off the floor. "I put this one here. A tiger, see, Daddy? Yellow and black."

It looked more like a bumblebee to John, but he nodded solemnly. "That's a fine tiger."

"It's scary. It roars so loud! *Roarrr!*"

Molly glanced his way. Her hair had gotten mussed, a few locks straying across the part to the other side, and her cheeks were as rosy now as they'd been outdoors in the cold afternoon. Something tightened in his gut when he caught her smile. "What do you think?" she asked. "A pretty nifty tree, isn't it?"

It was a splendid tree. It was the most beautiful tree John had ever seen, especially with Mike and Molly standing beside it. It was so magnificent, he didn't know what to say.

Molly didn't seem to notice. "Well," she said, checking her watch, "it's getting late, so—"

"I have some chicken," he told her, then swore silently at his ineptitude. Her quizzical expression forced him to clarify himself. "Leftovers from last night. I was going to heat them up. Would you like to stay?''

Her smile returned, not as bright as before but sweeter, somehow. "Leftovers. How appetizing.''

That sounded more like a no than a yes to him. Not that he blamed her. He'd taken over her entire afternoon, left her to watch Mike while he nursed his aching body, then offered a supper of reheated leftovers as a reward. Of course she wouldn't like to stay.

He covered his disappointment with a nod. "I'll take you home, then.''

"I love chicken," she said, her cheeks growing rosier. She studied the tree for a moment, but John could tell the tree wasn't on her mind. She looked as awkward as he felt.

This shouldn't be awkward. They were both adults. The way John felt about Molly right now—the way he'd been feeling about her for some time—was extremely adult. Why were they dancing around a discussion of leftovers? If it weren't for Mike, and for John's battered condition, he would gladly take her out for dinner someplace nice and then to a movie or a rock club where they could dance until 2:00 a.m. He would gladly take her home—her place or his—and make love to her.

But his arm was only semifunctional and Mike was in the picture, and it had been a long day. And the only thing Molly had indicated any love for was chicken.

Still, she hadn't said no. He would take what he could get, even if it was only her company for an hour longer. In the grand scheme of things, an hour spent in Molly's company was worth more than all the Christmas gifts John had ever hoped for.

"This is a tiger, too," Mike boasted, perching another yellow-and-black blob on a low branch of the tree. "I'm hungry. Let's eat now. Okay, Daddy?"

Why not? Any tree with two pipe cleaner tigers on it qualified as done in John's mind. Without waiting for a more definitive acceptance from Molly, he ran his fingers through Mike's hair and then strode into the kitchen.

By the time they took their seats around the kitchen table, John had yielded to Molly's superiority in food preparation. She microwaved three potatoes, then cut them open, sprinkled onion flakes and parsley on the softened white pulp and microwaved them again. While they were cooking, she warmed the chicken in the oven, then tore some greens into a salad bowl. John was reduced to keeping Mike out of her way and setting the table, two tasks he performed measurably better than cooking. Ever since Sherry left, he and Mike hadn't had too many hot meals. The only reason they happened to have half a cooked chicken in the fridge was because Bud Schaefer had insisted on buying one of those rotisserie birds at the supermarket on their way home from the tree stand.

John wondered whether his feelings for Molly had anything to do with her willingness to cook for him and watch his kid. He wasn't looking for a wife, not after his debacle with Sherry. He didn't want to be hurt again, and he sure as hell didn't want to hurt a woman. Given his performance as a husband the first time around, he didn't see himself inflicting that kind of damage on another woman any time soon.

Maybe if Molly didn't act so domestic around him, he'd be able to think of her strictly as a potential sex partner. Which seemed like a pretty piggish way to think about a woman, but it was safer than the other way.

He didn't talk much during dinner. His silence was a result of his irksome thoughts about Molly. His yearning for her—as a wife substitute, as a lover, as something else, something more, something he couldn't begin to understand—was a puzzle he wanted to solve before he did something he might regret. But Molly and Mike didn't seem to mind that he said little. They spent most of the meal engrossed in a vigorous analysis of Bert and Ernie's relationship on "Sesame Street," discussed in language Mike could understand.

Bert and Ernie could use a visit to the foam pit, John thought.

When they were done eating, John told Molly to leave the dishes, but she said she wouldn't mind putting them in the dishwasher as long as she had company. Mike volunteered to keep her company, and no way was John going to leave her alone in his kitchen to do the chores he ought to be doing.

He felt a twinge of guilt when she demanded that he sit. "If you want to watch, fine," she said. "But stay away from the sink. You shouldn't get your bandage wet."

"I can do things left-handed," he argued. "I can put a plastic bag around my right hand. How do you think I've been showering?"

"I'm glad to hear you *have* been showering," she teased, and then her cheeks blossomed pink again. John didn't think it would be wise to pursue that particular subject, especially with Mike in the room. So he sat and watched while she instructed Mike in the proper way to stack the plates in the dishwasher rack, the safe way to handle silverware, the importance of scraping food off the plates before he handed them to her.

John had never let Mike help him with the dishes before—not even his own unbreakable plastic plates and cups. The kid wasn't even two and a half years old. Could he really be mature enough for this?

Evidently he was. "I do it," he announced each time Molly gave him a new instruction.

She had pushed the sleeves of her shirt up to her elbows to keep the cuffs from getting wet. John observed the slender lines of her forearms, her delicate wrists, her small, star-shaped hands glistening with water as she rinsed each plate. He wanted to dry her hands, to straighten out her disheveled hair, to cup her face in his hands and pull her mouth to his. He wanted to thank her for teaching his son how to clear a table, and he wanted to get naked with her. He wanted to drag her into the shower with him, even if it meant getting his damned bandage wet.

She shook the moisture from her fingers, reached for a paper towel, and sent him a shimmering smile. His temperature shot up ten degrees. He wanted to kiss her smile, feel it against his cheek, turn that smile into a gasp of pleasure when he touched her.

Right. As if a man who'd lost his better hand to an acre of gauze bandaging could touch a woman with any sort of skill. As if a man whose arm was held together with surgical thread could hold a woman as tightly as he wanted to hold Molly. As if a man with a row of bruised ribs could make love with any sort of finesse.

As if he should be thinking about Molly in the context of making love.

"It's really getting late," she said, eyeing the wall

clock and wincing. "If you don't feel up to driving me home, John, I can call a cab."

"Don't call a cab," he said, aware of a desperate edge in his voice.

Mike began to skip in a circle around the table, chanting, "I do it! I do the dishwasher! I do it!"

Molly glanced at him and then lifted her gaze back to John. His left hand fisted with tension; he rested it against a chair and tried to will it to relax. He didn't want her to leave. Whether or not it was right, whether or not he had any rights when it came to her...

If she left, he would go crazy.

"Do you think you'll need help getting him ready for bed?" she asked, gesturing toward Mike.

"No." *Damn.* He could have kept her at the house for as long as it took to get Mike through his nightly routine if he'd pretended he couldn't handle it alone. But he didn't want to lie to Molly. And he didn't want her to stay for Mike's sake. He wanted her to stay for *him.*

Her gaze locked with his, direct and brave, even as her mouth wavered between a smile and a frown. "John?" she murmured hesitantly.

"Don't leave."

She searched his face. He hoped she saw the truth in his eyes. He hoped she knew what he really wanted to say, what he couldn't bring himself to come right out and ask.

Her mouth settled in an ambiguous smile, and she lowered her gaze to her hands, dabbing a stray bead of water from her wrist with the paper towel. "I guess I could stay a little while longer," she conceded. "I don't mind giving Mike a bath."

She was staying for Mike, then. She was staying to

help out the floundering father. And she was staying only a little while longer.

She had understood exactly what John was asking of her, and she'd given him her answer. He couldn't blame her. She'd made the smart, sensible choice. He ought to count his blessings that she didn't demand, right then and there, that he call her a cab.

He didn't want to count his blessings. Given the way he felt, he doubted he would be able to count much past zero.

He opened his mouth to offer her a lift home. No sense delaying the inevitable. If he drove her home now, while Mike was still awake, the kid could come along for the ride. Molly would love that. Mike was the only reason she'd sacrificed this day for John.

But before he could speak, Mike had grabbed her hand and was dragging her down the hall toward the bathroom. "Molly gives me a bath," he declared. "Make the fish, okay? Molly, you make the fish and I don't splash."

"Okay, Michael," she agreed, following him out of the kitchen. "I'll make the fish."

John had no idea what the hell they were talking about. All he knew was that he was left in the kitchen, alone.

And he wanted Molly even more. He wanted her because she was kind and she was generous and she was beautiful and because, on a Saturday night when she could be doing a million other things, she was going to make the fish for his son.

CHAPTER TWELVE

MICHAEL WAS ASLEEP.

After his bath, he swore he wasn't the least bit sleepy. He jogged several laps up and down the hall, screeching and giggling, until John snagged him and hauled him off to his room with the promise that they would read a book together only if Michael got into bed.

Smart move. Two pages into *Curious George*, Michael was snoring.

Molly watched from the doorway as John turned off the bedside lamp, kissed his son's forehead and picked his way across the toy-strewn floor to her side. Without speaking, they tiptoed down the hallway. His face remained hidden in shadow, his gaze straight ahead as they arrived at the entry to the living room.

What now? she wondered. She'd done everything she could do to help John with his son and his errands today. Surely he must have run out of favors to ask of her.

Not that she felt as if he'd taken advantage of her. Everything she'd done for him she'd done willingly, and she'd enjoyed it. In all honesty, she didn't think John had needed her for anything other than her expertise in choosing appropriate Christmas gifts for his son. He could have done everything else himself.

The irony, she realized, was that *she'd* been the one

who couldn't have accomplished any of the afternoon's pleasures without *him*. Without John, she couldn't have decorated a tree. She couldn't have shopped for tinsel and lights and spent hours draping them across the boughs of a fresh, fragrant pine. She couldn't have twisted pipe cleaners into colorful Christmas shapes and perched them on the branches.

Standing now at the entry to the living room, she admired the tree, which occupied the corner between the window and the fireplace, its small white lights twinkling like stars and causing the garlands of tinsel to sparkle. Once she went home she wouldn't have this. She wouldn't have a tree, or someone who loved her enough to leave presents beneath it the way John would leave presents for Michael. She wouldn't have a family to celebrate with her.

She'd stayed with the Russos all afternoon and evening because she'd needed this—the family, the tree, the joy of sharing the holiday with someone. But John and Michael weren't about to include her in their family. She shouldn't even want such a thing. She ought to leave before the wanting started to hurt.

"I'd better go," she muttered, risking a glance at John.

The tree's silvery lights danced along the lines and angles of his face, catching on the corner of his lip when he turned to her. His eyes were achingly dark as they searched her face. His gaze probed, questioned, pleaded—but she wasn't sure what he was asking, what he was pleading for.

"Will you call me a cab?" she asked.

"No."

He couldn't drive her home himself, not without first hiring a baby-sitter to stay with Michael. And finding an available baby-sitter on such short notice on a Saturday night would be impossible. A cab was the only sensible solution. "John, I think—"

"Don't go." He lifted his good hand to her cheek, his fingers digging into her hair. Sliding his hand around to the nape of her neck, he pulled her toward him and touched his lips to her brow. "Stay, Molly," he whispered. "For me."

For me. Not for Michael. Not for running errands, not for lending her assistance to a shopping expedition or helping out with the evening routines. For John. Just for John.

The heat of his kiss seeped slowly through her, caressing her mind, halting her breath, making her breasts tingle and her heart surge and her belly grow tight. She understood now what his gaze had been asking her. He wanted her to stay for the night, for sex.

But if she stayed, it would be for something more, something he hadn't offered: that sense of belonging, finding her place in John's world, in a house with a Christmas tree, in a home and a family that stood firm in the face of abandonment and loss.

That wasn't any part of his kiss. Molly shouldn't want it. She had a fine family of her own, and perhaps someday she would have a husband and children and a nice, cozy house. Ideally, she would have a husband whose line of work was safe and didn't launch her sister into paroxysms of rage. With luck, Molly would find a man who didn't carry the baggage of a failed marriage and an emotionally fragile son.

But she didn't want to think so far into the future. She wanted to think only about tonight, this minute, with John.

"Yes," she murmured, tilting her face up to him as

he leaned down to her. His mouth found hers, and her kiss answered *yes*, as well.

He kissed her gently. Deeply. Slowly. Thoroughly. His arms enveloped her, warming her, making her want to arch against him. She could no longer think of the holiday atmosphere she'd helped create in his home, or the special closeness between him and his son. All that mattered was John, a man so reserved in most things, but not now. When he kissed her he held nothing back.

His tongue swept her mouth, slid along her teeth, teased her lips. His fingers twined through her hair, massaged the nape of her neck, dipped beneath the collar of her shirt while his other hand, constricted by gauze and tape, came to rest at the small of her back, urging her against him. The heat he'd ignited with his first kiss grew brighter and fiercer, exerting a pressure so unbearably sweet she wanted to sigh and weep and beg for more. More kisses. More heat. More.

"Come," he said.

Stunned that he could command her response—and even more stunned that she could be so close to meeting that demand—she pulled back and blinked up at him. He slid his hand down her arm to weave his fingers through hers and motioned with his head toward the hallway.

Oh. He meant he wanted her to come down the hall with him. Abashed by her X-rated interpretation of his statement, she accompanied him to the door across from Michael's bedroom. He opened it, led her inside and closed it firmly behind him.

She considered briefly the room across the hall and the child asleep inside it. Did John expect her to spend the whole night with him? If so, what would Michael think if he found her there in the morning?

Probably not much, she decided. At two and a half years old, he wouldn't understand what a woman might do with his father overnight. He would simply think Molly didn't feel like going home—which was true. After the way John had just kissed her, the last thing she wanted was to go home.

Once she had assured herself that Michael wouldn't have a problem with her staying, she surveyed her surroundings. John's room was relatively neat, the closet shut, the bed made, the dresser devoid of clutter until John emptied the pockets of his jeans, removing his wallet, his keys and a handful of coins and tossing them onto the polished maple surface.

Watching a man empty his pockets like that seemed so domestic. So personal. So...intimate.

Turning from the dresser, he removed his sweater, easing the right sleeve past his bandages and withdrawing his arm, then whipping the sweater over his head and off his left arm. Molly's gaze lingered for a moment on the wide strip of gauze wrapped around his forearm. It stirred memories of the night she'd brought Michael to the emergency room in search of him, the gut-wrenching fear she'd suffered at the thought of him hurt, her new awareness of John as a man. She felt that awareness now, much more keenly. Beneath his T-shirt, she discerned the contours of his torso. Her gaze journeyed from his broad shoulders down his lean, sleek chest to the waistband of his jeans. Below the buckle of his belt, the denim was slightly faded along his fly.

He took a step toward her, his left arm outstretched, and she approached him. Compared to his beautifully proportioned height, she felt short and dumpy. She had always wanted to be tall like Allison—and never more than now.

But then his hand closed around hers, pulling her into his arms for another ravenous kiss, and she forgot about her physical imperfections. John obviously didn't think she was too short. His kiss indicated that he approved of her appearance quite heartily.

He loosened his hold on her and fingered the top button of her shirt. Fumbling with his left hand, he lifted his right to the button. But his thumb and index finger couldn't meet over the thick bandage.

She covered his hands with hers and drew them away. "I'll do it," she said.

He inched back from her, saying nothing, only gazing at her. His eyes glowed.

She felt a blush rise to her cheeks, and for a moment she fumbled with the top button as badly as he had. But then it came undone, and when she glanced up at him his smile shook her to her soul. It was both amused and aroused, daring her to continue.

She pushed aside her nervousness. Let him dare her; she'd never been one to back away from a challenge. Taking a deep breath, she unfastened the next button, and the next, and the next, until she reached the belt of her jeans. She unbuckled it and heard him sigh. Peering up again, she found his smile gone and his eyes dark with hunger.

She was not a particularly bold woman, and her experience with men couldn't fill more than a few pages of a dime-store diary. But John made her feel reckless. She wasn't sure why—he was a cop, for heaven's sake, and a responsible father, two of the most unreckless things a man could be. But the way he looked at her, the way he'd kissed her, the way he was standing before her, his hair rumpled and his head cocked slightly, his thumbs hooked on the pockets of his jeans...

Well, damn it, if he was going to dare her, she would be daring. "I guess I'll have to undress you, too," she said, her voice quavering only a little.

He sighed again, although there was a hint of a groan in the sound. "I guess you'll have to," he agreed, still watching her, his chest moving in slow, deep breaths as she closed the distance between them.

She gathered the fabric of his T-shirt in her hands and tugged it free of his jeans. Her knees felt shaky, but she kept going, lifting the shirt up, baring his stomach, his rib cage, the smooth, golden-hued skin of his chest, the subtle curves of his muscles. He obediently lifted his hands over his head, but she couldn't reach high enough to pull the shirt off. He bent his knees, enabling her to complete the task. As soon as his hands were through the sleeves, he lowered them to her waist, shoving back the unbuttoned edges of her blouse and pressing his lips to the skin below her collarbone.

She felt faint, as if all the blood rushed from her head downward to where his mouth touched her. Her hips grew heavy, her body trembled and she choked back a gasp as he traced a line downward with his tongue, refusing to stop when he reached the edge of her bra. He kissed her through the lace, gliding over the curve of one breast until he could close his mouth over the swollen nipple. In her heart she heard the echo of his husky voice, speaking the one word he'd uttered in the living room: *Come.*

"John..." His name emerged on a broken sigh.

He straightened up, capturing her gaze with his. "Take it off," he whispered.

Oh, God. She really wasn't *that* daring, was she? But her passion was greater than her panic.

Biting her lip, she slid her shirt from her shoulders, then reached behind her and unhooked her bra. It slid down her arms and joined her shirt on the floor. Anxious, she glanced at him.

He must have realized how much courage this act had required of her. A faint smile crossed his lips, grateful and frankly carnal, before he brought his mouth back to her. She felt the scratch of his bandages against her side, the seductive massage of his fingers against her other side as he took first one nipple and then the other into his mouth. She clung to his shoulders, trying not to dissolve into a seething puddle of sensation.

Sinking to his knees, he kissed a path to her navel, flicked his tongue over it, and rubbed his chin against the button at the waistband of her slacks. "I don't think I can do this," he said, making a desultory attempt to open the button with his left hand.

She gazed down at him, and he peered up at her, looking uncannily like Michael when he was trying to get away with something. John's expression was a bit naughty, a bit hopeful, and completely irresistible.

Unlike Michael, though, he also looked unbearably manly, his hair as dark as night, his jaw shaded with a day's growth of beard, his lips damp from kissing her. His eyes were as sharp and piercing as darts, cutting straight through her as if he could see her secrets, her deepest desires.

She couldn't deny those eyes.

She didn't want to.

Swallowing hard, she popped open the button and inched down the zipper. John did the rest, shoving her slacks and panties down her legs and then trailing his hands back up to her bottom. He kissed the curve of her belly and then lower, a light, tantalizing brush of his tongue between her legs.

A small cry escaped her, partly from shock and partly from the jolt of sensation that flared through her. He rose to his feet and gathered her to himself, taking her mouth in a long, dizzying kiss.

Somehow, despite his bad hand, he managed to remove his own jeans without any difficulty. He pulled her body to his, and she experienced another jolt of heat as he pressed himself to her. After a swift, hard kiss, he drew her toward the bed and down onto the thick burgundy quilt.

She needed to catch her breath—and so, apparently, did he. For a long, lovely moment they just lay side by side, facing each other, their heads settling into the pillows. He had the most beautiful face Molly had ever seen. It wasn't pretty or polished, but every feature was eloquent, conveying a blend of trust, affection and yearning. The combination was so potent, so poignant, she wanted to reassure him, open herself to him and promise him things he would never ask for.

Instead, she leaned forward and kissed his nose, the edge of his cheek, the point of his chin. He skimmed his hand along her side and forward, exploring the roundness of her breasts. She ran her hands up and down his back, and his muscles flexed beneath her palms. She kissed his throat and he sighed. She touched his nipples and he gasped. Her hands journeyed across his ribs and he gasped again, this time recoiling slightly.

"What?" she asked, worried that she'd done something wrong.

"Nothing," he murmured, nudging her hand away from his chest.

She realized that she'd touched his bruises, still livid so many days after his encounter with the thug. "I'm sorry, John. I forgot—"

"It's all right."

It wasn't all right. She slid down until she could kiss the discolored skin, wishing her kisses could heal him.

He pulled her back up to the pillow, rolling with her until she lay under him. His thigh nestled between her legs and he moved it against her, sending shimmering heat up into her.

She tried to concentrate on the mere feel of him, his weight and power and size, but she couldn't. There was too much else in this bed right now—his pride and stoicism, her profound longing, the ugliness and danger of his work, the pensiveness she felt about the holiday this year. The son he loved and his determination to do right by that son. Her own affection for his son and her concern for John's safety.

She loved him. She knew it and it frightened her because John had never offered a hint that he returned her love. But she couldn't lie to herself. She knew the truth when it punched her in the gut.

As if he sensed the change in her mood, he rose, propping himself up on his arms. His right arm buckled, and he collapsed against her and cursed.

"Are you okay?" she asked, horrified.

Groaning again, he slid off her and sprawled out on his back. "I'm fine. Just..."

"Just what?"

"Mortified."

"Mortified?" She pushed onto her side and peered down at him. A trace of a smile curved his lips, and she felt some of her concern ebb away. "Why?"

"Look at me." He shook his head, his smile failing to disguise his annoyance. "I'm operating at half strength." He raised his bandaged arm, then pointed to his discolored ribs.

Just hearing him admit his insecurity made her love him more. "If this is what you're like at half strength," she said, skimming her hand gently over his chest, "I don't think I could survive you at full strength."

"Molly." He gazed up at her, ran his thumb over the curve of her lip and smiled bleakly. "I'm really a lot better with two working hands."

That might be, but Molly was absurdly aroused by what he'd accomplished with just one hand—and two lips and a naughty tongue and his own arousal, which was definitely not at half strength.

Mustering what little courage she had left, she slid her hand down his body through the dark, wiry hair below his abdomen to his hard length. She skimmed him with her palms. "Do you want me to leave?" she asked with feigned innocence.

He closed his eyes and groaned at her touch. "No."

"Then you're just going to have to stay where you are and let me do the rest."

His eyes flew open and he stared at her, a daring, searing gaze that almost made her lose her courage. "I'm not so sure about that," he said, his voice a dark rumble.

"Why? You like to be in charge?"

"Yes."

That was blunt. "Well, tough luck, Detective Russo of the Arlington Police Force," she retorted, feeling a fresh burst of audacity. If he'd challenged her with his steamy gazes and his orders for her to undress, nothing had challenged her more than this.

Her sudden bossiness seemed to intrigue him. That hint of a wicked smile returned. "Tough luck?"

She tried to suppress a grin. "Oh, yes, John. Very tough."

"I think I'm worried." But he didn't look worried. He looked downright pleased—and, if possible, more aroused than before.

"Trust me," she said, wishing she could trust herself. She had no idea how to take charge in bed. She'd had a few boyfriends in her life, but just the past few minutes with John had proven to her that he was much better at this business than she was.

Then again, he seemed to be responding quite intensely to her gentle caresses. She tightened her hand and he responded even more intensely. A broken groan escaped him, and he eased her hand away.

"I thought I was in charge," she protested in a whisper.

"It feels too good." He lifted her hand to his lips and kissed it, then placed it on his chest. She could feel the rapid beat of his heart beneath her fingertips.

"What do you want me to do?" she asked, worrying that she'd failed somehow.

"Come on top of me," he murmured. "Let me feel you."

There were advantages and disadvantages to loving a man of few words. The main disadvantage was that he always left her wanting to know more. The main advantage was that he stated his wishes quite clearly.

She did as he asked, easing herself down onto him. He massaged her shoulders, her sides, the outer curves of her breasts, her waist. Then he drew her toward him, arranging her legs so she was straddling his hips. She braced herself on her arms and he touched her breasts. What he could do to her with one hand was astonishing.

His fingers glided down her body and she shuddered, her hips moving of their own volition, her fingertips digging into his shoulders. "Look at me, Molly," he whispered when she closed her eyes.

She obeyed, forcing her lids open and peering down into his face. His gaze stroked her soul as his fingers stroked her flesh. Her muscles tensed, her body needing more, needing him. She whimpered deep in her throat and arched her back.

"Are you still in charge?" he asked.

Through a haze of passion she saw his smile. She opened her mouth to answer, but he flicked his thumb against her in such a way that she could only moan. She might have been imagining it, but she thought she heard him moan, too, as if seeing her so aroused aroused him, as well.

"There are condoms in the drawer," he told her, gesturing with his right hand toward the night table beside the bed. He let go of her, and the loss of his touch chilled her. She groped frantically through the drawer, her hands trembling as she pulled out the box. She searched John's face, hoping he would take over from there. But he only lifted his bandaged hand and smiled again.

Anyone who could awaken such heavenly sensations inside a woman could certainly tear open a foil wrapper, with or without two working hands. But now, when she was on the verge of burning up, John was going to feign helplessness.

She did what she had to do, her fingers still shaking, her breath shallow. When she had him ready, she turned back to him and found his smile gone, his eyes luminous. He clamped his hands over her hips and pulled her down onto him, thrusting deep.

For a moment she refused to move. She wanted to savor the perfection, the glorious possession of his body. Soon she would want more, but this one moment, this first taste... It was heaven.

Her fingers curled against his shoulders and her breasts skimmed his chest as he rocked her body with his, helping her find her rhythm, angling her to take even more of him. She understood what he'd meant when he said it felt too good. What he was doing to her felt much too good, immeasurably too good.

Her body absorbed him, welcomed him, let him lead her onward. The boundaries between them blurred and vanished. John was part of her, his body locked inside her, carrying her with him until they were both on fire, exploding with pleasure, closer than two people could possibly be.

She sagged against him, too weak to move. He stroked his hand languidly up and down her back. She cuddled against him, cushioning her head with his shoulder. His skin was warm, satiny against her cheek. She could hear the rapid pounding of his heart.

A long while passed, neither of them moving, nothing said as their bodies slowly cooled off, their pulses slowed and they separated. John kept his arms snugly around her, giving her a sense of safety. She shouldn't feel safe. She'd just admitted to herself that she had fallen in love with him.

"Are you okay?" he asked quietly. He sounded weary.

Her emotions were raw, but other than that she was splendid. "'Okay' would be an understatement," she told him.

She couldn't see his smile, but she could picture it. "It's been a while for me," he said. "I hope I wasn't too rough."

She took a minute to digest his comment. She'd never before known a man who could say so much in so few words. In his statement she heard strains of his obsessive responsibility, worrying over how she was and whether he'd caused any problems for her. She also heard "It's been a while." For some reason, that surprised her.

"I'm sure it's been longer for me," she said. "I'm three steps short of being a nun."

"Three steps?" He chuckled, sliding his hand up into her hair and letting it spill through his fingers. "You don't seem like a nun to me. A nun would never take charge the way you did."

She laughed out loud, her lips bumping against his chest. "You're the biggest con artist in the world, telling me to take charge. You were in charge the whole time."

"Like hell." He rolled onto his side so he could view her. A lock of hair fell across her eyes, and he lifted it back into place. "You made me crazy, Molly. I could scarcely think, let alone control myself. You were running the show."

"Not quite." His face was so close to hers, it took vast amounts of willpower not to lean forward and kiss him. "I told you, I'm practically a nun. I wouldn't know how to run this particular show even if I wanted to."

"You're the sexiest nun I've ever seen." He kissed her tenderly and leaned back.

She studied his face in the dim light of the bedside lamp. He looked solemn in spite of his smile. "It's been a while," he'd said. Was she the first woman he'd been with since his wife had left?

And how in heaven's name could a woman leave a man who made love the way John did?

"Why did she leave you?" she blurted out, then clapped her hand to her mouth. "I'm sorry. It's none of my business. Forget I asked."

"It's all right." He stroked her hair again, tucking it behind her ear. "She left me because she didn't love me."

"That's the part I'm having trouble with," Molly said, figuring that since he hadn't kicked her out of his bed for being too nosy, or at the very least changed the subject, he must not mind talking about it. "She married you. She had a child with you. She must have loved you at some point."

He laughed mirthlessly. "I don't think so." He ran his hand through her hair again while he collected his thoughts. "We were dating, we were careless and she got pregnant. She wanted an abortion, but I begged her not to do that. I told her I'd marry her and we'd raise the baby together. I was persuasive." He paused for a minute, lost in thought. "It was never what she wanted."

Molly appreciated that he'd told her so much. But there was something missing, some flaw in his logic. Perhaps he'd been persuasive, perhaps his wife hadn't wanted marriage or a baby. But he was such a good man. If he could persuade her to marry him and become a mother, why couldn't he have persuaded her to stay with him?

He must have guessed her thoughts. "It wasn't what I wanted, either. We didn't marry out of love. I wasn't a good husband."

"You're the most responsible person I've ever met. How could you not be a good husband?"

The soothing pattern of his fingers through her hair would have lulled her into a trance if the conversation hadn't been so important to her. He sifted his words as his hand sifted her hair. "I was wrapped up in my work," he finally said. "I lived for it. I took the hardest cases, put in the longest hours. I was single-minded and aggressive. I was going to be the best damned cop in Arlington. In the world." He sighed. "I wasn't what she needed. I didn't do my share with Mike. She got stuck doing the hard stuff—the diapers, the feedings—while I was putting in the time and earning my shield. When I was home, my mind wasn't with her. It was on whatever case I was working." His hand went still and he stared directly into her eyes. "Cops don't make good husbands."

"That's ridiculous," she argued, but she sounded less than certain. For ten years she'd listened to Gail rant about cops, their power-hungry attitudes, their arrogance, their disregard for justice, their lack of compassion. Maybe cops made bad husbands because their work was so demanding and violent, but... No. She simply didn't want to believe John's statement was true.

She didn't want to believe it because she was in love with him.

She didn't want to let him believe it, either. She

was going to prove to this fine, honest, brave man that he was capable of anything: being a good father, being a wonderful lover—being the best cop in the world, if that was what he wanted. John could do it all.

If only she could convince him of it.

If only she could absolutely, without a doubt, convince herself.

CHAPTER THIRTEEN

AT NINE-THIRTY Monday morning, John swung into the glass-enclosed office overlooking the squad room and said, "I want to get back to work."

Coffey looked up from the stack of memos on his blotter. Squinting slightly, he scrutinized the tall, intense detective standing on the opposite side of his desk. John still had on his jacket; the morning's chilly air clung to him. He hadn't paused to admire the Christmas tree in the lobby downstairs or to shoot the breeze with the cops loitering in the squad room. He'd marched directly into Coffey's office, prepared to make demands.

Before coming to work, he'd spent a half hour with his doctor, having his stitches and butterfly clips removed. Before that, he'd dropped Mike off at the Children's Garden, where he'd seen Molly.

Just thinking about the two minutes they'd shared in the preschool's entryway made him grin. With other parents coming and going, he and Molly hadn't had the privacy he would have liked, but perhaps that was just as well. If they'd had privacy, he would have kissed her. And once he'd kissed her, he would have wanted to do a hell of a lot more. Only the swarm of parents kept him from ravishing her right there.

Coffey remained seated at his desk but didn't motion John to sit down. "What did your doctor say?" he asked, eyeing John skeptically.

"He said I was fine." Actually, he'd said John was healing well, which wasn't quite the same thing. But the doctor had only examined John's arm and his hand. He'd had no idea about how good the rest of John was feeling.

Molly. All he had to do was close his eyes and think about the way he'd held her, touched her, made love to her...and he felt as strong and spirited as a stallion. A couple of knife wounds were irrelevant.

"I don't want to do Santa, either," he added, feeling bold. "I want real work, Coffey. I want a case."

"I don't know." Coffey pressed his hands together, as if he were going to pray, and gave John a patronizing smile. "The Santa stint worked well. You got a lot of collars. And we know from experience that it was high-risk work. You've made a success of it, Russo—"

"You put me in a Santa suit because you thought I was stressed out," John reminded him. "Well, I'm not stressed out. I want real work."

"Undercover Santa wasn't real work?"

"No." It was, but John wasn't going to get his way by admitting it.

Coffey had assigned John to the Santa gig because he'd believed John was overwhelmed by the finality of his divorce and his child care crisis. If John wanted to get put on a case, all he had to do was persuade Coffey that neither of those issues were in play anymore. Thanks to Molly, they weren't.

But he wasn't ready to discuss her, not yet. He wasn't ready to tell Coffey about the woman who had helped him to understand his son, who had entered his house and transformed it into a home with her mere presence, who had spent the weekend with him, making him feel comfortable enough to talk about himself. He wasn't ready to describe the woman who had spent the night in his arms, so soft and lovely that Sunday morning he'd been aroused before he'd been awake. They'd made love again in the muted dawn light, warm and dreamy. They'd conquered worlds together. They'd glimpsed heaven. They'd become part of each other.

He could do anything now—run investigations, chase criminals, direct traffic, hold press conferences—anything except talk about Molly. That part of his life was too new.

"Trust me, Coffey," he said, trying not to beg. "Let me take a case. I'm ready."

Coffey looked dubious. But before he could speak, Bud Schaefer leaned in through the open doorway. "Coffey? I've got a shooting at a bar down on East Fifteenth. There's already some uniforms there. Who should I take with me?"

John knew Coffey wouldn't let Bud work the case by himself. Nobody went solo on a shooting. "I'll go," he volunteered, starting toward the door.

"Russo—"

"He'll be primary. I'm just backing him up."

"What kind of backup can you be?"

John held up his right hand, displaying the flat strip of adhesive with which the doctor had replaced the immobilizing wad of bandaging. He wiggled his fingers to show his dexterity. "I can do it."

Still doubtful, Coffey glanced toward Bud. "You want him partnering you?"

"If he says he can do it, he can."

Coffey turned back to John and shrugged. "All right. Keep me updated. And don't take any chances. The holidays always bring out the worst in people."

Anxious to get away from Coffey before he changed his mind, John strode out of the office ahead of Bud. He slowed as he neared the squad room door and checked his gun to make sure it was loaded. Tucking it back into the holster beneath his jacket, he waited for Bud to grab his cell phone. They left the squad room together.

Light flurries swirled through the air as they crossed the lot and climbed into one of the pool cars. Bud took the wheel and John settled into the passenger seat. All the pool cars had a similar smell, a mix of stale cigarette smoke and coffee and doughnuts spiced with a whiff of motor oil. John welcomed the distinctive fragrance. It confirmed that he wasn't playing undercover Santa anymore.

"So what happened?" Bud asked as he steered out of the lot.

"I told Coffey I wanted to get put on a case."

"No. Over the weekend."

John shot him a quizzical look. "What do you mean?"

"Something happened this weekend, Russo. You're a changed man."

It was John's habit to keep his private business private. But Bud had known him long enough to be able to read him. He considered refusing to respond to Bud's prying, but Bud might be insulted if he didn't toss him a scrap. "Mike and I did some Christmas shopping," he said. "We trimmed the tree. It looks good."

"You trimmed the tree?" Bud snorted. "Come on.

This is me you're talking to. Tell me what's going on.''

"We did trim the tree," John said, then relented. "Molly helped us."

Bud nodded, as if he'd known all along that Molly was the reason for John's vitality. "Hey, I think it's great. She's cute, she's a teacher, she works with kids. She's kind of on the short side, but nobody's perfect." He braked to a stop at a red light. There was no need to blast the siren and run traffic lights. Whatever had gone down in the bar was past tense; uniformed officers were already at the scene, and John and Bud had no cause for high-risk speeding.

"So," Bud probed, "what does Mike think of her?"

The question made John uncomfortable. He didn't want to admit that part of Molly's appeal was her rapport with Mike. If John thought of her in relation to Mike, he'd think of her in the role of a stepmother, and if he did that he'd think of her in the role of a wife. He couldn't let himself do that, not when he had so many misgivings about himself in the role of a husband.

He forced a smile. "At this point, it's too soon to matter what Mike thinks."

"Well, whatever else got trimmed besides that tree—" Bud glanced at him knowingly "—it's done wonders for you."

John didn't consider that remark worth acknowledging.

Bud lost his smirk. "If she's good for you, hang on to her," he advised. "I'm your partner, and I like you better when you're happy."

"I'm not happy," John argued just to be contrary.

A block ahead of them, they saw several black and whites parked in front of a bar, with a few onlookers milling around the sidewalk outside the door. "Who goes to a bar this early on a Monday morning?" Bud wondered out loud. "It's too early for people to be getting drunk and blowing each other's brains out."

"Let's find out what happened," John said, shoving out of the car as soon as Bud turned off the engine.

What happened, they learned after talking to the uniformed officers and interviewing the pale, trembling woman who owned the bar, was that she and the victim, a fellow she identified as Alvin Hampton, were setting up the bar for its ten-thirty opening when a woman barged in, screamed, "I'm gonna kill you, Alvin!" and shot him in the thigh. He had already been taken to Arlington Memorial, but one of the EMTs heard him mumble the name "Sheila." At first the bar owner insisted she had no idea who Sheila was, but eventually her memory sharpened enough for her to recall that the shooter just might have been Alvin's wife. A bit more prodding, and the bar owner also recollected that she and Alvin had been having an affair for three months.

John and Bud got Alvin's home address from the bartender and drove to the modest apartment building, where they found Sheila Hampton. She was thin, with disproportionately large hands and an odd shade of red hair with black roots along her scalp. When Bud told her he was going to bring her to the station for questioning, she insisted she'd done nothing wrong, but she left the apartment peacefully, locking the door behind her before John could see any farther into it than the front foyer. He and Bud were going to have to get a search warrant. He'd bet a week's salary there was a gun somewhere inside.

"Aren't you gonna read me my rights?" she asked as they escorted her to the car. She turned up the collar of her pea jacket and dug her hands into the pockets.

"You haven't been charged with anything," Bud explained. "We just want to question you."

"Yeah, well, I know my rights."

"Good for you," he said as John helped her into the back seat and shut the door.

"I'm not talking without a lawyer," she warned as they took their seats in front of her. "I'm just telling you that. I know my rights."

John noted that she hadn't asked what she was being brought in for questioning about—which implied that she already knew. She knew because she'd been the one to send her husband to the hospital with a gunshot wound to his thigh. If she'd shot him there, she'd probably been aiming at his groin. Scorned women were awfully predictable sometimes.

But all his hunches weren't going to put her behind bars. Procedures had to be followed. She'd have to be questioned, and if she wanted a lawyer, she'd get one.

Back at the station house, they ushered her through the lobby, refusing her the chance to admire the tree. They escorted her up the stairs, through the squad room and into an interrogation room. The last time John had been in this particular room, he'd been grilling two pint-size bank thieves. He had a feeling this interrogation wasn't going to be quite as much fun.

"I want a lawyer," Sheila Hampton reminded them, as if they could have forgotten.

"I'm going to get a search warrant," Bud whispered to John. "You deal with her."

John shrugged. He hated doing the paperwork necessary to secure a warrant, but he wasn't sure he
wanted to spend his morning with this phony redhead.
He waited until Bud had left the room, then said,
"Who's your lawyer?"

"I don't have one. You're supposed to provide me
with one. I know my rights."

"Okay." He left the room, locking her in, and
asked one of the clerks to contact the Public Defender's office. Then he returned to the interrogation
room. "You want some coffee?" he asked Sheila.

"Yeah. Cream and sugar. Lots of sugar. Three
packets."

Strolling down the hall to the lounge and preparing
a cup of coffee for her ate up a few minutes. He
brought her the steaming drink, then sat across from
her at the painted wooden table. It was an ugly thing,
the surface scratched and the legs scuffed, but it was
indestructible. John knew this from personal experience; more than once, he'd seen perpetrators kick the
table, hit it and attempt to lift it to throw at him. At
least Sheila Hampton didn't have enough meat on her
to try anything like that. The table probably weighed
more than she did.

"So," he said casually, letting her sip her coffee.
"Do you have a job?"

"What do you mean, do I have a job?"

"Well, it's almost eleven o'clock. I was just wondering if your boss might be expecting you at work."

"I called in sick," she said, then took another sip,
looking extremely proud of herself.

John kept his expression blank, but inside he was
grinning. Why would she have called in sick? She obviously wasn't ill. She'd planned to take the morning

off for a reason. The word *premeditated* flashed through his brain.

"What kind of work do you do, Mrs. Hampton?" he asked.

"I'm a secretary."

"And your husband? He works in a bar on East Fifteenth, doesn't he?"

Her gaze darted away. "I'm not saying another thing until you get me a lawyer."

He was grateful for the light rap on the door. Shoving back from the table, he opened the door and found himself face-to-face with a compact woman with straight blond hair and hazel eyes wearing a grim gray suit and carrying a bulging leather briefcase. She seemed to flinch when she saw him. Then she regrouped and glared at him, her gaze bristling with hostility. "You have someone in there for me?" she asked, her voice level enough for John to know that her hostility had nothing to do with their professional differences.

Her hostility had to do with him. "Hello," he said, unable to push a smile past his uneasiness.

"We need to talk," she snapped, then eased the door fully open. "Later. Right now, I'd like to confer with my client." She entered the room, right hand extended toward Sheila. "Hi. I'm Gail Saunders from the Public Defender's office." After shaking Sheila's hand, Molly's sister turned and reached for the doorknob. She directed a final, lethal stare at John, then slammed the door, shutting him out.

BY THE TIME Bud returned to the station house with the gun he'd found in Sheila Hampton's apartment, John was worn out from one of the most fruitless interrogations he'd ever conducted. The only glimmer of information he'd gotten out of Sheila was that her husband was a satyr, though she pronounced it "sayder," like the Jewish meal at Passover.

"A sadist, you mean?" he'd asked.

"No, a satyr. You know, one of those old goats that's always humping up against ladies." But she vehemently denied shooting him. "If I was gonna shoot anyone, I'd shoot the lady that messed with him," she offered before Gail Saunders told her to shut up.

Gail was the reason the interrogation was fruitless. She muzzled her client, censored her, interrupted whenever Sheila seemed on the verge of saying something useful. Once ballistics determined that Sheila's gun matched the slug the surgeons at Arlington Memorial had cut out of her husband's leg, she was booked on the charge of attempted murder. Not once in the course of the afternoon did she inquire as to her husband's condition.

John watched as she was cuffed and escorted through the squad room, destined for the detention cell in the building's basement to await her arraignment. He'd seen perpetrators walk that path many times before, and it always left him feeling bleak. He ought to be euphoric whenever he nailed one of the bad guys. He'd done his part to get a dangerous person out of circulation; he should savor the moment. But there was something pathetic in the sight, a feeling that in that bad guy's tiny corner of the universe, things had fallen apart disastrously, mechanisms had failed, the balance had been thrown off. It was sad, and he'd witnessed it enough times to be left with a bitter aftertaste.

Turning from the stairway, he started toward the

coffee room. Gail Saunders blocked the hall, her lips pursed and her eyes narrowed on him.

He was tempted to ask her to kindly step out of the way, but he knew she was waiting for him. She'd said they had to talk; he only wished he had a hint about what.

He gave her a tentative smile. "You want some coffee?" he asked.

"No, but I would like a few minutes of your time."

"Fine." He shrugged and gestured toward the coffee room at the other end of the hall. "I'm getting some coffee."

She fell into step beside him, accompanying him into the lounge. He filled his ceramic cup with the sludge left in the nearly empty pot, then motioned to one of the vinyl chairs placed around the small room. She remained standing, projecting height and mass even though she was no more than an inch or two taller than her sister. She gripped her briefcase in one hand and let the other hang at her side. Only someone trained to pick up clues through body language would have noticed the tension in her furled fingers.

He wasn't sure why she seemed to resent him, unless it was because she'd been unable to crack him with her cross-examination when he'd testified during that murder trial a couple of weeks ago. But whatever the reason, he didn't want to alienate her. She was Molly's sister.

He took a sip of coffee, trying not to grimace at its burnt flavor. Leaning against the counter, he watched her. She was the one who wanted this conversation, so she would have to begin it.

She bought a minute by gazing around the lounge, skimming the jumble of messages tacked to the bulletin board on one wall, glancing up at the buzzing fluorescent light, making note of the antiquated refrigerator and the worn linoleum tiles checkerboarding the floor. Then she turned her attention back to him. "I had dinner with Molly last night," she said. "She told me she spent the weekend with you."

John saw no need to confirm or deny it. If Molly wanted to talk about it with her family, he wasn't about to object.

"I'm her sister and I love her," Gail continued. "I want to know what's going on."

"Don't you think that's her business?" he suggested, granting Gail a point for loving Molly but deducting a point for her nosiness.

"I'll tell you what I think, Detective Russo. I think Molly is awfully naive when it comes to men. I also think cops have the ability to induce trust where it might not be warranted."

Her words were like an assault. He held himself still, trying to tamp down his anger. But inside, he was seething. Who the hell was she to be making such absurd generalizations about cops?

She was a public defender, which—he supposed— gave her certain access to cops. They were her professional adversaries, arresting and testifying against the scum it was her job to defend. But that had nothing to do with his private life or her sister's.

"I think Molly is a lot smarter than you're giving her credit for," he said quietly, filtering the indignation out of his voice. She could bait him all she wanted. He wasn't going to bite.

"I know Molly is smart," Gail retorted. "I also know she's a soft touch. You're a single father with a kid, and she can't resist kids."

"You think she spent the weekend with me because of my son?" he asked, quirking an eyebrow.

Gail pursed her lips, obviously not a fan of irony. "I think she spent the weekend with you because she loves you. She has no idea who you are or what you are, or whether you can think past tomorrow—but she loves you. I know cops better than she does, Detective. You pour all your energy into getting your collars. That's the most important thing."

He wasn't going to get into a debate with a public defender about the way he did his job. "What does this have to do with Molly?"

She opened her mouth to speak, then reconsidered and sorted her thoughts. "My experiences with cops have not been good, Detective Russo."

"I know we're opponents on the job, but—"

"I'm not talking about the job. I'm talking about my life. My experiences with the police don't give me much reason to trust you. You're welcome to change my opinion if you can. Promise me you're going to take good care of my sister and never hurt her. Promise me you're not just going to enjoy her for a while and then send her on her way." Her voice cracked slightly as she added, "I'm Molly's big sister, and I love her, and I don't want her to get hurt. Promise me you won't hurt her."

He closed his eyes and sighed, knowing damned well that he couldn't promise Gail Saunders any of those things. He might have argued that neither he nor Molly—nor Gail herself—could see into the future. For all any of them knew, Molly might choose to dump him before he even figured out where he was going with the relationship.

But even if he said as much to Gail, he couldn't

overcome the truth in her words. He couldn't promise that he would never hurt Molly. He couldn't promise it to himself. He certainly couldn't promise it to Molly's sister.

"Life doesn't come with a guarantee," he reminded her. He'd tried to be a good husband and he'd failed. He was trying to be a good father, but the jury was still out on that one. Saturday night with Molly, he'd been as good a lover as he could be, minus a fully functional hand. But he couldn't tell Gail what she was demanding to hear: that he would always be good to Molly, always good for her.

Gail nodded. Her nod didn't express agreement so much as confirmation. She looked as if she'd decided that John was every bad thing she'd expected, and he was going to destroy her sister without mercy. He couldn't begin to guess where the enormous chip on her shoulder came from. Even after toiling a few years in the office of the Public Defender, she didn't have the right to be more cynical than he was after ten years in the police department.

"I appreciate your caring so much about Molly," he said, acknowledging that he hadn't done himself any favors by being honest.

"I wish I could say the same about you," Gail muttered. She pivoted on the stack heel of her sensible shoes and headed toward the door leading out to the hallway. "Have a good night, Russo. I'll be spending it fighting for reasonable bail for Sheila Hampton."

He watched her stalk out of the lounge. She had fire in her, just like Molly. And she was pretty, like her sister, although the resemblance between the two women wasn't obvious. They were both smart and quick on their feet and not afraid to speak their minds.

But there the similarity ended. Gail Saunders dressed in dark, dowdy clothes and exuded chilly brilliance, whereas Molly...

Molly was soft, gentle, warm. Kind. Forgiving. Vulnerable to a man who was himself far too vulnerable.

He wondered, for a minute, what had happened to Gail, what unnamed experience had scarred her. And then he abandoned that thought for a far more essential question: what was going to happen to Molly if she stayed with him?

He knew he was going to hurt her, just as Gail had predicted. He was going to hurt her, and he ought to protect her from that hurt by sending her away now.

CHAPTER FOURTEEN

"I JUST CAN'T BELIEVE she did it," Molly muttered, jamming a star-shaped cookie cutter into the dough. She pressed it through and wrenched it, then lifted it and shook a perfectly shaped star of dough onto the cookie sheet. "My own sister. How could she do such a thing?"

Allison spread green sprinkles onto the star and sighed. The kitchen still held the scent of onions and soy sauce from the spicy pepper steak dinner she'd cooked. Although she had more or less moved into Jamie's place on the west side of town, she still spent a great deal of time in this house, her home since childhood and still her grandmother's residence.

She'd phoned the Children's Garden that afternoon and invited Molly to join her, her grandmother and the baby for supper. "Jamie's backed up in his work and he's bribed me to take Samantha and disappear for the evening so he can catch up," she'd explained.

"I hope it was a decent bribe," Molly had teased, although an evening with Jamie's darling seven-month-old daughter and Allison's feisty grandmother was reward enough.

The bribe, it turned out, was an official engagement ring. The emerald flanked by pavé diamonds was dazzling. Grammy had observed that any man who would present his fiancée with a ring that expensive-looking probably expected her to perform kinky sexual acts. Allison, used to her grandmother's off-color jibes, beamed and said she certainly hoped that was what Jamie had in mind.

Now Grammy was in the living room with Samantha, trying to teach the baby the alphabet by making her watch "Wheel of Fortune." And since Allison knew Jamie needed at least another two hours to finish writing his weekly column, she had decided that she and Molly should bake Christmas cookies.

Why not? Molly had thought. She didn't have anything better to do, anywhere better to go. Besides, she was frustrated and angry, and Allison was the kind of friend who would listen to her grumble without complaint.

"It's been three days," she lamented. "Three days, and all he's done is say hi and give me this funny smile when he drops Michael off or picks him up. He hasn't asked me to have dinner, hasn't invited me back to his house.... I thought things were so right between us. And I swear, I didn't do anything that would make his feelings change. It must have been Gail."

Deep in thought, Allison added some red sprinkles to the green and awaited the next raw cookie. Molly plopped it onto the baking sheet, and Allison lifted the tub of red sprinkles again. "Do you know what Gail said to him?"

"She told me she more or less asked him what his intentions were. His *intentions*. I mean, come on! Just because my folks are in Ohio doesn't mean she has the right to act like my guardian."

Allison shook some sprinkles onto the dough. "Your sister has a hang-up about cops, Molly. From the first time you mentioned John she's had qualms

about him. He could be any man in the world, but as
long as he's a cop she's going to have trouble dealing
with it.''

"She's a narrow-minded busybody,'' said Molly.
"Yes, she has a hang-up about cops, but so what? I
have a hang-up about men who hate children, but if
Gail started dating a guy who hated children, I
wouldn't intervene.''

"She's your big sister. She's just looking out for
you.''

"I don't want her looking out for me!'' Molly was
so angry, she mangled the dough in the cookie cutter.
Sighing, she flattened it with the heel of her palm and
pressed the cutter into it again. "John isn't just a cop.
He's a brave, kind man with only one big flaw, as far
as I can tell—he takes too much responsibility for
things. Which is a heck of a lot better than some of
the losers I've met who could drive a car straight into
a tree and blame it on the tree.'' She cut a neat star
and placed it on the baking sheet. "And John doesn't
hate kids. He's a Daddy School student. That's worth
a whole lot of points in my book.''

"Mine, too,'' Allison said with a smile. Setting
down the sprinkles, she added, "You know, Grammy
put Jamie through the wringer a lot when I first started
seeing him—and she's still putting him through the
wringer, even though we're getting married. It doesn't
matter that he's going to be my husband—she still
calls him a bum. She's ten times worse than your sister.''

"Your grandmother's full of nonsense. Nobody
takes her seriously when she teases like that.''

"A man who wasn't sure of his own feelings might
very well take her seriously,'' Allison argued gently.

Molly's stomach knotted. She searched Allison's face for a sign that Allison hadn't meant what she'd implied. But she saw no indication that Allison was joking. "In other words—" Molly tried not to choke on the words "—you think John doesn't feel anything for me."

"I'm sure he feels *something*, Molly."

"But his feelings are too weak to matter. That's what you're saying, isn't it? He doesn't care enough about me to get past whatever the hell Gail said to him."

Allison covered Molly's floury hand with her own, her fingers stained red and green from the food coloring in the sprinkles. "I don't know if that's true. But if he was really in love with you, do you think Gail could stop him?"

"Gail could stop anyone," Molly muttered, her eyes burning with tears. Allison was right, of course. All she'd done was give voice to the thoughts and doubts that had been plaguing Molly for three days. If John felt as strongly about her as she did about him, he would have let her know that three days after she'd awakened in his bed, she was on his mind, in his heart.

It was only bad luck that John had been allowed to resume his usual duties so soon after he'd been stabbed, that he'd participated in the arrest of a woman who had allegedly shot her husband and that, despite the fact that Gail had dozens upon dozens of defenses to prepare, she'd gotten sent to the police station to defend that particular woman.

Gail had told Molly the woman was innocent. But if the woman's husband had broken her heart, Molly wouldn't blame her for shooting the guy. At the moment, Molly was very sympathetic to scorned women.

"I know John must be fond of you," Allison said. Molly shot her a scathing look, but Allison didn't flinch. "Maybe he's just rethinking the situation before he pursues it further. Maybe he feels awkward because you run his son's preschool, and he's trying to figure out how to balance everything. And with his divorce so recent—"

"His wife left him six months ago—and their marriage was disintegrating long before that. The only recent thing was formalizing the breakup."

"But who's to say how long it will take him to recover? Maybe he wants to be completely healed before he gets involved with you."

Molly thought of how unhealed he'd been Saturday night. His right arm and hand had been out of commission, but it hadn't stopped them from making love....

The knot in her stomach unwound, sending ripples up into her throat, where they reknotted into a tight lump. Surely making love to her must have meant something to him. Surely it had been as significant to him as it had been to her.

"You know what?" Allison picked up the snowflake cookie cutter and pressed it into the dough. "If it really matters to you—and I know it does—you could ask him."

"Ask him what?"

"Ask him why he's steering clear of you. He might say something you don't want to hear, but you're already assuming the worst. If you want, I'll go with you. We could drive to his house right now and confront him."

"Oh, God, no!" Molly laughed in spite of herself. "He's probably giving Michael a bath right now. He's probably drenched in water from the tub even as we speak. This would definitely not be a good time to confront him.''

But Allison was right. Molly was doing herself no favors by stewing at home while John avoided her. The only way she was going to find out what was going on in his mind was to ask him.

His answer might be painful, but not knowing was agony. Nothing he could say to her could make her feel worse than she already felt.

"Let's get this batch in," Allison said, carrying the sheet to the oven. "I want to send you home with a plate of cookies. You might need them for comfort."

Molly smiled sadly, not bothering to point out that if John told her he wanted nothing more to do with her, the most delicious holiday cookies in the universe weren't going to do any good.

SHE DIDN'T HAVE the opportunity to talk to him over the next two days. When he dropped Michael off at school both mornings, the entry was crowded with parents, and John's faint smile barely reached her through the swarming adults and children in their clumsy boots and snowsuits. When the students were picked up in the evening, he seemed to slip in and out, as well.

She could have telephoned him. But to learn over the phone that he wanted nothing more to do with her would be too cold, too impersonal. If she couldn't see his eyes while he talked to her, she wouldn't know whether or not to believe him.

Shoving herself out of bed Saturday morning, she acknowledged that the moment of truth had arrived. If John didn't attend today's session of the Daddy School—the final class of the year—she wouldn't have to confront him and ask what the hell was going on between them. His absence would be her answer.

She tried to convince herself not to dress for the occasion. The truth was, she had no idea what the occasion would be: something on the order of a funeral, a grand, passionate reconciliation or a nuclear-powered blowup.

She put on jeans, a shirt and a patterned wool sweater, figuring they'd suit any of the three alternatives. Her appetite had been a sometime thing all week, but she forced down a half a grapefruit, a cup of coffee and one of the buttery Christmas cookies Allison had sent her home with Wednesday evening. Then she brushed her teeth, slapped on a neutral lipstick, grabbed her keys and headed out to her car.

At ten o'clock, her students began to arrive with their youngsters in tow. Gordon showed up with Melissa, the four-year-old in the throes of terminal sibling rivalry. Hank showed up with his son Joey. Avery with Keisha clasping his hand and managing to skip in her bulky fireman-style boots. Rick and his daughter Rebecca. Lance and his son Brett.

Shannon was on hand to watch the children for the duration of the class. As soon as the children had been liberated from their outerwear, she trooped them up the stairs. Molly watched them go, then turned back to the small group of fathers, feeling her spirits sink.

John wasn't there. She had her answer, and it was the one she'd dreaded.

"Well," she said with forced cheer, "I'm glad you all managed to make time for today's class, what with the demands of the holiday. Why don't we all go into the Pre-K room and—" Hearing the squeak of the front door opening, she paused. "Oh, wait—it sounds like we've got a straggler."

Two sets of footsteps echoed down the hall, one heavy and adult, the other the quick, light trot of a child. Michael's voice pierced the room. "Where's the children, Daddy? I wanna go with the children!"

The Russo men entered the room, Michael bubbling over with energy and John lagging a few paces behind him. Michael looked exuberant; John looked wary. His leather jacket hung open to reveal a pale gray sweater above brown corduroy jeans. His hair was wind-tossed, his hands buried in his pockets. His eyes went straight to her, dark and troubled.

"Hello, John," she said. The presence of the other fathers compelled her to greet him as if he were just another student. "The children are upstairs with Shannon," she told Michael. "You can go up and join them."

"I go with the children!" he announced, not bothering to remove his jacket before he vanished up the stairs.

Her gaze moved back to John. He was still staring at her. She couldn't interpret his expression, except to recognize that it was grim. He wasn't thrilled to see her. He wasn't even pleased to be attending the Daddy School class. But he was here—whatever that meant.

"Let's go into the Pre-K room," she repeated for his sake. She wasn't going to find out why he'd come until after class, if at all, so she figured she might as well get the class started. She waited until they had all settled their bodies on the floor cushions and ledges and then began. "Given what's going on at this time of year, I thought we'd talk about being a good father during the holidays. Are any of you having any problems with your children that relate to the holidays?''

''My kid wants every single toy they advertise on TV,'' Lance moaned. Everyone laughed, and a few of the men nodded in agreement.

''Have you considered turning off the TV?'' Molly suggested. This brought more laughter. John almost smiled, she noticed. ''Of course it's up to the parents to decide what—and how much—your children should get. It's not up to the TV, and it's not up to your children. It's up to you.''

''I'd like to be reasonable about the gift giving,'' Avery said. ''But it's hard when everyone else is giving so much more. It makes you feel like a lousy father if all you're giving your kid is a doll, a few games and some books. My brother is giving his kids their own computers. It makes me feel…I don't know… deficient.'' He shrugged.

''Well, first of all, I don't think any child at this school needs her own computer. I'd wait until Keisha's in first grade, at least.'' She smiled again to show she was joking. ''Remember that when it comes to Christmas giving, the parents are allowed to set limits, and it's no one else's business.'' She held up her hands to silence the fathers before they could dispute her.

''I know it's hard, but there are many ways to explain your decisions to your children. Talking about peer pressure is going to go over their heads. But instead, why don't you think about establishing your own family's holiday traditions? This is a really important part of becoming a parent. You probably have all these memories of your childhood holidays, and your wives have their memories, and now you've created your own family and it's time to establish some new traditions. You can establish a tradition of giving mostly homemade gifts. Or a tradition of picking out a gift to leave beneath the tree at the police station. Those presents are distributed to needy children, aren't they?'' she asked John.

He nodded. ''We collect them. The fire department distributes them.''

She tried not to respond to the sound of his voice, low and dark, painfully familiar. She tried just as hard not to respond to his eyes, his crooked half smile, the lean contours of his torso beneath the sweater. It was torture not to grab his hand and march him down the hallway and into the storeroom next to her office, where they could close the door and hash things out in private...or kiss and let their passion burn their problems away.

But she had a class to conduct. Inhaling sharply, she tore her gaze from John and addressed the rest of the fathers. ''When I was growing up, my family lived in a house without a fireplace. I thought Santa would never come to our house, because I knew he entered houses through the chimney, and our chimney was connected to the furnace, and you sure wouldn't want Santa dropping into your furnace.'' The men laughed. ''My parents told me that if we left our stockings somewhere else, Santa would enter our house where the stockings were. We hung them along a windowsill in the kitchen, near the back door, and lo and behold, Santa managed to get into our house just fine. This is what I mean by setting your own traditions, doing things your own way.''

''I've got a different problem,'' Rick spoke up. ''We celebrate Chanukah. Rebecca wants to know why Santa won't visit her. She thinks it isn't fair, because she's been a good girl all year.''

"That's a hard one," Molly agreed. "It's difficult to see so many people celebrating Christmas when it isn't your holiday. Do you give her presents for Chanukah?"

"Yes, but she says it's not the same. How can I get her to be proud of who she is when it looks like everyone else is having more fun than she is?"

"You could try coming up with some family traditions, too. Maybe you could donate some time at a homeless shelter or a nursing home on Christmas Day. Or take a drive in the country. If you do something special that none of Rebecca's Christian friends are doing, she might feel like *they're* the ones missing out on all the fun."

And so it went, the entire two hours of the class devoted to making the holidays meaningful and happy for all the children. The fathers traded information on which toys were hot and which were worthless. They discussed ways to involve their children in various holiday preparations. They talked about how to maintain discipline when visiting relatives doted on the children and spoiled them. They even swapped laundry tips: cranberry sauce stained pretty badly, but sweet potatoes washed out all right if you pretreated the stain.

John listened without contributing too much. Molly had no idea whether he cared about wash-day challenges, and she knew he had already done most of his gift shopping for Michael, so maybe this class was of limited interest to him. Still, he stayed.

At exactly noon, she heard tiny feet stampeding down the stairs, accompanied by giggles and the babble of shrill voices. The children spilled into the Pre-K room, all of them chattering at once: "We went in the foam pit!" "Joey has a hole in his sock!" "I jumped way, way, way high! I jumped the highest!"

That last boast came from Michael.

The next few minutes were a jumble of children struggling into coats and boots, fathers searching for missing mittens and exchanging best wishes for the holidays. Molly noticed that Michael was seated in the midst of the chaos, patiently putting on one of his boots. He didn't ask for help, didn't whine, but just sat on the floor, wriggling his foot slowly into the stiff rubber boot.

When he'd first come to the Children's Garden, he would have quickly grown frustrated and demanded assistance. He had matured a great deal in the past few weeks. Molly was proud of him. And then she wondered whether she had the right to be proud—not simply as a professional early childhood educator but as someone who cared personally about his tender emotions. He had endured so much in his short life, yet he'd somehow developed the ability to face a challenge and try his best.

Her vision misted. She experienced more than a teacher's satisfaction with a successful student. Her pride in Michael was maternal—and she had no right to feel that way about him.

Abruptly turning away, she spotted John reaching for the zipper of his jacket. Had he come here only for the class? Was he really going to leave without talking to her?

She'd slept with him, for crying out loud! She'd shared herself with him, body and soul—and he'd shared himself with her. Was he actually going to walk out without a word?

If Michael could face a challenge so courageously, so could she. Squaring her shoulders, she crossed the Pre-K room to John. Standing so close to him made her uncomfortably aware of his size...his virility. When he was this near, her mind came alive with memories of every minute they'd spent together, every word they'd spoken, every thought they'd exchanged, every kiss, every touch.

"We have to talk," she said.

"Okay."

She would have preferred for him to say, "Yes, you're absolutely right, I have things to tell you." And then, of course, she would have wanted him to tell her what she longed to hear: *I love you, Molly. I needed a few days apart from you to make sure, but now I know. Now I can say it.* As if he'd ever say so many words without prompting. As if he'd say *those* words.

But at least he was willing to give her a hearing. Now she had to figure out what to say.

She waited until all the other fathers and children departed, leaving Molly and John alone—except for Michael. Not wanting to impose on Shannon, who was still upstairs, probably straightening out after the foam pit jamboree, Molly hunkered down next to Michael, who had gotten his second boot about three-quarters on. "Would you like to do a puzzle?" she asked. "I've got a great animal puzzle."

"A big puzzle?" He looked interested.

"Yes. Would you like to do it?"

"I like a big puzzle." He yanked his boot fully on and pushed himself to his feet. "Where's the big puzzle?"

Molly led him into the Young Toddlers section and pulled a box down from a shelf. "Here it is," she said, emptying the pieces onto one of the low tables and pulling out a chair for him. Within minutes, he was immersed in the task of fitting the pieces together.

Satisfied that he wouldn't interrupt her and John for a while, she walked out of the classroom to where John was waiting on the other side of the partition. They could watch Michael over the wall while they talked.

John clearly wasn't going to begin the conversation. She'd been the one who wanted it, so she was going to have to get it started. Ignoring the panic that gnawed at her, she took a deep breath and lifted her gaze to him. "My sister told me she had a word with you on Monday." She wished her voice didn't sound so thin, so anxious.

John glanced at Michael, then turned back to her. He lifted his hand, no longer bandaged, and shoved back his hair. When he lowered his hand she saw the red line of his slowly healing wound across his palm. His wariness fell away, leaving behind a pained expression. "Yeah," he said. "We had words." The way he said it implied that they'd fought.

"And ever since then, you haven't—" she swallowed the catch in her throat "—you just backed off from me, John. I don't know..." Her eyes were beginning to burn and she blinked, desperate not to cry in front of him.

He wrapped his arms around her and pulled her gently against him. She wanted to resist, but she needed the strength of his embrace right now. She needed his warmth. Her nerves were shivering.

"I don't know what she said to you, John, or why

it was so meaningful to you that you could just—just run away from me—"

"Your sister only pointed out the truth," he murmured. "She wanted me to promise that I'd never hurt you. That's a promise I can't make. I *will* hurt you."

The soft wool of his sweater was damp, and she realized the dampness had been caused by her tears. She hated herself for weeping, but she couldn't help it. Stupid though it was, she felt that falling apart was a safe thing to do as long as John's arms were around her.

"Why do you think you'd hurt me?" she demanded.

"I hurt the last woman I cared for," he said.

Her tears halted as she felt the impact of his words. Had he just admitted he loved her? Wasn't that implicit in what he'd said?

Before she could fully grasp his statement, he continued. "I can't make the kind of promises you deserve."

"What promises have I asked for?"

He sighed. "My work makes me hard. It makes me cold. I carry a gun, Molly."

"I know you carry a gun," she stated. "And I'm not thrilled about it. But when you got hurt..." She swallowed again and leaned back so she could see his face. "When that creep hurt you, all I could think of was that I wish you'd shot him. I know, that's a terrible thing to say." Her voice crumbled, and she felt her eyes grow wet again. It was scary to think how much she loved John—so much that she would wish a violent punishment on anyone who hurt him.

He pulled her back against him. "That's what I'm saying," he explained. "If you get involved with a cop, it's going to change the way you think. It's going to suck the sweetness right out of you.''

''Maybe it's too late to be worrying what it's going to do to me. I'm already involved with a cop.'' Her voice gained strength. She'd said it, said everything she had to without using the word *love*. Her convictions gave her strength. ''You're afraid you might hurt me. Well, that's a chance I'm willing to take. Love doesn't come with a guarantee, and that's why you have to be brave to try it. I can be brave if I have to.'' She angled her head to view him, and his dark eyes found hers. ''I've seen how brave you can be, too. So I know you can do it if you want.''

His lips twitched into a hint of a smile. ''You're a lot braver than I am, Molly.''

''I don't think so.''

''And you're stubborn and reckless—''

''Stubborn, yes. Reckless, no.''

His smile solidified, reaching his eyes, reaching her heart and warming it. He bowed and brushed her mouth with his. ''I guess I could learn to be brave if that's what it takes to make this thing work.''

''We'll make it work,'' she vowed, wondering whether that was a promise either of them could keep. Perhaps he'd been right in calling her reckless. He was careful and self-protective enough not to promise anything.

But she *would* keep this promise. She would do whatever she could to keep it, because she loved him. And when he kissed her again, a long, leisurely kiss that held promises of its own, she knew that the love they had was worth it.

''I finished the puzzle!'' Michael hollered, startling them. They sprang apart and glanced over the wall, where Michael was beaming at them, the completed animal puzzle spread across the table next to him. "A very hard puzzle. I worked it out. Everything fits. All the pieces!"

Yes, Molly thought, her love expanding to include him. All the pieces fit and the puzzle was solved. Like Michael, she and John could work it out. If John wanted the pieces to fit as much as she did, they'd get it done.

CHAPTER FIFTEEN

"SHE'S BEAUTIFUL," John whispered.

"You're telling me," Jamie whispered back.

Through the open door John could hear laughter, conversation and the occasional clink of glasses touching. But Jamie McCoy, the host of this Christmas Eve party, had insisted on marching John down the hall to the nursery so he could admire the baby whose life he'd saved—or so Jamie claimed.

She wasn't as small as she'd been when John had seen her last June. Then, she'd been barely a month old. Now she was a gorgeous little girl, clad in white pajamas with little pink kittens printed all over them, sleeping on her tummy with her diaper-padded rump in the air and her thumb in her mouth. Her hair was pale and downy, her eyelashes silver-white and her mouth pursed as she sucked on her finger.

"You realize," Jamie murmured, gently spreading her blanket over her compact body, "that I owe you big for this."

John didn't believe the citizens of Arlington owed him anything more than the generous salary and benefits package he received for doing his job. He was glad when a case came out well, but it was his professional responsibility to make that happen whenever he could.

If anything, he owed Jamie. It was thanks to him

that John had gotten the name of Allison Winslow, who'd referred him to Molly.

A swell of laughter from the living room reached the nursery, which was lit only by the dim green glow of a frog-shaped night-light. John listened for Molly's warm, rolling laughter in the sound. Wanting her so much still frightened him, but he was trying hard to be as brave as she thought he was.

Molly made it hard to be a pessimist. She refused to let him carry the weight of their relationship on his shoulders. She had actually gotten him to accept that the collapse of his marriage hadn't been all his fault. "It takes two to make a relationship succeed," she argued. "And it takes two to make a relationship fail."

If this relationship with Molly failed—and against his better judgment, he believed it might not—at least the issue that broke them up wouldn't be his job. Molly seemed to understand that police work wasn't always a nine-to-five thing, that sometimes he worked late and sometimes he brought his work home, not in a briefcase but in his heart and his gut, where it would gnaw at him long into the night.

Only four days had passed since she'd persuaded him to take a chance on loving her, and in those five days she hadn't seen him at his worst. She hadn't witnessed what he could be like after spending a night trying to erase from his mind the vision of a murder-suicide. Molly had no idea how bad it could be. But she was prepared to defy the odds, and so was he.

"It was good you could come tonight," Jamie remarked, leading him from the nursery. They paused to adjust to the bright light of the hall, then proceeded to the even brighter kitchen. "But I wasn't exactly expecting you. You've screwed up my plans."

John didn't know how to respond to that. Molly had assured him he would be welcome at the party; she'd asked Allison if she could bring him and, according to her, Allison had sworn that she'd be in big trouble if she *didn't* bring him.

He remained silent as Jamie dug into the refrigerator and pulled out two chilled bottles of beer, one of which he passed to John. "See, I had this idea of setting Molly up with a friend of mine," he explained as he wrenched off the cap and took a swig from the bottle. "You want a glass?"

John shook his head, both intrigued and appalled by the thought of Molly with another man.

"Allison hates it when I drink from the bottle," Jamie griped. "She's trying to civilize me. She thinks she understands guys, but she doesn't. You tell me, am I an expert on guys or what?"

John smiled. He read Jamie's weekly newspaper column, "Guy Stuff," and found most of his observations right on the money. When it came to guys, Jamie *was* an expert. "Tell her beer tastes better from the bottle," he suggested. He himself couldn't recall the last time he'd drunk beer from a glass.

"That might work." Jamie took another drink, then lowered his bottle and gave John a good-natured smile. "My buddy, Steve—you met him, didn't you? He's the guy moping in the corner by the tree. He's in a funk because I'm getting married. He thinks my getting hitched is a betrayal of everything I stand for. I had this notion that if I introduced him to Molly, he'd feel the sting of ol' Cupid's arrow and maybe understand that falling for a woman isn't such a terrible thing."

John had felt that particular arrow's sting, and while

he wouldn't call it terrible, he wasn't quite convinced that it was good. It was good for him, certainly, but was it good for Molly? Would it be good for her once she realized what cops were like on a bad day?

He had to stop being so fatalistic. She loved him; maybe she'd be able to deal with the rest. "I'm sorry I ruined your plans," he said.

"Well, for Molly's sake, I guess I'll forgive you." Jamie tapped his bottle against John's. "Here's to her. Make her happy. She and Allison are like sisters, you know. If Molly isn't happy, Allison grieves."

John smiled impassively, his thoughts on Molly's real sister and her angry honesty. If he'd listened to her and kept his distance, he would have done his part to guarantee Molly's happiness. But he hadn't kept his distance, and he could only hope this thing worked out the way Molly was certain it would.

Sipping his beer, he followed Jamie back into the living room. In one corner stood a towering spruce, its boughs decked with tinsel and metallic silver and gold balls. A glum-looking fellow hunkered down on an ottoman next to the tree—Jamie's disappointed pal, Steve. Molly stood amid a cluster of guests, relating preschool stories. "One of the kids told me she'd seen Santa Claus at the mall, but she knew he wasn't the *real* Santa Claus. She insisted that the real Santa Claus was living in a condo in Tampa. She said he was spending Christmas Day at Walt Disney World, and she wished she was, too. I swear, I don't know how kids come up with this stuff!"

"It makes more sense than what we tell them," one of the women near her observed. "If you were Santa, where would you rather live, the North Pole or Tampa?"

"No contest. Tampa's got football," a man joked.

Molly's gaze snagged on John and she smiled—not the smile she'd worn while regaling the other guests with tales from the Children's Garden, but a smile just for him, a smile that told him she trusted him and loved him and believed in him.

He trusted her, too. He was close to admitting he loved her. And yes, he believed in her. The trouble was, he wasn't sure he believed in himself.

But right now, in the cozy room redolent with the scent of the tree and the fire blazing in the fireplace, with Molly's smile and her lovely eyes bewitching him, he could believe in almost everything—even the possibility that loving Molly was the right thing to do.

SHE WAS GOING to have a tree for Christmas, after all. John's tree, John's and Michael's.

"Are you sure you want me to spend the night?" she asked as he steered down Jamie's winding driveway, the tires of his car crunching on the snow-glazed gravel.

John shot her a quizzical glance. "Why wouldn't I?"

"It's Christmas Eve. Michael's going to wake up at 6:00 a.m. tomorrow."

"Why would he wake up so early?"

"Christmas," she said with a laugh, even though the reality of having to pass this precious night alone in her own bed depressed her. "Nobody under the age of fifteen sleeps past 6:00 a.m. Christmas morning," she explained.

John mulled over her statement and shrugged. "So he'll wake up early. What's the problem?"

"I'll be there," she said quietly. "In your bed." It

wouldn't be the first time she'd stayed all night at John's house. But she and John had always risen before Michael. By the time he'd climbed out of bed, they'd been dressed and in the kitchen, fixing breakfast. Michael was too young to realize what they might have been doing before they'd reached the kitchen. All he cared about was the fact that Molly was having breakfast with him, which seemed to please him immensely.

She hadn't yet dealt with the possibility that Michael might blab about her presence in his home to his classmates at the Children's Garden. The school was closed for the holidays. Once it opened again, after New Year's Day, she and John would have to reassess their situation.

But that was more than a week away, and Molly didn't want to think about it now. If she thought about it, she would start hoping that by the end of that week a bond would exist between her and John, something as strong as her love for him—and then the rest would be easy.

If the bond didn't form, if it was too soon, too fast for John to acknowledge it...well, she might have to be more discreet about spending time with John. Which would be awful.

She wouldn't dwell on it tonight. Not when the black winter sky was strewn with stars and the scent of snow danced in the air. Tonight was Christmas Eve, and tomorrow would be Christmas. There would be time to worry about the future when the future arrived.

The high-school girl John had hired to baby-sit sat in a stupor in the den, her eyes unfocused and the TV tuned to a low-budget space flick. Stirring herself to life when John and Molly entered, she reported that

Michael had thrown a fit when she wouldn't let him have a second ice-cream sundae but calmed down when she warned him that Santa only visited good little children. John pressed a very large bill into her hand and helped her on with her coat. Once he had departed to take her home, Molly collected the pile of wrapped gifts she and John had hidden in his cellar and arranged them under the tree. She slipped into the pile the two presents she'd gotten John, smuggled into his house inside her overnight bag. She'd purchased a Shetland wool sweater in burgundy, because he looked so handsome in sweaters, and a book about fathers, filled with soul-baring poems, amusing anecdotes and beautiful photographs of fathers and their children. She camouflaged her two presents among the wrapped gifts for Michael, then headed down the hall to John's bedroom.

She liked the room. She liked his house. She felt almost too comfortable in his kitchen, his living room, his bed. If Santa could bring her only one gift this year, she wished it would be that John felt for her what she felt for him—and that he trusted his feelings.

She slipped out of her dress and went into the bathroom to wash. When she emerged wearing only her slip and nylons, John was in the bedroom, his tie undone and dangling from his collar, his shirt unbuttoned, and his eyes seductive as he scrutinized her. The heat in his gaze ignited tiny fires inside her, fires that grew hotter and brighter as he crossed the room to her. And then his hands were on her, his touch burning through the silk of her lingerie, his mouth claiming hers, and she knew that even if Santa couldn't give her her heart's desire for Christmas, she would at least have John's love tonight.

"HE CAME! SANTA CAME!" Michael screamed through the door. "Daddy, get up! Santa came!"

Molly opened one eye and groaned softly. "What time is it?" she whispered.

John twisted to peer at the clock on the night table behind him. He cursed softly. "It's 6:02."

"I warned you," she murmured, cuddling closer. He reflexively closed his arms around her and slid one leg between hers. While John had been an outstanding lover with only one working hand, he was even more incredible when he wasn't healing from stab wounds. Last night he had loved her with his agile hands, his graceful fingers, his mouth, his body. And this morning she didn't want to break from him.

But Michael was whooping and hollering on the other side of the closed bedroom door. John must have locked it; given how hyper Michael was, he would have stormed into the room if he could.

"Go wait in the living room," John yelled, releasing Molly and sitting. "Give me a minute and then we'll have a look at what Santa brought you."

"He came, he came!" Michael shrieked, his voice fading as he ran down the hall to the living room.

John leaned over and dropped a kiss on Molly's lips. Then he swung out of bed. She tried to shake off her languor—and she tried to resist the urge to ogle him as he strode naked to the bathroom and shut himself inside. She considered staying in bed while John went to the living room to watch Michael dive into his gifts. Rolling over and burrowing under the covers might be easier than emerging from John's bedroom and facing his son at this ungodly hour.

But then she would miss the thrill of watching as Michael giggled and jumped up and down and tore the wrapping paper to shreds. The joy of Christmas wasn't getting gifts. It was witnessing the pleasure of others getting gifts.

When John stepped out of the bathroom, she dove in. A quick swipe of her mouth with a toothbrush, a fast splash of water, and she returned to the bedroom and scrambled into the jeans and rugby shirt she'd packed in her overnight bag. John made a halfhearted attempt to straighten his disheveled hair with his hands, then gave up and opened the door.

Patience wasn't Michael's forte. By the time they'd reached the living room, Michael had ripped apart the package containing the toy plane puzzle and snapped the pieces haphazardly together. He was standing on the sofa cushions in his pj's, waving the plane back and forth and making growling engine noises.

"Hey, Mike—off the couch," John chided.

Michael leaped down and raced across the room to his father. "Look what he bringed me, Daddy! Look what Santa bringed!" His gaze took in Molly, lurking nervously behind John, and he smiled. "Look, Molly! Look what Santa bringed! It's a airplane!" With that, he turned and zoomed the plane back toward the tree.

Well, that was simple enough. If only everything could be so simple. If only John could be as accepting of what was blossoming between him and Molly as his son was.

The next several minutes were a blur of tattered paper, jubilant cries—"A boat, Daddy! I go sail the boat in the sink!"—the forest fragrance of the tree and John's gratified smile. He handed Michael package after package—"Look, Daddy! A sweater! I can wear it!"—and slowly eroded the mound of gifts under the tree. As the pile shrank, she caught glimpses of the presents she'd hidden behind Michael's last night. She wondered when John would notice them, whether he would like them, whether she'd presumed too much by placing them under his tree.

He did notice them. He glanced at them, then at her, and quirked an eyebrow. She smiled shyly, and he smiled, too, a lot less shyly. He watched Michael twirl around the room, moving his plane in death-defying loops and figure eights before navigating the vehicle into the den.

They were alone for the moment. John turned back to Molly. "What's that?" he asked, gesturing toward the packages.

"There's one way to find out," she murmured, doing her best to ignore the anxiety that nibbled at her. Those were the last two presents under the tree. He hadn't gotten her anything. She shouldn't have given him anything, either. Now he was going to be embarrassed, and he'd resent her for making him feel guilty, and—

"It's great," he said, folding back the tissue paper that lined the box containing the sweater. He lifted it and shook out the folds, then ran his hands over the soft wool. "Or should I say, 'Look, I can wear it!'"

His eyes sparkled. Maybe he wasn't suffering from embarrassment or guilt.

And maybe he should be if he'd neglected to get a gift for her.

She kept her misgivings at bay as he unwrapped the book. "Wow," he murmured, lifting the book into his lap and leafing through the pages. "This is nice. Very nice." He inched over to where she was seated on the floor, leaning back against the couch, and arched his arm around her. "Thank you, Molly. Merry Christmas."

"Merry Christmas," she muttered, half furious with him for not giving her a present and half suspicious that he was up to something.

He relaxed beside her, his legs extended, the book and sweater in his lap and his arm draping her shoulders. "I guess Mike liked his loot."

"I guess so." She choked on the words.

And then her suspicions were confirmed. He frowned, squinted and pulled away from her. "Uh-oh. It looks like there's something on the other side of the tree."

She saw nothing behind the low boughs, but John crawled over the carpet to the tree, lifted some branches out of his way, and retrieved a cube-shaped box. "Look at that," he drawled, handing it to her. "It's for you."

Her anger fled, replaced by laughter. "You're a terrible actor, John."

"Yeah? I had you going for a minute." He settled on the carpet next to her and leaned back against the cushions. "Go ahead, open it."

She did, much more carefully than either of the Russos. She eased off the tape, lifted the corners of the paper and removed it from the box without tearing it. Then she pulled off the lid of the box. And scowled in bewilderment. Inside were tiny tufts of foam rubber.

"It's a foam pit," he told her. "I made it."

"It's...very nice," she managed to say, fingering the top layer of foam and wondering how to hide her disappointment.

"I like the foam pit at your school."

"Yes..." The foam pit was where they'd kissed the

first time. It was where she'd realized how attracted to John she was, how much she could care for him if she let herself. But to fill a plain cardboard box with bits of foam?

"Maybe you ought to let go and jump around in it," he suggested.

She glanced at him in bewilderment. He was smiling slyly, and she began to suspect that he was teasing her again. Shaking her head in feigned annoyance, she tilted the box and plunged her fingers into the foam. She felt something.

Gingerly she lifted it out. A bracelet, simple gold links with two charms dangling from them. The charms resembled small gold stick figures, one a girl and one a boy, the way a young child might draw them. They hung close enough together on the chain that their stick arms touched, as if they were holding hands.

"Oh, my God," she breathed.

His smile waned slightly. "You don't like it?"

"I love it!" She flung her arms around his neck and kissed him hard, then soft. She wound up half on his lap, leaning back against his chest while she fidgeted with the clasp. Her hands shook—with excitement, with love, with the giddy panic that came from accepting all the implications of a gift of jewelry—but somehow she managed to get the bracelet on. "Look at it, John! It's perfect!"

"I saw it and thought of you."

She jiggled her wrist and watched the stick figure girl and boy dance. When they finally grew still, they seemed to be holding hands again. They reminded her of the drawings her students created at the Children's

Garden...but they also reminded her of John and herself. Side by side, touching.

"So," he said as he closed his arms around her and drew her back against his chest. "You like it."

"Almost as much as the box of foam," she said solemnly.

He laughed. She smiled. She'd never felt more content, more serene...more in love. Santa Claus seemed to have brought her exactly what she wanted.

IN THE EVENING, after a dinner of ham and potatoes, an eggy bread, a spinach salad and peppermint-stick ice-cream, John drove her home. She'd packed only one night's worth of necessities into her bag, and she wanted to give Gail a call at the ski lodge to wish her and her friends a merry Christmas. Michael asked if he could come for the ride, but, as John had complained to Molly, he hadn't had a moment alone with her since 6:00 a.m. The high school girl he'd paid so generously last night was more than happy to come back to John's house and watch Michael for a couple of hours.

A couple of hours. In a couple of hours, she could invite John into her home, into her bedroom. Or maybe not the bedroom. Without Michael to interrupt them, they could make love anywhere. On the living room floor. On the kitchen table. Well, no, it wouldn't bear their weight, but the counter would.

She was astonished by how deeply, how crazily, how single-mindedly she wanted him. But then it occurred to her that the reason she was so drawn to him physically was because she was so drawn to him in every other way. Roasting a Christmas ham with him had seemed so natural. Playing with Michael in the den, where they all watched a video of Frosty the Snowman, had felt so right. Waking up with John that morning had been as glorious as going to bed with him the night before. Adorning her wrist with the bracelet he'd given her made her feel magical.

He was wearing the burgundy sweater. She doubted it made him feel magical—sweaters didn't have the same powers as bracelets—but she was touched that he'd put it on, and it looked splendid on him. In fact, she couldn't wait for him to take it off.

"That's my street," she said, pointing to the plank sign bearing the name of her condominium development. It stood on the corner, nestled into a cluster of rhododendrons half buried beneath the most recent snowfall.

John nodded and turned onto her street. It meandered in a picturesque route past staggered rows of shingled town houses with sloping roofs and vest-pocket front yards.

"My unit is just around the curve in the road. See where all those cars are?" She noticed at least a dozen cars parked along the curb in front of her home. "Someone must be having a party."

John was forced to park half a block away. As soon as she shoved open her door, she heard rock music pounding through the open front window of the unit directly across the street from hers. She knew the family who lived there, a usually quiet middle-aged couple with a son away at college.

He was obviously home from college now. "That must be Andy and his friends," she said. She'd seen a fair amount of Andy last summer when he'd lived with his parents and taken a job at a sporting-goods shop in town. He was a jock, according to his parents, attending college on a lacrosse scholarship.

"What a racket," John muttered.

"I'm sure they're just having fun," Molly said. "Andy's a good kid."

"Why does he have the window open? It's twenty degrees out."

"It's probably ninety degrees inside. Look how crowded it is in there." They could see a mass of silhouettes against the drape covering the window and hear dozens of voices shouting to be heard above the loud music.

Molly doubted she and John would be bothered by the noise once they got inside. She was going to keep her windows firmly shut, and if the temperature rose to ninety degrees in her home, passion would be to blame. "Forget it," she cajoled John, who seemed distracted by the rowdy bash across the street.

He followed her up the steps to her front porch, glanced over his shoulder one final time, then turned his back on the noise and eased her key from her hand. He slid it into the lock, twisted the doorknob—and flinched at the sound of crashing glass.

They both spun around. Someone had thrown something through the window and onto the street. A beer bottle, it appeared.

She sensed energy coiling inside John. His hand fisted around the doorknob as he stared at the shards of green glass scattered across the asphalt, glinting in the light of a street lamp. "Those kids are drinking. How old is Andy?"

"Eighteen, but they probably—"

"Someone's going to get hurt. Are the parents home?"

"I have no idea, John. Come inside. If you're really concerned, we can call the police."

He turned back to her, his expression stern and stone-hard. "I *am* the police."

"Yes, but—but you're off duty. Come inside, please. We'll call and let someone else handle it."

"Molly." He pushed open her door and nudged her inside. "You stay here. I'm going to go over and break up the party before someone gets hurt."

"Do you have to?" She sounded plaintive, practically begging. She didn't want him to break up Andy's party. Neighbor relations were a delicate thing. She'd never had a problem with Andy or his parents before, and she wanted to keep it that way. "Maybe someone else has already called the police. You don't have to go over there."

"I do. It's my job." Another bottle flew through the window, followed by gales of obstreperous laughter. The bottle failed to reach the street, but landed in the snow with a dull thud. "Go inside and close the door," he commanded. "I'll be back in a few minutes."

Fear nibbled at her. Why did she have to go inside and close the door? Was it so dangerous to break up a teenage party that she needed to be shut behind a protective wall? "Maybe I could go with you," she suggested, wishing she didn't feel so frantic—or at least wishing she knew *why* she was feeling frantic. "I know Andy. I could talk to him."

"Go in the house and stay there." The words were terse and blunt.

"What are you going to do?" she whispered.

"I'm going to my car to get my gun, and then I'm going to talk to your good neighbor Andy."

His gun? He had a gun in his car? He'd driven her home in a car with a gun in it?

Her heart pounded. Her mind spun. She recalled the first time she'd seen him, when he'd worn a gun in a shoulder holster under his jacket. She recalled telling him she didn't like guns.

He was a cop, and cops used guns. It didn't matter that she loved him. All that mattered was that he had a gun in his car and he was going to use it.

Before she could say something—before she could even find the right words to say—he had nudged her across the threshold and closed her door, leaving her alone and filled with dread.

CHAPTER SIXTEEN

SHE STOOD AT THE WINDOW, unable to drag her gaze from the disaster unfolding outside. She watched John walk past the row of parked cars until she could no longer see him, and she watched him come back into view, sauntering down the sidewalk until he stood in front of her town house, his back to her as he scrutinized the noisy house across the street. He looked no different to Molly, but she knew he had changed. He had his gun now—under his jacket, tucked into the waistband of his jeans, up his sleeve, in his hand, somewhere. All she could see was the back of his head, his dark, shaggy hair, the smooth surface of his leather jacket and his long legs. But she knew the gun was with him.

When he didn't immediately cross the street and raid Andy's party, she experienced a glimmer of hope that he'd changed his mind. That hope was dashed within a few minutes, when a police cruiser rolled to a silent stop in front of him. Double-parking alongside one of the cars, the driver climbed out. So did the officer in the passenger seat.

Three cops. Three of them, probably all carrying guns, were going to bust Andy's party. It was more than overkill. It was bullying—a trio of arrogant policemen squashing a lively gathering of kids. Yes, the kids were too loud. Yes, some of them were evidently drinking, which was against the law. But for heaven's sake, it was Christmas and people liked to celebrate. Even people a few years younger than the legal drinking age. Did such a situation really require three cops? With guns?

After a brief conference, John broke from the other two and strode up the steps to Andy's front door. They waited for him at the bottom of the porch steps, alert and apparently ready to spring.

John must have rung the bell or knocked, because the door opened. He went inside.

Her heart pounded. She was scared for him, scared for the revelers—mostly scared that something was going to happen, something ugly, something that would change the way she felt about the man who had given her a foam pit, a charm bracelet, a night of slow, deep lovemaking.

The door was left ajar, but no one emerged. The two uniformed cops climbed the stairs and entered. And then a thin, wiry young man crawled headfirst through the window's narrow opening.

One of the cops emerged from the house, charged down the steps and tackled the skinny kid as he pulled himself to his feet. The cop had to weigh at least sixty pounds more than the kid, who wasn't wearing a jacket. Molly wondered why they were tussling. Couldn't the cop just escort him to the police car?

More kids streamed out of the house, along with John and the third cop. Through her window she heard muffled shouts. Some kids tried to run, but the snow slowed them down, and John and the other policeman easily snagged them and hauled them back to the front of the house. The kids were lined up and told to press their hands against the clapboard edifice.

None of them had on a jacket. Molly saw puffs of vapor emerge from their mouths as they breathed. The cops patted them down, one at a time, and Molly shook her head. What on earth did John think these young folks had on them? Why was he treating them like common criminals?

One of the youths suddenly reared away from the wall and lunged at the cop who'd been frisking him. The cop tumbled backward into the snow, and then John dove toward the youth, grabbing him, slamming him into the snow and straddling him. In John's hand was a revolver. She could see it more clearly than the faces of the kids, more clearly than John's face. She saw John fist his hand around the back of the kid's neck and twist his head until he could see the gun, just inches from his face.

The entire scene seemed to shift into slow motion. The party guests turned, dazed and stiff. The cop who'd been knocked down stood slowly, awkwardly. He handed John a pair of handcuffs that had been hooked to his belt, and John manacled the wrists of the kid underneath him.

Molly closed her eyes. She couldn't turn away, but she couldn't bear to watch, either. She couldn't bear to see the man she loved brutalizing a drunk teenager. She felt tears slide down her cheeks, but she couldn't even move to wipe them away. She simply let them fall.

She heard an echo of Gail's warnings about cops, about how they abused their power and bullied people, how they waved their guns around to make people submit to them. John was doing just that.

Where was the man who was so concerned about doing right by his son? The man who had created a toy-size foam pit for her? The man who had kissed her in the real foam pit, and kissed her again in his bed, and made love to her with such tenderness she wanted to weep with pleasure?

Not here. She was weeping, but that man was not here.

An eternity seemed to pass before another squad car arrived. The rowdiest of the youngsters were crammed into the two police cars and the more sober of them were sent inside. Glancing at her watch, Molly was astonished to find that only twenty minutes had passed from the moment John had left her front porch to the moment he returned, ringing her bell.

She didn't want to let him in when she was so upset. But the intricate gold links of the bracelet weighed on her wrist, her own romantic handcuffs, shackling her heart. She opened the door, stepped back and let him enter.

He brought the biting cold of the night in with him. Even after he closed the door, Molly couldn't stop shivering. Gathering her courage, she lifted her gaze to his face. The iciness in his eyes made her shiver even more.

He said nothing. She should have expected that. John never said anything unless he was forced to.

"Why did you do that?" she asked, her voice taut with rage and sorrow.

"They were drinking. Things were out of control."

"So? You think college-age kids should be banned from having a few beers on Christmas Day?"

"It doesn't matter what I think. If someone breaks the law, I go in."

"You didn't have to go in! For God's sake, John!

You could have just telephoned from here and told Andy to send everyone home!''

"Some of those kids were too drunk to drive. I couldn't let them get behind the wheel.''

"Then why didn't you leave it to the other cops?'' Her voice rose; she was raging. She stormed in a circle around the living room, trying to burn off some of her anger so she could speak more normally. ''Why did it have to be you?''

"I was there.''

"But it's your day off. You're not working today, John. Why couldn't you have let those other cops handle it?''

He opened his mouth and closed it again. She felt his eyes on her as she paced the room. He seemed to be waiting for her to stand still before he spoke. She wasn't sure she wanted to hear what he had to say, but she came to a halt near the sofa and glared at him.

"A cop is always working,'' he said quietly, measuring each word. ''It doesn't matter if you're off duty. You're always a cop.''

She filled her lungs and emptied them. She knew what he was telling her: not just that he was a cop, but that he would never stop being a cop. Not on his day off. Not on Christmas. Not when he was being a father to Michael or a lover to her. He was always, always a cop.

All right. Maybe she could accept that. But why did he have to be a violent cop? Why did he have to intimidate unruly youngsters with a gun?

"You terrorized that boy,'' she murmured.

He didn't retreat. He held her gaze, looking neither defiant nor contrite, but stony and sure. ''He posed a threat to one of the uniforms.''

"What?"

"One of the other cops. He threatened him, he hurt him, so I took him down."

Rage bubbled up inside her again. Unable to stand still, she crossed to the fireplace and back to the sofa, praying for her heartbeat to slow down and her mind to speed up. "How—" Her throat tensed, and she swallowed to free her voice. "How could that drunk kid threaten anyone?"

Again John checked himself before answering. He ran his hand through his hair and sighed. "Does it matter?"

"Of course it matters! You were shoving your gun in his face!"

"He impeded the officer. He hurt him. He said things I'd rather not repeat. There was a dangerous situation, so I took him down." He paused, frowning. "You've seen me do that before."

"Yes, but—" She shuddered, remembering the visceral fear she'd felt when John had slammed the pickpocket into a brick wall.

"The pickpocket was just some stranger," she argued. "This was my neighbor's guest."

"That punk on Dudley was someone's neighbor, too, Molly. When kids are doing something wrong, you stop them before anyone gets hurt."

"No one was going to get hurt here."

"Someone did. The uniform got hurt. And that kid *didn't* get hurt. All I did was subdue him."

"With your gun. You subdued him by waving your gun around like—like—"

"Like what, Molly?"

Like the cop who had waved his gun at her sister. Like any man who got a firearm in his hand and believed that made him a god. Like the sort of thug from whom John was supposed to be protecting the citizens of Arlington. If someone waved a gun at her, she'd be subdued, all right. Subdued and full of hatred.

"When a cop is threatened, other cops defend him," he explained. "It's a code we live by. The kid was lucky. It could have been worse."

Maybe the kid was lucky, but Molly couldn't imagine anything worse than this. John Russo had transformed right before her eyes. He had gone from being a kind, thoughtful man to a robot with limited responses: a cop is a cop. When one cop is threatened, all cops defend him.

Where was the humanity in him? Where was the kindness, the thoughtfulness, the gentle humor, the fierce passion?

Not here, not in this stranger with a gun tucked into the waistband of his jeans.

"Please go," she whispered, forcing her gaze from his gun to the window. Through her ghostly reflection on the glass she saw Andy's town house. Despite the lights glowing inside, the house appeared vacant. The party was over.

John hesitated for a moment, then pivoted and stalked to the door. He wasn't going to argue with her or try to persuade her that he was still the man she adored. He knew who he was, and now she knew, too.

She waited to hear the click as the door closed behind him. Then she sank onto the sofa and let her tears come. Around her wrist jangled the bracelet, a gift from a man she loved, a man who seemed to have vanished like a dream.

HE SHOULD HAVE expected it. He had expected it. But when it actually happened...it hurt. Bad.

He'd let himself believe what he and Molly had would continue. If he'd held on to his own understanding of reality, if he'd clung to his experience and refused to accept that this time—this woman—might be different, he wouldn't be reeling with pain right now. He would have been prepared for this right from the start.

He blamed himself, not her. She'd made her promises with good intentions, unaware of the demands of loving a cop. If she hadn't seen him jump on that punk, that foul-mouthed piece of crud who'd hurled himself at John's colleague, his knee slamming against the cop's crotch and his mouth spewing obscenities between vows to bite the cop's finger off, she would have heard John talk about it. If he didn't talk about it awake, he would have mumbled about it in his sleep.

If he hadn't talked about it, he would have dwelled on it, anyway. She would have taken him in her arms and he would have had to say, "Not now," because his head would still have been in the ugly scene at the town house. When he was like this, he couldn't be reached. Not even by Molly.

Maybe it was just as well that she'd found out now, before the notions that had been swimming in his head for days could find their footing on solid ground. Notions about what a joy it would be to wake up beside her every morning for the rest of his life. Notions about what a fine mother she would make for Mike—and for any children she might have. Notions that she might have those other children with him.

It wasn't meant to be. John had known that going in. He'd simply chosen to forget the reality for a while.

But now, driving home from her house, his arm twinging where another son of a bitch's knife had left a scar, his head thudding and his heart aching, he could no longer forget.

CHAPTER SEVENTEEN

MOLLY WAS GRATEFUL for the holidays. She wasn't ready to face John, and once the new year started and the Children's Garden reopened, she would have to see him. She needed a few days to build up her strength.

But she resented the emptiness of her time. She had nothing to do, nothing to distract her from her misery. She didn't even have a Christmas tree to take down. The tree was at the Russo house. In fact, everything that mattered was at the Russo house.

When she closed her eyes, she could sometimes picture herself in John's home, loving him, playing with Michael, eating breakfast with them, being part of their lives. Other times when she closed her eyes she saw only the melee outside her window, the ferocity with which John had tackled that young man, the way he'd pointed his gun.

She couldn't spend the rest of her life with a man like that. She couldn't be part of that bitter world.

She spent a quiet New Year's Eve with Gail and one of her friends from the Public Defender's office. They rented a bunch of frothy thirties comedies starring Cary Grant and Clark Gable, men who didn't need guns to get the girl—at least not in those particular movies. The three women drank champagne and ate popcorn, and at midnight they turned off the movies and toasted the new year. Molly spent the following day gearing up to go back to work.

She loved her career. She loved the children, the school, the staff. And she reminded herself of that repeatedly, as if she could convince herself that January 2nd was going to be a day like any other. She clung to the consolation that the second fell on a Friday, so she would have to see John twice at most—once in the morning and once in the evening—before the weekend rescued her. Then she'd have two days to recover before their next confrontation.

Then, too, Michael might not come to school Friday. Many parents had decided to extend their vacations through the weekend, and Molly expected a low turnout. Most of her staff had requested a day off on Friday, too. Shannon would be there, and Molly had arranged for a substitute teacher to help out. Arlene was in her fifties, but she'd taught in a nursery school before retiring to raise her own children, and she was patient and creative. She'd worked at the Children's Garden many times, and Molly considered herself lucky to have been able to hire her for the day.

Fifteen children showed up Friday morning. Molly divided the children into two groups, one younger and one older. She had some Disney videos on hand, a lot of modeling clay, the foam pit and—including herself—three sturdy adults to keep the children occupied. She was determined to get through this ghastly day. She would survive this, even though Michael Russo was one of the fifteen children present.

She'd managed to avoid John during the morning drop-off, but she hadn't reckoned on how hard it was going to be to see Michael, to hear his voice, his delicious giggle, his familiar whine. "Molly!" he shrieked when, after a safe interval, she emerged from the supply room where she'd been hiding and joined the others in the big room at the end of the hall. "Molly! Hi!" He dashed over to her, his arms outstretched, and she had no choice but to hug him.

As her arms closed around him, she felt tears gather along her eyelashes. John wasn't the only Russo she loved. She adored Michael, too. But now she could be only his teacher, not his friend. Not a woman who shared a life with his daddy.

The day dragged for her—and it raced by before she had a chance to brace herself for pickup time. If she once again resorted to hiding in the storeroom when John entered the building, he would consider her a spineless wretch—which, admittedly, she was. But if she remained by her desk, greeting the parents as they came in to get their children, she would have to see him. And the minute she saw him, she would probably start blubbering.

She glanced at her watch. One week ago, that wrist had held the most magnificent charm bracelet in the world. Now it felt naked, deprived. The bracelet was lying on her night table so she could torture herself by letting it be the last thing she saw before she fell asleep and the first thing she saw when she awakened. No, she couldn't face John, not yet. She hadn't even glimpsed him, and already her eyes were beading with tears.

As soon as the door opened at five, signaling the arrival of the first parents, she waved Arlene toward the entry. "You go greet the parents," she said. "I'm going to help Shannon keep the kids occupied."

Nodding, Arlene headed down the hall to the front desk while Molly joined the circle of children sitting

on the floor singing "The Wheels On The Bus."
Molly had her back to the hall, but her gaze lingered
on Michael. Once he bellowed "Daddy!" and leaped
up, she would know John was there. Waiting for that
inevitable moment made her head ache.

Arlene came to fetch Abigail first. Then Keisha let
out a whoop and raced to the entry shouting,
"Mommy!" Taylor was the next to depart.

Across the circle from her, Michael wore a toothy
grin and bounced on his bottom, singing, "The people
on the bus go up and down, up and down, up and
down!"

For the zillionth time that day, Molly had to fight
the urge to dissolve in tears.

"The Wet Wipes on the bus go *swish, swish,
swish,*" he belted out, "all through the—Daddy!"

A sharp pain seared through her heart and em-
bedded itself in her soul. Even before Michael announced John's arrival, she'd felt his nearness sublim-
inally. Without turning, she'd known he was there, just
a few feet behind her, breathing the same air.

She could be a coward and remain in the circle. She
could be even more of a coward and sprint for the
back door. Or she could pretend to be composed and
confident. The third choice required her to stand up,
turn around and smile politely at John.

She could not recall ever attempting such a difficult
task, but the cowardly choices didn't sit well with her.
Inhaling deeply, she pushed herself off the floor,
wiped her suddenly damp palms on the legs of her
jeans and turned.

Oh, God. He looked wonderful and terrible all at
once. He looked as if the most sorrowful piece of her

soul had split from her and infected him. In his eyes she could see her own pain mingled with his.

She could also see resignation. He wasn't going to ask her to forgive him—as if there was anything to forgive. He was what he was, and that wasn't going to change.

He looked gaunt and tired, his hair mussed and his hands clenching and unclenching at his sides. His mournful eyes locked on to her. He showed no sign of backing away from her, but he didn't appear inter-ested in starting a conversation, either.

"Daddy, I saw Molly!" Michael boasted. "We played all day. I had a new teacher and we played all day, and we saw movies! We saw *The Lion King!*"

John spared his son a quick glance, then lifted his eyes to Molly. Tension hardened his jaw as he moved his lips. She prayed for him to say something, but he didn't. Not with his mouth, anyway. His eyes com-municated all sorts of profound messages—if only she could translate them.

"I made a dog with the clay," Michael prattled, tugging at his father's pants. "I made a doggie."

"Very good," John managed to reply, his voice barely audible above the chorus of children singing about the wipers on the bus going *swish-swish-swish.*

"It got a big tail," Michael continued. "I'm gonna put on my boots. Can Molly come with us?"

"No," John said softly, his eyes searching her face. What should she say? That she would gladly come with him only if he got rid of his gun and quit police work?

He wouldn't give up his career. And she couldn't ask him to.

A sharp scream from the other end of the front hall

jolted them. John spun around, groping under his jacket. "Don't!" Molly whispered, fearing that he was going to draw that horrible gun again. Whoever was screaming—a mother, from the sound of it—didn't call for John's macho cop routine.

Pushing past him, she hurried down the hall. Elsie Pelham, Abigail's mother, stood at the front desk shouting unintelligible curses at Arlene.

Molly clasped Elsie's shoulder and eased her away from the dismayed teacher. "Elsie, what's wrong?"

"That idiot—" she wagged an accusing finger at Arlene "—let Abbie leave with my ex-husband! He's kidnapped my baby! He's stolen her!"

Molly turned to Arlene, who shrugged helplessly. "He came in and said he was Abigail's dad. And then Abigail saw him and shouted 'Hi, Daddy!' I just assumed—"

"That bastard doesn't have custody of my daughter," Elsie wailed. "He told me if I didn't give him custody, he'd take it! Oh, my God, oh, my God!" She broke down, sobbing, sagging against the wall as if her legs could no longer hold her up. "Oh, my God, I'll never see her again! My baby!"

"What kind of car does he drive?" John's voice, though muted, cut through her hysterics and captured her attention.

She blinked at him through tear-filled eyes. "What?"

"What kind of car does he drive?" John pulled a notepad and pen from an inner pocket of his jacket. When Elsie continued to blink dazedly at him, he added, "I'm a police detective. We can track the car down if you tell us what he's driving."

"A '94 Cavalier," she said, her voice dulled by her sobs. "Dark red. Maroon, actually."

John scribbled on his pad. "Do you know the plate?"

"No." She shook her head. "It's a New York plate. He moved to New York and he's going to take her across the state line and I'll never get her back. He said there's a judge there who'll give him custody. He told me—he warned me—he was here for a holiday visit, and I thought he was leaving today, but he stayed. He stayed just to do this. He stole my baby." Her voice shattered into a low howl of rage.

"What's his name?" John asked, as calm as Elsie was frantic.

"Who? Oh. Frank. Frank Pelham."

"Description?"

"He's about five-foot-ten and he has brown hair. Everyone says he looks like Robert Downey, Jr."

John didn't seem to recognize the actor's name, but he dutifully wrote it down. "And you're sure he has your daughter with him?"

"Of course he does! She doesn't know there's a custody fight. She doesn't know the kind of man he is. I let her see him, but I know he'll never let me see her if he keeps her. He hates me. He's going to keep her from me forever!" She succumbed to sobs again.

"All right." John clicked his pen shut and turned to Arlene. "When did they leave?"

She shrugged again. "Five minutes ago. Molly, I'm really sorry...."

Molly's heart pounded, but she tried to keep her head clear, her anger under control. She kept files filled with detailed instructions regarding who was and wasn't allowed to pick up a child, and everyone on her staff, including substitutes, was required to memorize the information. She'd gone over the rules with Arlene before, but Arlene had obviously forgotten. "I'm really sorry" didn't begin to compensate for the possible damage Arlene's carelessness had caused.

"What are you going to do?" she asked John, her worry about Abigail Pelham pushing aside her selfish worries about her broken heart.

"I'm going after him. If he's heading for New York State, he'll likely be on I-84. I'll radio a description of the car and we'll see if we can stop him."

"Abbie won't come with you," Elsie Pelham warned. "She thinks her dad is fine. She doesn't understand the custody arrangement. She won't leave her dad's car for a stranger." She lifted her chin, though she still seemed barely able to stand. "I'll come with you. If she sees me, I—"

"No," John said so quickly Molly would have smiled if the situation hadn't been so grave. She couldn't imagine John trying to chase down Frank Pelham's car with Elsie bawling and babbling next to him.

"I'll go," Molly volunteered. "Abbie knows me. Arlene, you keep Michael here, okay?"

"Anything," Arlene said, clearly shaken by her error. "Whatever you want."

"Go to the police station and wait," John ordered Elsie. He eyed Molly dubiously, then shoved his pad back into his pocket and strode toward the door. Molly grabbed her jacket from the coat tree behind the desk and chased him out of the building.

Neither spoke as he opened the passenger door of his car. He pulled from the floor near her feet a bulky, hemispheric object trailing a wire. A flashing red light, she realized as he lifted it through the window and fastened it to the roof of his car. "You can roll up the window, but don't crush the wire," he said as she sat.

She rolled the window halfway up, then folded her hands in her lap and waited while he revved the engine, tore out of the lot and lifted a radio handset from the console. He flicked a button and spoke into the mouthpiece, describing the car, the circumstances, the passenger. "I'm on him, but if there are any Staties out there, I think I-84 is our best shot," he said before hanging up.

The light on the roof of the car splashed a pulsing red wash across the windshield and hood. John navigated the rush-hour traffic aggressively, crossing the double yellow line, running red lights until he reached the entrance ramp onto the interstate. The highway was also sluggish with traffic, but he wove deftly among the cars, paying attention not only to the hazards of the road but to the license plates of the cars around them.

Molly studied the plates, too: Connecticut, Connecticut, Connecticut. Up ahead she saw a dark red Cavalier...Connecticut.

John tapped a switch on the dashboard and a siren began to bleat. Molly flinched, her heart pounding from the noise and John's manic driving. It occurred to her, somewhere in the deeper recesses of her mind, that like the night she'd lost him, John was currently off duty. And like that night, he wasn't letting his being off duty stop him from doing a job. He was a cop, and regardless of the fact that he'd finished his working day, he was doing his job now. This time it wasn't to flush some inebriated kids from a neighbor's house, though. It was to rescue a little girl from her pigheaded father—and to save Molly's butt.

Up ahead, she saw a pair of flashing blue lights above a sedan. "Statie," John murmured, veering onto the shoulder and accelerating to catch up to the state trooper's car.

"Do you think he's on Frank Pelham's tail?" she asked, wide-eyed in spite of herself.

"He can't be after a speeder. I'm the fastest car on the road, and I'm barely pushing fifty." Remaining on the shoulder, he pulled up alongside the trooper's car, rolled down his window and shut off his siren. "Have you seen him?" he shouted.

"Not yet. If he gets past the city limits, he's gonna fly. The road gets empty about five miles west of here. Any chance he took another route?"

"Yeah," John yelled into the winter wind.

"Well, if he thinks he can outsmart us by going through Massachusetts, we've got men all over the roads. Maybe we'll intercept him."

"Let's hope," John hollered, then rolled up his window and tore ahead of the trooper's car.

Amazed that he could converse from speeding car to speeding car, amazed that law enforcement was so quick to respond to the crisis, amazed that she was in the middle of it, even exhilarated by it, Molly returned her attention to the cars clogging the road. She nearly jumped when she spotted a non-Connecticut license plate, then sagged when she saw it was a Rhode Island tag. John turned the siren back on and continued down the shoulder.

"Thank you," she said quietly, still searching the license plates.

John shot her a quick look, then steered around a

pile of trash someone had dumped on the side of the highway. "Don't thank me. I haven't done anything."

"You've offered to help. You didn't have to—"

"Yes, I did," he said, cutting her off.

Because it was his job? she wondered. Or because he was a father who loved his son, who had to help a mother whose daughter was missing? Was he helping because he was a cop or because he was a good man?

Maybe there wasn't such a huge difference between the two.

"There!" she cried out, spotting a New York license plate on a car stalled in traffic about twenty feet ahead of them. The plate was attached to a dark red sedan, and the silhouette of a man's head rose above the driver's seat. If Abigail was in the car, she was too short to be visible.

"Where?"

"There!" Molly pointed emphatically. "Right there!"

"Got it." John cruised along the shoulder until he was astride the car behind the Cavalier. He signaled with his directional light to pull into the traffic lane, and then flashed his lights and honked for the Cavalier to pull off the road.

As John followed the Cavalier onto the shoulder, Molly held her breath. What if it was the wrong car? What if they lost precious minutes dealing with this car while Abigail and her father were speeding toward some other border crossing?

Leaving the motor running, John yanked on the parking brake. "You stay here," he commanded. "If I go like this—" he made a beckoning motion with his hand "—come over."

Molly nodded. She wished she could find a hint of

personal emotion in his gaze, something meant for her. But at the moment, he was strictly a cop. Nothing else—not even his and Molly's star-crossed romance—mattered to him.

Sighing, she unclipped her seat belt and watched him stalk over to the other car. He held up something in front of the driver's-side window—his shield, she guessed—and then peered into the car. Without looking at her, he made the beckoning sign with his hand.

She hurried out of the car and jogged over. The driver glowered and clung to the wheel, as if determined not to let anyone drag him out of the driver's seat. Behind him, in the back, sat Abigail Pelham. "Hi, Abbie," Molly called through the partially open window.

"Molly!" Abigail giggled, wiggling her booted feet. "This is my daddy! We're going to New York!"

"Not tonight," John muttered. The air began to pulse blue along with the red of the light on John's car, and the state trooper's car coasted past the two cars before pulling onto the shoulder, boxing the Cavalier in. While the trooper sauntered over, John murmured to Molly, "I'm going to have the trooper take them back to the station. Explain it to Abbie so she doesn't get scared, okay?"

Molly nodded, swallowing a lump in her throat at his consideration for the little girl. While John and the trooper talked with Frank Pelham, Molly told Abigail that she and her father would be going in another car and that her mommy would be waiting for her once they reached their destination. Suitcases were removed from the trunk of the Cavalier, which was locked up, and the trooper escorted the Pelhams to his cruiser. They got in and drove away, leaving Molly and John

on the side of the road, as alone as they could be on
a highway at the heart of rush hour.

She felt shaky as the reality of what had just happened sank in. She'd been involved in a police chase.
She'd helped save a girl from a custody battle kidnapping. She'd sat beside John, and she'd felt bold, determined to right a wrong. And now that the wrong
was in the process of being righted, she felt
drained...but good. Very good.

She lifted her gaze to John. He was studying her,
his face glowing red and then falling into shadow, red
and then shadow as the light continued to flash on the
roof of his car.

"You're never off duty, are you?" she said.

"No."

She gave herself a moment to digest that truth.
"Were you on duty even when we were making
love?"

Something flickered in his eyes, something warm,
comprehending. One side of his mouth twitched up-
ward in a vague attempt at a smile, but his voice was
solemn. "When we were making love, you got all of
me, Molly. You got everything."

And she'd loved everything, all of him, his body
and his soul, his tenderness and his fierceness, his ret-
icence and his strength. She'd seen and felt and loved
all the many facets of him.

She still loved him. Even if she was frightened by
what he did, frightened by what could happen to him.
She loved him, and that wasn't going to change.

"I'll never feel comfortable about your gun," she
warned.

"The gun isn't me, Molly. It's a tool I sometimes

use in my work." He risked a step toward her. "It isn't me."

"I think I understand," she whispered, moving toward him. "But I don't like it."

"There are things I don't like about you, too," he admitted, his smile widening slightly.

"Name one," she challenged him.

He lapsed into thought for a minute, then said, "You're quick to judge people."

"Who, me?" she scoffed indignantly.

His smile grew even bigger. "Right. And in your judgment, I'm—"

"A wonderful man," she finished, taking the final step that obliterated the distance between them. He spread his arms and she sank into them. It felt like coming home. "I love you, John," she whispered, hoping he could hear her through the rumble of traffic and the muffling tightness of his embrace. "I wish you didn't have to do what you do, but it's who you are. It's part of everything."

"Yes."

"It won't change."

"No."

She closed her eyes and held him closer. "I can't bear the thought of your hurting someone or getting hurt. It's scary."

"Not nearly as scary as falling in love," he argued.

She peered up at him. "Falling in love scares you?"

"More than you know," he confessed. "But I love you so much, I'll just have to overcome the fear."

She reached up and cupped his face in her hands, then pulled him down to her. They kissed, their hearts beating in a strong, steady rhythm while the red light throbbed above them and the cars of a thousand weary commuters rolled by.

John and Molly kissed, fearless in each other's arms.

Take 4 bestselling love stories FREE

Plus get a FREE surprise gift!

Special Limited-time Offer

Mail to Harlequin Reader Service®

3010 Walden Avenue
P.O. Box 1867
Buffalo, N.Y. 14240-1867

YES! Please send me 4 free Harlequin Superromance® novels and my free surprise gift. Then send me 4 brand-new novels every month, which I will receive before they appear in bookstores. Bill me at the low price of $3.34 each plus 25¢ delivery and applicable sales tax, if any.* That's the complete price and a savings of over 10% off the cover prices—quite a bargain! I understand that accepting the books and gift places me under no obligation ever to buy any books. I can always return a shipment and cancel at any time. Even if I never buy another book from Harlequin, the 4 free books and the surprise gift are mine to keep forever.

134 BPA A3UN

Name	(PLEASE PRINT)	
Address	Apt. No.	
City	State	Zip

This offer is limited to one order per household and not valid to present Harlequin Superromance® subscribers. *Terms and prices are subject to change without notice. Sales tax applicable in N.Y.

USUP-696   ©1990 Harlequin Enterprises Limited

HARLEQUIN WOMEN KNOW ROMANCE WHEN THEY SEE IT.

And they'll see it on **ROMANCE CLASSICS**, the new 24-hour TV channel devoted to romantic movies and original programs like the special **Romantically Speaking—Harlequin™ Goes Prime Time.**

Romantically Speaking—Harlequin™ Goes Prime Time introduces you to many of your favorite romance authors in a program developed exclusively for Harlequin® readers.

Watch for **Romantically Speaking—Harlequin™ Goes Prime Time** beginning in the summer of 1997.

If you're not receiving ROMANCE CLASSICS, call your local cable operator or satellite provider and ask for it today!

Escape to the network of your dreams.

See Ingrid Bergman and Gregory Peck in *Spellbound* on Romance Classics.

©1997 American Movie Classics Co. "Romance Classics" is a service mark of American Movie Classics Co.
® and ™ are trademarks of Harlequin Enterprises Ltd.

RMCLS-R

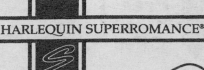

As Seen on TV!

Free Gift Offer

With a Free Gift proof-of-purchase from any Harlequin® book, you can receive a beautiful cubic zirconia pendant.

This stunning marquise-shaped stone is a genuine cubic zirconia—accented by an 18" gold tone necklace.
(Approximate retail value $19.95)

Send for yours today...
compliments of ✦HARLEQUIN®

To receive your free gift, a cubic zirconia pendant, send us one original proof-of-purchase, photocopies not accepted, from the back of any Harlequin Romance®, Harlequin Presents®, Harlequin Temptation®, Harlequin Superromance®, Harlequin Intrigue®, Harlequin American Romance®, or Harlequin Historicals® title available at your favorite retail outlet, together with the Free Gift Certificate, plus a check or money order for $1.65 U.S./$2.15 CAN. (do not send cash) to cover postage and handling, payable to Harlequin Free Gift Offer. We will send you the specified gift. Allow 6 to 8 weeks for delivery. Offer good until December 31, 1997, or while quantities last. Offer valid in the U.S. and Canada only.

Free Gift Certificate

Name: _____

Address: _____

City: _____ State/Province: _____ Zip/Postal Code: _____

Mail this certificate, one proof-of-purchase and a check or money order for postage and handling to: HARLEQUIN FREE GIFT OFFER 1997. In the U.S.: 3010 Walden Avenue, P.O. Box 9071, Buffalo NY 14269-9057. In Canada: P.O. Box 604, Fort Erie, Ontario L2Z 5X3.

FREE GIFT OFFER   084-KEZ

ONE PROOF-OF-PURCHASE
To collect your fabulous FREE GIFT, a cubic zirconia pendant, you must include this original proof-of-purchase for each gift with the properly completed Free Gift Certificate.

084-KEZR

**A showgirl, a minister—
and an unsolved murder.**

EASY VIRTUE

Eight years ago Mary Margaret's father was
convicted of a violent murder she knew he
didn't commit—and she vowed to clear his
name. With her father serving a life sentence,
Mary Margaret is working as a showgirl in Reno
when Reverend Dane Barrett shows up with
information about her father's case. Working to
expose the real killer, the unlikely pair also
proceed to expose themselves to an unknown
enemy who is intent on keeping the past buried.

**From the bestselling author of
LAST NIGHT IN RIO**

JANICE
KAISER

Available in December 1997
at your favorite retail outlet.

**MIRA
BOOKS**

The Brightest Stars in Women's Fiction.™

**Don't miss these Harlequin favorites
by some of our bestselling authors! Act now and
receive a discount by ordering two or more titles!**

HT#25720	A NIGHT TO REMEMBER	$3.50 U.S. $3.99 CAN.	☐
	by Gina Wilkins		
HT#25722	CHANGE OF HEART	$3.50 U.S. $3.99 CAN.	☐
	by Janice Kaiser		
HP#11797	A WOMAN OF PASSION	$3.50 U.S. $3.99 CAN.	☐
	by Anne Mather		
HP#11863	ONE-MAN WOMAN	$3.50 U.S. $3.99 CAN.	☐
	by Carole Mortimer		
HR#03356	BACHELOR'S FAMILY	$2.99 U.S. $3.50 CAN.	☐
	by Jessica Steele		
HR#03441	RUNAWAY HONEYMOON	$3.25 U.S. $3.75 CAN.	☐
	by Ruth Jean Dale		
HS#70715	BAREFOOT IN THE GRASS	$3.99 U.S. $4.50 CAN.	☐
	by Judith Arnold		
HS#70729	ANOTHER MAN'S CHILD	$3.99 U.S. $4.50 CAN.	☐
	by Tara Taylor Quinn		
HI#22361	LUCKY DEVIL	$3.75 U.S. $4.25 CAN.	☐
	by Patricia Rosemoor		
HI#22379	PASSION IN THE FIRST DEGREE	$3.75 U.S. $4.25 CAN.	☐
	by Carla Cassidy		
HAR#16638	LIKE FATHER, LIKE SON	$3.75 U.S. $4.25 CAN.	☐
	by Mollie Molay		
HAR#16663	ADAM'S KISS	$3.75 U.S. $4.25 CAN.	☐
	by Mindy Neff		
HH#28937	GABRIEL'S LADY	$4.99 U.S. $5.99 CAN.	☐
	by Ana Seymour		
HH#28941	GIFT OF THE HEART	$4.99 U.S. $5.99 CAN.	☐
	by Miranda Jarrett		

(limited quantities available on certain titles)

TOTAL AMOUNT		$ _____
DEDUCT: 10% DISCOUNT FOR 2+ BOOKS		$ _____
POSTAGE & HANDLING		$ _____
($1.00 for one book, 50¢ for each additional)		
APPLICABLE TAXES*		$ _____
TOTAL PAYABLE		$ _____

(check or money order—please do not send cash)

To order, complete this form and send it, along with a check or money order for the total above, payable to Harlequin Books, to: **In the U.S.:** 3010 Walden Avenue, P.O. Box 9047, Buffalo, NY 14269-9047; **In Canada:** P.O. Box 613, Fort Erie, Ontario, L2A 5X3.

Name: _____

Address: _____ City: _____

State/Prov.: _____ Zip/Postal Code: _____

*New York residents remit applicable sales taxes.
Canadian residents remit applicable GST and provincial taxes.